FALCON
iN THE GLASS

ALSO BY SUSAN FLETCHER

THE DRAGON CHRONICLES
Dragon's Milk
Flight of the Dragon Kyn
Sign of the Dove
Ancient, Strange, and Lovely

OTHER BOOKS BY SUSAN FLETCHER:
Alphabet of Dreams
Shadow Spinner
Walk Across the Sea

FALCON IN THE GLASS

A NOVEL BY

SUSAN FLETCHER

✦ ✦
✦

MARGARET K. McELDERRY BOOKS
New York ✦ London ✦ Toronto ✦ Sydney ✦ New Delhi

MARGARET K. McELDERRY BOOKS
◆ An imprint of Simon & Schuster Children's
Publishing Division ◆ 1230 Avenue of the
Americas, New York, New York 10020 ◆ This
book is a work of fiction. Any references to
historical events, real people, or real locales
are used fictitiously. Other names, charac-
ters, places, and incidents are products of the
author's imagination, and any resemblance to actual events or locales or
persons, living or dead, is entirely
coincidental. ◆ Copyright © 2013 by
Susan Fletcher ◆ All rights reserved,
including the right of reproduction in
whole or in part in any form. ◆ MARGARET K.
McELDERRY BOOKS is a trademark of Simon
& Schuster, Inc. ◆ For information about special discounts for bulk purchases, please contact
Simon & Schuster Special Sales at 1-866-506-
1949 or business@simonandschuster.com.
◆ The Simon & Schuster Speakers Bureau
can bring authors to your live event. For
more information or to book an event, contact the Simon & Schuster Speakers Bureau
at 1-866-248-3049 or visit our website at
www.simonspeakers.com. ◆ The text for this
book is set in Centaur MT. ◆ Manufactured
in the United States of America ◆ 0813 FFG
◆ 10 9 8 7 6 5 4 3 2 ◆ Library of
Congress Cataloging-in-Publication Data ◆
Fletcher, Susan, 1951– ◆ Falcon in
the glass / Susan Fletcher.—First edi-
tion. ◆ p.   cm. ◆ Summary: "Eleven-
year-old Renzo must teach himself
to blow glass with the help of a girl
who has a mysterious connection to
her falcon"—Provided by publisher. ◆ ISBN
978-1-4424-2990-1 (hardcover) ◆ ISBN 978-
1-4424-2992-5 (eBook) ◆ [1. Glass blow-
ing and working—Fiction. 2. Human-animal
communication—Fiction. 3. Birds—Fiction.
4. Murano (Italy)—History—Fiction. 5.
Italy—History—Fiction.] I. Title. ◆ PZ7.
F6356Fal 2013 ◆ [Fic]—dc23 ◆ 2012022468

For my brother, Bruce

PROLOGUE

It was a ghostly sight, so startlingly strange that for some time afterward the captain wondered if he might have imagined it. It appeared out of the fog, out of the hush of the still waters before him, as he guided his ship among the haze-shrouded islands of the lagoon.

At first it was a faint, darkish smudge on the water. As it grew near, the smudge thickened into the shape of a small, sail-less boat, filled stem to stern with . . .

Children, was it?

Children and birds?

The little craft rode low in the water, packed tight with its odd, silent cargo. The birds, varied in size and shape, perched on shoulders, on arms, on wrists, on fingers, on heads.

As the boat passed hard by his ship, a girl looked up and caught the captain's eye. Her face was heart-shaped, elfin. Her eyes were fierce. For a long moment they gazed at each other, captain and girl. Then the little boat slid away behind him and vanished in the mist.

PART I

FALCON

• • •

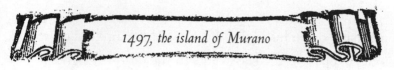

I.

Stranger in the Glassworks

Something rustled in the dark — a sound so faint, Renzo barely heard it at all, but it told him he was not alone.

Out of the corner of one ear, he heard it. His eyes and mind and heart had belonged entirely to the glass before him, and not to the signs of danger.

It glowed copper-orange, the glass — a veined and stunted sun blazing in the gloom of the workshop. Renzo had gathered it, molten, on the end of the blowpipe; he had rolled it on the stone *malmoro*; he had shaped it in the *magiosso* mold. He had set the pipe to his lips and breathed — just long enough and hard enough to belly out the glass in the slightest curve and begin to make it *his*.

Of sounds he'd taken no notice. Not the roar of the furnace, nor the splash of water when the *magiosso* dropped into its bath, nor even the soft, secret *whoosh* of his breath inside the pipe.

He heard them but did not mark them. Not until the new sound came — the rustling, faint and quick.

He stood still as stones now, waves of prickling gooseflesh

coursing down his back. This was a different kind of sound, out of place in the glassworks in the dead of night. It was a sound an assassin might make, hiding deep in shadow, his legs beginning to cramp, not wanting to move but forced by pain to shift position. Or a hesitation sound, perhaps. The assassin wondering, Shall I make my move now, or later?

It was a sound Renzo's father might have heard these many months since, on the last night of his life.

It came again:

Rustle-shiver-scritch.

Above!

Renzo peered up into the shadows, where the furnace's glow flickered across the rafters.

And beheld a bird.

Renzo's knees went weak; his breath escaped in a sigh of relief.

Only a bird.

He wanted to laugh then, at his foolishness. At his heart, still clattering between his ribs. At the glass, now a misshapen lump—darkening as it cooled, crumpling in upon itself.

Only a bird. A little falcon—a kestrel.

He watched it for a moment, breathing, waiting for his heart to settle. The assassins would not return, he told himself. They'd done what they'd come to do. And whatever befell his traitor of an uncle, it would be far from here.

The falcon rattled its feathers. Better get it out of here. The *padrone* did not tolerate birds in the glassworks. What if a feather—or worse—should fall on the smooth surface of a newly worked cup or bowl?

Renzo knocked the blowpipe against the rim of the pail at his feet; the glass cracked off and clattered among the heaped remains of his earlier failures. Simpler forms gave him no trouble, but the complicated ones . . . Sometimes he wished he had three hands.

He set the blowpipe on the rack beside the other pipes and rods, then made his way across the wide, open floor of the glassworks and opened the oaken door.

Outside, still waters lapped against stone. The chill winter breeze touched his face, carrying the smells of the lagoon: fish, and salt, and tar. Mist rose from the dark canal and crept like smoke along the lane, blurring the silent houses, making them wavery, gauzy—homes for ghosts. The sweat grew clammy on Renzo's body and made him shiver. His shoulders and arms and back all ached; a dark pool of weariness pressed down on the crown of his head and seeped into his eyes.

Nothing had gone well tonight. And he was so far behind.

He stepped back inside, clapped his hands, shouted at the bird. But it must have felt snug there, high up in the rafters. It did not budge.

He scooped up a handful of pebbles from outside and tossed one at the bird. It let out a hoarse cry and took off flying. He pursued, throwing more pebbles, not trying to hit it, just drive it out the door.

"Cease with that! *Basta!*"

Renzo's heart seized. He whirled round to see who had shouted.

The figure came hurtling out of the shadows behind the woodpile. Came so fast, Renzo barely had time to put up his hands to defend himself before she was raining blows down upon him. He might have lashed out, except that she was smaller than he, and he saw that she was a girl. No more than twelve or thirteen years old, he thought. No older than he, himself.

She dealt him one last shove and then bolted toward the open doorway. She twisted back and sent the kestrel a look — a strange look, like a summons. The bird sailed out of the workshop behind her.

Astounded, Renzo stared after them — girl and bird fleeing together, dissolving into the dark, into the mist. Before they vanished entirely, he thought he saw the kestrel swoop down and come to perch upon her shoulder as she ran.

But he must have imagined that.

2.

Prophecy

R enzo! Did you hear me?"
  The *padrone* was frowning, his face etched deep with
unhappiness.

"What is amiss with you? Have you gone deaf? I told
you to remove this bowl to the annealing chamber."

Renzo leaned his broom against the stacked crates of
finished glass. He crossed the floor toward the furnace, the
bright-hot roaring core of the glassworks, where the *padrone*
and two other masters worked the glass. The heat licked
at Renzo, drawing sweat from his brow; he picked up the
goblet bowl with the lifting irons and hurried toward the
rear of the furnace.

Her face still swam before him — the girl from the night
before.

All that morning it had done so — in the slivers of glass
he swept from the floor, in the mounds of sand and soda
in the poisons room, in the surfaces of the worked glass he
bore to and from the annealing chamber. He had glimpsed
it for a moment only, that face. But now, in memory, Renzo

found he could capture and explore it, discover far more than he had grasped in the quick blink of an eye when she had stood before him in the flesh.

It was a small face, and thin. From the size of it he might have thought it belonged to a younger child, in her tenth year or maybe eleventh. But he had seen something older in her eyes—green eyes, intensely green—and something terrible, too.

Terribly afraid. Terribly fierce. Both at the selfsame time.

He had not seen her before. He would have remembered.

Renzo set the bowl in the annealing chamber, high in the dome above the main furnace. Thinking back, sifting through his recollections. A dark, ragged cloud of hair. A thin cloak, shaggy with tattered threads and fringes.

"Renzo! Pick up the *tagianti* and fetch them here. No, not those. The rounded ones. Have you gone blind? Pay attention! And the compass, if I may disturb you to bestir your feet. *Presto!* The glass will not wait for you; it is cooling as I speak."

The *padrone's* habitual thin-lipped scowl deepened as Renzo handed him the tools, but Sergio, the *padrone's* eldest son and apprentice, was smiling. A mocking smile.

Renzo lingered to watch as the *padrone* stretched out a long, narrow cord of glowing glass. He was not a large man, but he was strong; ropy muscles stood out on his arms and neck. Renzo drew closer, until the heat came at him in waves, as the *padrone* handed Sergio the *borsella* and instructed him how to persuade the glass to transform itself into something new.

It would be a wineglass stem, Renzo saw—a lovely,

delicate thing shaped like two interwoven vines. His weariness lifted as he watched Sergio's hands, clumsy at first, and then slowly learning what was required of them as the vines twined upward, seemingly hungry for sunlight. Renzo fixed every movement into memory, his own fingers itching to work the glass.

He recalled what it was to stand in the savage, shimmering heat with his father close beside him. To breathe the familiar smell of wood smoke, to hear Papà's voice, above the deep throb of the furnace, rumbling in his ear: *Just a little twist, Renzo, is all that is required here. Then pull. Now, now, now, just now, but more fluid with the twist. Do you see it? Do you see?*

Renzo swallowed. Cleared the thickness from his throat.

Sergio glanced up. "The furnace needs stoking," he said.

Renzo waited. It was not his duty to stoke the furnace. That was for Anzoleto, who had stepped out to obey the call of nature. Renzo was a laborer, a drudge, but it was possible to go lower. Cutting wood and feeding the fire were the lowest jobs in the glassworks.

"Perhaps," Sergio said, "the drudge prefers not to work himself. Perhaps we should hire a drudge for the drudge."

He laughed, but the *padrone* did not. He grunted, then glanced up as Anzoleto appeared in the doorway. "Tend to your own work, Sergio," the *padrone* said. "Do not disappoint me. You must do better than this." He broke Sergio's wine stem from the *pontello* and flung it into the bucket of broken glass. The *padrone* turned to Renzo and Anzoleto. "Everyone! Tend to your work."

So then it was back to sweeping the floor, to sorting and crushing the broken glass, to grinding the soda to powder.

Back to wondering about the girl.

After she had left, Renzo had searched all through the glassworks trying to discover how she had broken in. He had found his answer in a small storeroom at the rear, where a narrow window opened onto an alley. The shutter hung crookedly from a single hinge, unlatched.

Renzo had told the *padrone* about the broken hinge but not about the girl. He ought to have reported her. She might be a spy. Always there were spies near glassworks, sent to ferret out secrets of the craft. Even worse were the government spies sent by the dreaded Council of Ten to make sure the glassmaking secrets never left the lagoon.

Spies—and also assassins.

As Renzo knew only too well.

Yes, the *padrone* would want to know about the girl. He would want to catch her, discover who she was and what she'd been doing.

Still, Renzo hesitated. If he told, others might come into the glassworks with him at night. Everyone knew that Renzo worked the glass when all but the night furnace tender had left; that was not the problem. But they might shunt him aside; they might foist other chores upon him. They would almost certainly disrupt his work.

And he was way behind.

He glanced back toward them, the *padrone* and his son. Sergio was looking at him again. Suspicious. As if to say, *Don't think I don't know what you are doing. That you're trying to take my place.*

But if Sergio thought that, he was wrong. Renzo didn't want Sergio's place.

He wanted his own.

• ◆ •

"Lorenzo, did you hear me?"

He sat bolt upright, tried to pretend he had not just nodded off on the bench at the table. But Mama had twisted away from the oven to frown at him, and he could tell by her look that she knew.

"Lorenzo, when did you leave for the glassworks last night? Tell me the truth. Was it midnight again? Don't even try to lie to me; I will know."

"Yes, Mama," he said. "But—"

"But me no buts. What have I told you of this? Do you listen only to humor me? Do I get any respect from my only son? Any at all?"

Renzo sighed. "Yes, Mama."

"Yes, you listen? Or yes, you will obey?"

"I listen, Mama." He turned to her, looked straight into her worried eyes. "I do."

"Still you are determined," she said, "to leave long before you ought. To deny yourself hours of sleep and put yourself at risk. Your father would not approve of this, Lorenzo. He would not."

Renzo sighed. This was true. In his mind he could hear Papà's voice: *The glass will not give up its secrets to a man who is not alert, and it may well cut or burn him.* But now, three days before the New Year, Renzo didn't have the luxury of sleep. Just two months until the test, and he still had far too much to learn.

The first time he'd been tested, Renzo had failed miserably. The glass had slumped in his hands; it had spilled on the floor; it had cracked; it had splintered; it had burst. The few cups and bowls that had survived his clumsiness had been lumpish, crooked things, fit only to be returned to the crucible.

It was true that he had been grieving and had not been able to fully mind his work. It was true that he had been tense, with so much at stake. In all of Murano this was the only glassworks that had offered him work after Papà had died. The others wanted nothing to do with his family, nothing to do with the disgrace.

But none of that mattered. What mattered was that he had failed.

The *padrone* had been disappointed. Angry, even. Renzo realized that the *padrone* had counted on Renzo taking up the blowpipe and beginning to produce forthwith. Maybe he had hoped that Renzo had brought some secret skills learned from Papà, who had been *padrone* of a rival glassworks.

Mama had begged the *padrone* to give Renzo a lowly job so that he could practice at night, and to give him another test when a year had passed.

The *padrone* had consented, grudging Renzo a pittance for his work, enumerating the skills he expected Renzo to master. More skills than could be claimed by any apprentice

Renzo had ever heard of. Skills nearly impossible to learn on his own. In the meantime Renzo had his other duties, and was not to interrupt the glassworkers to ask for help. No one — not even old Taddeo, who fed the fire at night.

Renzo suspected that the *padrone* enjoyed watching his old rival's son perform menial chores. If Renzo could prove that he could do a master's work for an apprentice's pay, well and good. If not . . .

If not, he would never get the chance to apprentice. He would be a drudge forever.

Now Mama set three steaming bowls of stew on the table. She called for Pia, who was feeding the chickens in the yard. Pia skipped into the cottage, threw her arms around Renzo, and settled herself lightly on the bench beside him. Mama gave him a pointed look, as if to say, *See who else you are jeopardizing with your foolishness?*

If she only knew, Renzo thought, what jeopardy they were in. How much he still had to learn, how slow his progress. How impossible it was to learn what he needed to know without an extra pair of hands to assist him. If she could only see how the glass wobbled at the end of the blowpipe, or hardened before its time, or sagged and dropped to the floor.

But he couldn't bring himself to tell her.

A shaft of sunlight slanted through the window and warmed the goblet at his father's place, making it glow like gold. Mama set four places at the table every meal, as if she expected Papà to come striding through the doorway, twirl her in his arms, and sit down to carve the roast.

"Renzo, did you hear me?" Pia looked up at him reproachfully.

"No," he said. "I'm sorry. What did you say?"

"I saw the bird children. In the marketplace today."

Bird children? He saw it again in his mind's eye — the girl's summoning look, the bird following, seeming to perch on her shoulder before they disappeared into the fog and the dark.

"Bird children?" he asked.

"The ones who talk to birds! They tell them what to do."

"What do you mean, 'They tell them what to do'?"

"I saw a boy call five pigeons from a rooftop. They flew down to his arm."

"That's no great feat," Renzo said. "Those birds are gluttons; they'll do anything for food."

Pia was indignant. "There was no food! And then a littler boy stood on the other one's shoulders, and he held out a basket, and a big bird flew by and took the basket in its claws. It flew all around above the *campo*, and then it gave back the basket to the boy."

Bird children. Performers.

Renzo looked at Mama. "Do you know about this?" he asked.

She regarded him, half-amused and half something else, something he couldn't quite place. "Of course," she said. "And you would too if you didn't live so deep inside that head of yours."

Renzo opened his hands in silent admission.

"They came to Venice in the summer. A few adults but mostly children, I think. They did tricks with their birds in the Piazza San Marco, and were a good amusement, I hear tell."

"But why have they come to Murano? What happened?"

"Winter happened. They slept in doorways, cut purses, begged for food. They wouldn't stay where they were told. They kept their birds with them, uncaged. They were . . . indecorous. The Ten were not pleased and took steps to let them know they were not welcome in the city. Apparently the children scattered to the four winds, and two or three of them fetched up here."

Mama rose from her bench, cleared the bowls from the table.

The girl's face rose up again before him; Sergio's voice echoed in his ears:

A drudge for the drudge.

And a new thought began to glimmer in Renzo's imagination. What if *she* could chop wood, stir the melt, and feed the fire? What if she could act as his assistant? She could bring new glass from the furnace, so he could attach a handle or a stem to a glowing-hot cup or bowl.

But . . .

Females were *never* allowed in the glassworks. Worse still, she was a foreigner. If she were caught helping him . . . Disaster!

Still, there was no one else he could ask. A grown beggar would be dangerous, and there were no other homeless children that Renzo knew of. And, among people who lived here — impossible. In the world of glassmaking in Murano, everyone knew everyone. Word would get round to the *padrone* that Renzo was asking for help, which the *padrone* had expressly forbidden. But this girl . . .

She was a stranger, an outcast. She had come to the glass-works for warmth, for a safe place to shelter. If he offered food as well, in exchange for work . . .

Surely she'd leap at the chance!

Wouldn't she?

From outside the window he heard a rippling of water and the scrape of a boat against the wall of the canal. Then voices: a wife greeting her husband, children greeting their father. The weariness pressed down on him again — seeping through his scalp and into his shoulders, into his heart. The sunlight had shifted away from the table to huddle in a small corner of floor. He looked at the goblet at Papà's place — a goblet Papà himself had wrought. It stood gray and dim and cold.

Renzo remembered rising with him before sunrise every morning. They'd break their fast and walk together along the quiet, dark canals to the glassworks where Papà had been *padrone*. Renzo had labored over one pitiful artifact after another, not keeping any but returning them to the pail when they were done. Listening to Papà tell him that there would never be a greater glassmaker than Renzo himself would be, that he had the eye and the hand and the heart for greatness, that he would bring honor to the family, that they would build on Renzo's legend for centuries.

And Renzo had believed him. The maimed little things he'd returned to the pail troubled him not at all, even though he could see that they were abortions. Because he'd believed his father, believed with all his heart that his prophecy would come to pass.

He believed it still.

Papà's curse had been fulfilled. Why not his prophecy, too?

3.

A Drudge for the Drudge

The idea clamped on to him like a rat on a string of sausages:

A drudge for the drudge. Such a simple plan!

Renzo lay on his cot, listening to rain rattling on the roof. He had dozed but briefly, and then awakened in the dark, his mind restless, astir.

Perhaps, he thought, he could contrive a way for the girl to slip into the glassworks every evening. It would have to be after the daytime crew left, and the man who mixed the batch—but before Renzo himself arrived in the middle of the night. He could leave the shutter closed but unlatched when he left for the day. Who would ever notice? And deaf old Taddeo likely wouldn't hear her come in. She could steal in through the window; she could stay warm and dry in the little storeroom while Taddeo, none the wiser, fed the furnace and nodded off in the heat.

Renzo jumped up, wrapping his blanket about him. He padded across the cold floor tiles, following the red-orange glow of embers to the fireplace. He paced before the fire, warming one side, then another.

He would have to watch her, make sure she wasn't a thief or a spy. He would have to judge whether she could keep a secret. He would have to send Taddeo home early; someone else would have to chop wood and feed the fire. And it was possible the girl would refuse to work at all.

But still. Maybe . . .

Renzo stared into the fire. He ached to take up the blowpipe, to stand in the heat of the furnace, turning a lump of molten glass into a vase or a goblet or a plate of such surpassing beauty that people would stand before it and gape in mute astonishment.

When he had watched Papà at this work, it had seemed a kind of sorcery. But Renzo knew it was a sorcery that must be earned, early and late, by diligence and hard labor — labor he could not do without help.

A drudge for the drudge.

But how could he find her to make his offer? Would she return?

If only he hadn't thrown those stones! If only he had talked to her, or . . .

A wind gust shook the house. The rain grew suddenly violent; it thundered on the roof. A damp chill prickled at his neck, his shoulders. He shivered.

This storm, though, was all to the good. She would be *forced* to seek out shelter.

Wouldn't she?

He tiptoed to the bedroom, opened the door a crack, peered inside. Dimly he could make out the shapes of Mama and Pia on the bed. He hoped Mama was asleep. She'd be distressed that he was leaving so early, well before the midnight bell. But there was no point in his staying here, wide awake.

He waited. Mama did not stir.

He shrugged on his tunic and found the pouch of food Mama had left for him. At the door he pulled on his boots and cloak. He fastened the cloak pin at his neck, fingering its smooth silver surface.

Papà's pin.

Now off to the glassworks. If the shutter had been repaired, he would unlatch it and leave it ajar. If not . . .

She might be in the storeroom right now!

A drudge for the drudge!

She was homeless. Likely hungry. Surely cold.

How could she refuse?

•   •   •

Taddeo sat hunched on the *padrone's* bench. His wrinkled eyelids drooped; his mouth hung open; a string of spittle dribbled down his grizzled chin. But the fire blazed hot in the furnace, so he must not have been sleeping long.

Renzo searched the rafters but saw no sign of the kestrel. He listened, but heard only the roar of the furnace. He peered back toward the storeroom door, in the deep shadows, untouched by firelight.

Taddeo snorted, startling himself. His arms thrust out;

his eyes popped open. He blinked at Renzo a moment, and then the long, thin folds of his face settled into an expression of reproach.

"I . . . couldn't sleep," Renzo said.

"Nor I," Taddeo grumbled. "People standing over me. Waking me up. Can't close my eyes for an instant."

"Listen," Renzo said. "Have you seen or heard anything unusual tonight? A bird, maybe?"

"A bird?" Taddeo looked puzzled. "I never seen no bird. Seen, nor heard one neither. Birds, they can be very quiet. It's not always you can hear a bird." He narrowed his eyes, peered up at Renzo. "Why do you want to know?"

Renzo hesitated. He didn't want to tell him about the girl. Didn't trust him, entirely. "I thought I heard something the other night. Likely it was rats."

Taddeo shivered. "Rats! I dislike 'em, rats. Better it be a bird." He unfolded himself slowly, rising to his feet. He moaned—a protracted *ooh*, and then three staccato *aah*s. A little louder and more dramatic than necessary, Renzo suspected.

"Why don't you go home now?" Renzo said.

Taddeo twisted round to stare at him. "Now? What hour is it?"

"Not yet midnight, but you look weary. I can feed the fire."

Usually Taddeo stayed to tend the fire after Renzo came. He was not supposed to leave before dawn—the *padrone* would not like it. In a couple of hours, though, Taddeo would offer one ailment or another as an excuse. He would whine for a while and then depart.

Renzo never told. Taddeo wouldn't stir himself to help Renzo, but he often hovered and criticized his every move. It was easier to work when he was gone.

But now Taddeo seemed suspicious. "Why?" he asked.

Because I have to talk to her. Because I can't wait to see if she's here.

Renzo shrugged. "You . . . just seem weary," he said again. "You, um, deserve a little rest."

Taddeo narrowed his eyes. He stepped toward Renzo, brushed his hand across the shoulder of Renzo's cloak. "Wet," he said. "You'll send me out in the pouring rain, will you? And me with the bone-ill that hates the damp?"

Renzo squelched his exasperation. No matter what you did, Taddeo would find something to complain about.

Taddeo shook his head. Muttering, he shuffled across the wide floor of the glassworks and out into the dark.

Renzo watched until the door shut behind him. Long ago Taddeo had been one of the most sought-after assistants on Murano. They said there was no one quicker; they said he never missed a thing. But now, with his eyes and ears grown dim and his body slow, he was reduced to hauling wood.

Renzo plucked a torch from a wall cresset. He lit it in the furnace and headed back toward the storeroom, beyond the stacked crates of finished glass and into the gloom. He breathed in the acrid smoke, tasting burnt pitch at the back of his mouth. Carefully he pushed open the door. The torch flame leaped; the chill thread of a breeze whipped across his face. He held the light up toward the window.

The shutter—still hanging from a single hinge. Still unlatched. No one had fixed it yet.

"Hello?" he called.

No answer.

Slowly Renzo moved into the room. Darkness parted before the torch, revealing bags of sand and soda, stacks of folded tarps.

"Are you there?" he called.

He stood. Listened.

The muted roar of the furnace. The crackling of the torch. The *whuff* of wind. The patter of rain.

"I will not harm you, I promise. You nor your bird. I have food. We can share it."

The torch popped. Long, wavery shadows leaped to either side.

No one there.

Renzo searched through the glassworks, talking quietly— about food, about shelter, about warmth. He hunted through the poisons room, then looked behind the woodpile, behind the stacked crates of finished glass, behind bins of stones and glass shards. He stood on a bench, thrust up his torch, and peered into the thick darkness that gathered in the rafters. He stepped down again and, crouching low, scoured the floor for feathers or droppings.

But by then he was certain he would not find them.

There are times, Renzo knew, when you can feel a

presence, or an absence. If you pay attention, if you strain your senses out past the edges of your skin, you can sense whether there is another being breathing silently in a room with you.

The glassworks felt empty tonight.

Renzo had come to like being alone in the glassworks. When he was alone, working the glass, he could imagine Papà there beside him. Giving him encouragement. Giving him advice. But now he felt hollowed out, bereft.

"Hello?" he called again. "If you're there, please come out. Hello?"

4.

The Marsh Boy

Five days later a messenger came into the glassworks. The *padrone* looked up from his work. "Well?" he demanded.

He had been more than usually harsh all morning, snapping at Sergio, criticizing his work, calling him lazy and sloppy and slow. Though Renzo wouldn't have hesitated to take Sergio's place, he couldn't help feeling a bit sorry for him.

"The shipment's here," the messenger said. "The quartz."

Ah! Renzo looked at the *padrone*. Someone would have to go to the dock, pick up a load of the quartz-rich sand required for the finest glass, and return it here.

"I'll go," said Sergio. Surprising no one. Who wouldn't crave a respite from his father after such a morning?

The *padrone's* scowl deepened as he regarded his son, considering his request. It was well known that Sergio took suspiciously long to return from such errands. It was said that he tarried through the marketplace, trading stories with fishermen, coaxing marzipan or fruit from the vendors, flirting with pretty girls.

Usually Renzo looked forward to the times when Sergio went out on errands, because there was a chance that *he* might be asked to take up the blowpipe and assist the *padrone*. But now Renzo longed to go out himself. He had searched the glassworks in the small hours of every morning, but the girl had not returned. He had searched the marketplace every afternoon when the glassworks had closed for dinner. Still, few people were out and about at dinnertime; he'd seen no sign of the girl.

But if he could get away now, he could take delivery of the sand and detour through the marketplace at the height of business.

"No," the *padrone* told Sergio at last. "You have too much to learn, and you're too slow in learning it. You stay with me. Renzo will go."

Sergio muttered under his breath; Renzo tried to hide his elation. He fetched the handcart from its place in a far corner of the glassworks; in a trice, he was out the door.

Tattered clouds blew in across the lagoon. The water was gray and ridged and sullen; even the seabirds looked cold. Renzo hunched against the rasp of the January wind and pushed the bulky old cart toward the Faro dock, maneuvering it awkwardly through alleys crowded with craftsmen, servants, magistrates, and fishermen. He kept a sharp lookout for signs of the girl—a tattered cloak, a dark tangle of hair, a kestrel nearby.

In vain.

The ship lay rocking gently, serene above the hubbub all around it. Porters, hefting heavy burlap bags and barrels, wove in and out among the crush of sailors and peddlers and dogs. Carters shoved through the throng, making for the ship; a donkey drover pushed back in the opposite direction, herding his braying charges toward town. Merchants haggled over stacks of cargo, a knot of sailors laid wagers on a cockfight, and troops of small boys ran screaming through it all.

It could take an hour, Renzo guessed, to push this clumsy cart through the press and take his turn to receive the heavy bags of sand. By then it would be dinnertime, and Mama would be expecting him.

But what if he went hunting for the girl now and returned later? By then much of this crowd would have dispersed.

He headed for a nearby patch of marshland, the empty cart rattling on the paving stones. He shoved it through the reeds at the dry edge of the marsh until he came to a clump of sedge. He hid the cart within it.

Then he hastened toward the marketplace. He wandered, searching, among the knots of shoppers at the stalls—the butcher's, the farmer's, the confectioner's, the baker's.

Not a green-eyed waif among them.

He eyed the drifts of pigeons pecking at the paving stones. Gulls soared and cried overhead, and on the rooftops, here and there, he spied a blackbird or a sparrow or a lark.

Not a kestrel in sight.

Renzo sighed. What now?

Pia had said that the bird children were performing tricks. They would want a crowd to watch them, to offer food or coins. Where else might you find a crowd?

The *campi*.

He set off, running now, for the gathering places outside the main churches on the island. First the church of Santo Stefano. The girl wasn't there. Next the church of Santa Chiara. No luck there, either. His hopes rose as he approached the basilica of Santi Maria e Donato. There, in the *campo* outside, a cluster of well-fed matrons stood gossiping. The usual assortment of pigeons and gulls clucked and strutted across the pavement. No kestrels. No raggedy children with birds.

Renzo felt all within him sag. He leaned against a pillar, breathing hard. Sweat had begun to dry and cool beneath his shirt. The group of matrons dispersed; a fine rain began to fall.

It was time to fetch the cart and return to the dock for the sand. He had already been gone too long.

• • •

By the time he reached the marshland, the rain was pelting down in cold, heavy drops. He followed the trail of trampled reeds to the clump of sedge. He peered beneath it . . . and blinked.

The cart had been upended.

He looked about him. No people. No animals that he could see, save for birds. Nothing but the backs of a few scattered warehouses, and then marsh, stretching out to the lagoon.

He bent down, hooked his fingers over the edge of the cart, and yanked, tipping it over.

Something fluttered up into his face. He swatted at it, and it veered off — a long-legged, speckled bird — swooping low above the rushes.

Something cried out.

Renzo looked down. It was a boy. Small. Curled on the ground. Wearing a tattered cloak. He gazed up at Renzo with wide, startled eyes.

Green eyes.

Bright green.

Like the girl's.

"Hey!" Renzo said. "Do you — "

The boy leaped to his feet and bolted. He cut nimbly round the cart and ducked into a wall of reeds. Renzo lunged for him, caught him by the collar. The boy lashed out and struggled to get free, but he seemed only six or maybe seven years old — about Pia's age, Renzo guessed. He clamped an arm about the boy's middle and held him close. "Stop," Renzo said. "I won't harm you. Just — "

"Leave go!" the boy wailed. He flailed about and kicked Renzo's shins — surprisingly hard, considering he had only rags for shoes.

"I'm looking for a girl," Renzo said. "She had a kestrel with her. She is maybe thirteen years old, and her eyes are green, like yours. Is she your sister? Your cousin?"

"No!" the boy said, launching a new volley of kicks with his sharp little heels.

"She was hiding in the glassworks. I only want to talk to her; I promise not to hurt her bird. Do you know where I might find her?"

"No! Leave go!"

The boy gave a sudden lurch. He sank his teeth into Renzo's arm. Renzo cried out; the boy twisted from his grasp and plunged into the reeds.

Renzo let him go. The boy soon disappeared. But a speckled wading bird with long, red legs erupted from a tuft of rushes and skimmed low over the marsh in the direction the boy had gone.

◆ ◆ ◆

Later, after he had delivered the sand, after he had apologized to Mama for being late for dinner and caked with mud, Renzo pondered his encounter with the boy. The bright green of his eyes. The strips of ragged cloth stitched to the shoulders of his cloak. The bright red legs of the little gray-brown wading bird. Clearly this boy was one of the bird children. Renzo had frightened him; he had seized him, held him against his will.

The girl would never trust him now.

But in the small hours of the following morning, shortly after Taddeo had left the glassworks, Renzo heard a fluttering up above. He whirled around. A slender figure stood behind him in the gloom. She stepped into the light of the furnace and pointed a blowpipe in his direction, wielding it like a spear.

"Back with you," she said. "Stay back!"

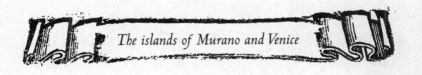
5.

The Dungeon

The little owl flew south over the marsh at the rim of the island and angled into the edge of the wind. One leg dragged on him a bit—the leg with the weight tied on. He tucked it up tighter and adjusted his wings. Soon the sounds of land faded away behind; he tilted in the air currents, drinking in the clear taste of sky. He followed the thin thread of kenning across the wide water—pumping, pumping his wings—until another island drew near, an island thick with glimmering lights and buzzing with the sounds of men. And now the kenning grew stronger, until it thrummed in his bones. The owl flitted between the encroaching cliffs of buildings; he swooped low over a ribbon of liquid moonlight. Then he slipped between iron bars and hurtled down into the dark.

. . .

The bird startled them, brushing by. Its feathers did not touch them, but they felt a stirring of air and glimpsed a quick gray blur in the moonlight before the bird shot between the window bars of the second-floor landing and disappeared down the dark stone passage to the cells below.

The guard named Guido spoke first. "It isn't a crime," he said. "Birds may come and go as they please."

The guard named Claudio replied, "True."

"They can't be faulting us for birds," Guido said. "We're not the jailers of birds. And our job is to prevent escape. Those who wish to *enter* the dungeon of the Ten, welcome to it!"

Claudio chuckled. "Yes," he said. *"Benvenuto!"*

Voices drifted in, faintly, from outside. In a moment Guido heard the wake of a passing boat—the splash of waves, one after another, against the sides of the canal below.

There was a problem, Guido knew, with his argument. True, they were not the jailers of birds. They were the jailers of men and of women. But if a bird were to go in and out, carrying messages for a prisoner, and if this were to be discovered . . . Well, excuses counted for nothing with the Ten. Less than nothing. Even reasonable excuses. Heads could roll.

His own head, for example.

Ordinarily it would not occur to Guido to be suspicious of a bird. Pigeons from time to time found their way into the dungeon. Once he had seen a wren, deep inside, pecking at crumbs on the floor. But this one tonight had seemed a *purposeful* bird. Not just fluttering in by chance but arrowing straight through the passage as if it knew exactly where it was going, like a dog sent to fetch a stick.

The bird had seemed no larger than his own hand, but

its head was wide. An owl, a tiny owl. And this was the third time Guido had seen it since the woman had arrived.

The bird woman.

Might she be a spy . . . or a witch?

"I didn't see a message capsule," Guido said. "Did you?"

"No," Claudio said.

"She couldn't be sending messages," said Guido. "Where would she hide the ink?" It was true that they hadn't actually searched her person when she'd come in. The way she'd looked at them . . . No. They had not wanted to touch her. But they had thoroughly eyed her over. "We would've seen an ink pot if she had one," he said. Though possibly not an ink stone—but Guido didn't want to think about that.

"Just so," Claudio said. "We would have seen."

Guido sometimes wished that Claudio brought more to the discussion. Talking with Claudio was like having a conversation with a wall. He did not argue or contradict, and yet the exchange was somehow unsatisfying. Was he dim-witted? Guido couldn't tell. It might be instead that he was canny.

It might be that he was a spy.

Guido glanced at Claudio—the hooked nose, the pitted brow, the thin frizz of hair. Claudio's eyes lay deep in shadow, lit neither by moonlight from the window nor by the torches set in cressets behind them on the wall.

Unreadable.

"On the other hand," Guido said, "I've seen owls like this twice before since the woman came. Maybe one of us should go down and search her."

Claudio nodded sagely. "Maybe."

"Good," Guido said. "Then I'll do the rounds, and you look to the bird."

Claudio did not answer. He opened the pouch at his waist; he shook something into his hand. A ducat. "*Cristo* or doge?" he said.

Blast! "No, you go on to the woman," Guido said. "You'll be done in two shakes. I don't mind the rounds. Truly! Go on!"

Claudio did not withdraw his hand. "*Cristo* or doge?" he repeated.

Guido silently groaned. "*Cristo*," he said.

Claudio tossed the coin, caught it, slapped it onto his wrist. He removed his upper hand and held out the coin for Guido to see.

In the moonlight Guido beheld the dim shapes of the old doge and San Marco.

Blast!

◆　　　◆　　　◆

The moonlight evaporated behind him as Guido descended the narrow stairs to the ground floor. The harsh glare of his torch sent shadows lurching across the walls. He smelled damp stone and burning pitch and, increasingly as he walked, other, more unpleasant things. Excrement. Sweat. Fear.

Sounds echoed strangely in this place—moans and murmurs, and from time to time a shriek. You couldn't tell if the sounds came from a cell nearby or from another, far away.

Guido reached the bottom of the stairs and set off along the dark corridor. He searched the floor for feathers or droppings—signs that a bird had flown past. The stench thickened; his gorge rose sour in his throat. Farther along, the passage forked and twisted, but he knew the way. He peered into the small, barred openings in the doors of the cells—the thief huddled in his corner, the madman pacing and muttering, the murderer with the scar on his cheek.

No bird. But he hadn't truly expected one. Until at last, he crossed the threshold to the women's part of the prison, and came to *her* cell.

She sat cross-legged in the center of the floor in the patch of light cast by the small oil lamp. Despite her age she held herself as straight as a gondola pole. Guido felt for the key on the ring and thrust it into the lock; the door creaked open. Cautiously he stepped inside. The woman turned to regard him, unafraid. There was nothing of the evil eye about her gaze, but it seemed someway unnatural to Guido, disturbing in its calmness.

He held up his torch and surveyed the cell—the floor, the walls. The stonework was rough; here and there a block thrust out beyond the others, forming a niche where a small owl might perch.

But no. It wasn't there.

Or at least he couldn't see it.

Still, the torch couldn't penetrate every dim pocket of gloom. And she might have hidden the bird inside her cloak. Or behind her. In the corner. On the floor.

She watched him with those eyes of hers. Those bright green, witchy eyes.

Guido was torn. She could likely curse him with a glance, that one. If he forcibly searched her, bad things could happen. He pictured himself with boils all over his body. With one arm broken and hanging. He pictured himself dead.

On the other hand, there was the Council of Ten. If she was sending messages, and they found out . . .

Guido cleared his throat. "Stand," he said. "Step to one side."

Slowly, she rose and moved over. Such a sliver of a woman! It seemed unmanly to fear her so.

Guido crept nearer. "Take off your cloak. Hold it up, then set it on the floor."

Silently, she obeyed.

"Now lift the pail. Let me see behind it."

She did.

There was nothing behind her, nothing in her cloak, nothing behind the waste pail. Nothing that he could see, though the torchlight didn't penetrate the thick shadows massed in the far corners of the cell.

But Guido had had enough. He edged backward, not taking his eyes off the woman. He slammed her cell door behind him, locked it, and hastened back along the passage. When he had nearly reached the stairs, a sound drifted to his ears — a run of high, clear, fluted notes, echoing eerily down the corridor.

The owl.

Guido shivered. Something so chilling about that sound!

Should he go back?

No. He'd never find it.

Since the day she'd arrived in the dungeon, the old woman hadn't given him a lick of trouble. But he would heave a sigh of relief when she was gone from here—whether banished or hanged, it was all the same to him.

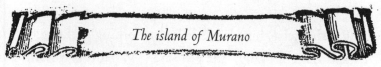

6.

Skin of a Bubble

Renzo gaped at her. Then, "You're here," he said.

She didn't budge, neither to acknowledge that he'd spoken nor to turn aside the end of the blowpipe—still aimed straight at him.

He set down the *tagianti*, filled with a strange, sharp gladness. He moved toward her, away from the blistering heat. From habit he had unlatched the shutter, though he had nearly given up hope of her return. "Did the boy tell you I was looking for you? Because—"

"Get back!" She brandished the blowpipe.

Renzo halted.

Her face looked just as he remembered. Pale, heart-shaped, small-boned. Surrounded by a tangle of dark hair. Almost elfin, she seemed. And those eyes: bright green, unnatural. She wore a ragged, threadbare cloak with strips of fringed and tattered cloth sewn to each shoulder. Like the boy. Her foreignness— wildness—struck him now, more forcibly than before.

He peered up into the shadows of the rafters and made out the shape of the small, dark bird.

Was this wise, his plan? He knew nothing of her.

"You came looking," the girl said. "What d'you want?"

If he said "work" right away, she might flee. "I, ah, want to help you," he said. "To give you shelter and food——"

"Don't lie. You've no cause t' help me. What d'you want?"

She had an odd accent that he couldn't identify. Renzo turned up his palms to show he held nothing in his hands. "Truly, I want to help."

She thrust the blowpipe at him. "No. You don't. There's none that purely wants to help — not ever. Not 'less they're kith or kin. And any who says elsewise is a liar. So I ask you: What d'you want?" She took a soundless step toward him. He glanced down at her feet and saw she had wraparound rags for shoes, like the boy.

She was shivering.

It came to Renzo, of a sudden, how her life must be. Begging and stealing food, sleeping in dark corners. Looked down upon by respectable citizens, and driven off when it suited them. Perhaps from time to time some had *claimed* to want to help her. Men, perhaps. Perhaps they had betrayed her . . .

The furnace heat beat at his back; he grew warm — too warm.

"Help me keep the fire and stir the melt. And help me with the glasswork itself, when I need a second pair of hands."

"Why me?" she demanded. "So you can play at being master? So you can have a slave to toy with?"

"No! It's not that. It's——"

She narrowed her eyes. He felt her slipping away from him.

"There's . . . no one else," he admitted. Hating that he had to say it, that he had to show her his need.

"Why not? What of the day workers?"

"I can't ask them."

"Why not?"

"It's a long story."

"I've got all night."

Renzo glowered. What business was it of hers?

But she was backing away. Leaving.

"My father . . . ," he began.

She hesitated. Flicked the blowpipe as if to say, *Go on*.

"My father was the *padrone* of another glassworks, one of the finest on the island. I want his skill, his mastery. I want to carry out his . . ." *His prophecy. His legacy.* But he *wouldn't* tell her that.

"So you're wanting t' be a big man, like your father."

Renzo bit back a sharp retort.

"Whyn't you work there, then?" she asked. "In your father's glassworks?"

Because it no longer existed. Because it had to be sold to pay off the debts. Because . . . The old glassworks swam into his memory, ravaged and bare—stripped of its iron tools, its shelves, its bins of sand and frit and soda. Even the furnaces were gone, taken apart stone by stone by stone and reassembled elsewhere for another *padrone*.

"He died," Renzo said. "And now I have to prove myself

here. There's to be a test in a couple of months, and I've got much to learn. I'm not allowed to keep the other glass-workers from their work, their sleep, or their families, and I'm not allowed to bring outsiders in."

"*I'm* an outsider."

"Yes, well. I'm breaking the rule."

She regarded him for a long moment. He breathed in deep, waiting, filling up with the familiar smells of wood smoke and melting glass.

"Why *me?*" she repeated softly. "You could smuggle someone else in here, a friend or —"

"If a friend stole in here night after night — even if he told no one — his family would sooner or later catch him leaving or notice he was gone. And then the secret would be out. But you —"

"Oh, no one'd miss *me*. At least none who matters. Is that it? And I can't be telling your secret, 'cause if I did, your constables or your thugs would come for me. Is that what you think?"

Her voice had gone harsh. He'd angered her. But what could he say?

Slowly he nodded. The furnace roared behind him. His bloodbeat throbbed painfully in a spot just above his right eye.

"Well, then," she said, "show me what work you're want-ing from me, and I'll think on't."

Renzo let out a silent breath.

The girl cast a glance toward the rafters. The kestrel flut-tered down out of the darkness. It alit on a strip of tattered cloth on the girl's shoulder and trained a wild black eye on Renzo. Something . . . odd about that bird. Some bond between it and the girl, more than just the bond between performers.

The girl feinted at Renzo with the blowpipe. "My bird stays here with me. And if you throw rocks at her again or harm her howsoever, I'll run you clean through."

He didn't think she could. She didn't look strong enough. He would have bet a week's wages that he could grasp the blowpipe, wrest it from her, and pin her against the wall.

But still, with the bird glaring as if to pluck out his eyes, and the girl herself so wild and strange . . . He wouldn't want to try.

◆　　◆　　◆

She did not set down the blowpipe straightaway but kept it pointed in Renzo's direction while ordering him about.

First she demanded food. He hadn't brought an extra portion this night, not imagining that she would come. But Mama had packed him a small repast, wrapped up in a napkin: sausage, cheese, and a hunk of barley bread.

The girl took the food—all of it—but did not eat. She backed away from Renzo, still holding the blowpipe before her, and set it on a shelf near the door.

"Show me the work," she said.

He did. He chopped alder wood and fed the fire, show-ing how to tell from the color of the flames when it was hot enough and when it must be fed again. He moved in close to the furnace and, as waves of heat leaped out and threatened to blister his skin, stirred the melt in the crucible with a long iron rod. He stepped back, strapped a strip of wood to the front of his right thigh, and held out a hand for the girl's blowpipe.

She eyed him levelly, refusing to give it up.

He sighed, took another blowpipe from the rack, gathered a mass of molten glass from the crucible, and rolled it back and forth on the stone *malmoro*. Then he sat on a bench and, resting the blowpipe against the strip of wood on his thigh, spun the pipe. With his free hand he picked up the *tagianti* and pulled at the glass to elongate it.

All this he did while explaining what he was about, at the end of the girl's well-aimed blowpipe. Mostly she stayed behind him; he couldn't see her while he worked and had to twist round from time to time to talk to her. He began to wonder if she was paying heed to him at all. He began to wonder if she had any intention of helping him, or if she only relished watching him work, treating him as her slave.

Who was whose drudge now?

The next time he looked back, she had slumped down on the *padrone's* bench, eyes shut, the tip of the blowpipe resting on the floor. The bird, now a speckled gray puffball on her shoulder, had tucked its head beneath a wing.

Was she listening? Had she heard a single word he'd said?

Renzo sagged, feeling all his hopes collapse within him. How had he ever imagined that this half-wild, ignorant girl could be of use?

"Go," he said. "Take the food, I don't care. Just go."

She didn't stir.

He moved toward her and reached for her shoulder to shake her awake.

The kestrel roused and hissed at him. Its eyes, with dark vertical stripes beneath them, were eagle-fierce.

Renzo drew back. Who knew what that bird might do?

The girl, now awake, lifted the tip of the blowpipe to point at him—but absentmindedly, with no threat behind it. She seemed to be thinking. Then, "Why d'you keep the fire so hot all night? Whyn't just stoke it up next day?"

"Because. The glass won't be right if you don't keep the fire hot."

She frowned at him, seeming unsatisfied. "Why d'you stir the glass? It's already well melted, yes?"

"To prevent seed and cord."

"Seed?" she asked. "Cord?"

"Bubbles," he said, "and stringy lumps."

"Hmm." She chewed her lip, seeming to consider. "And the *malmoro*? For what purpose is that?"

The *malmoro*? She remembered the *malmoro*? So she had been listening, after all!

"To shape the glass, make it even."

"But then you go pulling at it with those pliers. Doesn't that do the same?"

Renzo wasn't certain which was more annoying—when she paid too much attention or not enough. "No. Both steps are necessary."

She narrowed her eyes at him, chewing her lip again. She

pointed at the smaller furnace, a little way across the floor. "Is that for when you're making little things?"

"No. That's the *calcara*. It's for the first melt."

"The first . . . You mean, you melt the glass twice?"

Renzo nodded.

"Always?"

"And often more than twice."

"Why?"

"To get rid of impurities, to add certain ingredients, to make the glass more workable and consistent."

These were basic questions that she asked—things well known in the glassmaking world, not things a spy would wish to know. Still, Renzo felt his irritation rising. What was this, an inquisition? She was supposed to be listening to him—learning—not questioning the ways of the trade.

"So many steps!" she said. "I'm thinking you could cut one or two to save time."

"No step is too many! You don't understand. We pull vessels from the fire and shape them with our breath, as fragile as the skin of a bubble. No pits or bumps or nicks must mar them. They must be perfect, without flaw."

She quirked an eyebrow, regarded him appraisingly. "So," she said, "it's not only your wanting t' be a big man, like your papà. You crave to make them . . . beautiful."

Renzo shrugged, discomfited. He had said too much. Revealed too much. Not of glassmaking—of himself. "So will we do this?" he demanded.

For the first time he saw a smile flicker across her face.

She feinted at him with the blowpipe. Playfully now. The kestrel hissed at him again, flapped its wings.

Renzo flinched.

"I'll ponder on't," the girl said. She stood, set the blow-pipe on the stand beside the other iron rods. She picked up the napkin of food from the shelf and headed for the door. There she turned to face him. "Next time bring more food. Unless you're wanting t' go hungry again."

7·

A Shadow in the Trees

Pia!" Mama dropped back, away from Renzo, forcing the line of departing churchgoers to bend its course and flow around her.

Renzo scanned the crowd for Pia. He caught sight of her as she handed a coin to a ragged beggar who hunched against the wall beside the path.

"Pia," Mama called again. "Come here!"

The beggar closed his knobby fingers about the coin. Pia smiled at him, then hurried, half-skipping, half-dancing, to join Mama and Renzo.

Mama took Pia's hand and firmly tugged her along the path. "You were supposed to put that in the alms box. If you don't put the coins where I tell you, I won't give them to you anymore."

"But he's hungry," Pia said.

"The church will take care of him," Mama said. "If you squander our money on beggars, we'll soon be hungry too."

Renzo recalled a time when Mama had a quick smile and a spare coin for beggars after mass. Now the corners of her mouth turned down in a habitual worried frown, and twin furrows etched themselves between her eyebrows. She never spoke to Renzo of money, and he didn't know how long theirs would last. But he knew that unless he got himself an apprenticeship, his family would certainly go hungry, in time.

If only the girl would return to the glassworks! He hadn't seen her since two nights before, when she'd said she'd consider his offer. He hoped he hadn't scared her away.

They turned off the path, squishing across the sodden grass toward a group of somber gravestones standing in a row in a corner of the churchyard. Tree branches sagged with the weight of the chill rain that had fallen earlier. The air was fragrant with the sharp smells of the cedars and the sea, and gravid with rain yet to come.

It was no longer new, the stone they sought, but showed a year's worth of weathering — a dullness in the surface from the mottled crust of mud, drips of cedar resin, and tiny pockets of moss that clung to bumps and crevices at the top and sides of the stone — a kind of settling-into-the-earth that made the marker seem permanent and natural, not so raw. The carved words and numbers were crisp, though, as if they had been cut out this very morning.

ANTONIO LORENZO DORO. 1457 — 1496. RIPOSA IN PACE.

Papà.

Renzo's heart shrank to a hard, sore knot in his chest. Papà's face, in memory, had grown dim. But Renzo could see his father's hands as if they were before him still. Large, muscular hands, with patches of thick, yellow calluses, as stiff as the horn in a lantern window and begrimed with ancient dirt. Then there were the burns—one on his left thumb and another a puckered, crescent-shaped scar on the back of the selfsame hand. *That* time Papà had had to go bandaged for two weeks; he had nearly bitten off the heads of his assistants until the dressing came off and he could work the glass again.

Now another hand, small and smooth, slid into Renzo's. Pia gazed up at him.

As busy as he was, Renzo hadn't been the comfort to her that he should have been. He squeezed her hand. "Well, Pia. We have work to do. Come with me and help."

They cleared away the scattered leaves and branches on the grave; they plucked out the stubborn, withered weeds that sheltered in the lee of the stones. Then Mama spread a folded cloth upon the ground; they knelt there together as she prayed.

She prayed for Papà's soul—that he had found his way through purgatory and into heaven, that they would all meet him there one day.

But she did not pray for Renzo's uncle Vittorio, who was surely also dead. By now the assassins would have found him.

The priests, thought Renzo, they say we must forgive. Yet how do you forgive someone who has stolen your father? Someone who has recklessly thrown away all he built up, leaving you pitied or shunned by neighbors, leaving you nearly destitute and wholly bereft?

How can it be right to forgive such a one?

Damp wicked up through the cloth and into Renzo's

knees as Mama prayed. Something hard poked his knee from beneath the cloth; he shifted to find a comfortable position, remembering the quarrel in the old glassworks. Uncle Vittorio raging at Papà for taking credit for *his* designs. Papà bellowing that *he* was *padrone*, that everything in the glassworks was made in his name. Vittorio retorting that they should be equal partners, share the burden. Papà shouting that Vittorio had little to contribute.

Renzo had crouched behind the woodpile, wanting to clap his hands over his ears, but he couldn't help but listen. Then the pitcher, hurtling across the space between them. The *thud* as it hit Papà's brow. The cry of outraged pain, the shattering glass. Then Papà's curse, ringing out across the glassworks:

"Damn you, Vittorio! God keep you from me; may I never lay eyes on you again."

That night Vittorio had left. Knowing full well that glassmakers were not allowed to leave the lagoon, that they must stay within the borders of the republic to guarantee they wouldn't spread the secrets of the glass. Knowing full well that by leaving he was risking his own life and destroying the family's honor. Knowing full well that because of him Papà would be a pariah among the other glassmakers.

And after that . . .

No, Mama never prayed for Vittorio. Never mentioned his name.

Still, Renzo knew, lifting his bowed head to regard the tombstone, that Vittorio had never intended *this*. He was headstrong, quick-tempered, careless, but never before had the assassins exacted such a price. The one who left . . . *Him* they would seek out and kill. But never his family. At least never before.

Renzo recalled how Vittorio used to play his lute for him and Pia, regaling them with silly songs that made them rock with laughter. "Another, Uncle!" they would plead. "Uncle, please?" Vittorio used to sneak them sweets that Mama did not approve of. He had loved sweets, and had the waistline to prove it. Renzo recalled how, when he was small, Vittorio would take him up on his shoulders and let him ride. As if Renzo were a great explorer, like Marco Polo, astride a tall stallion. Both of them — horse and rider — laughing all the way to China.

"Amen." Mama rose to her feet; Renzo and Pia did likewise. Mama picked up the cloth, brushed it off, folded it. A wind gust lifted the branches of the cedars, turning up their pale undersides and loosening the frigid rainwater that had clung to them since nighttime. A spray of droplets rattled down. Something stirred in there, among the trees, half-hidden behind a wide trunk.

Renzo stared.

It was a shadowy figure — a man — not easy to make out in the sun-dappled gloom. Standing perfectly still.

The hair rose on the back of Renzo's neck, and the familiar fear came upon him, the fear that came when a man stood too long near their house; or when a footfall sounded behind him in the dark; or when, in the marketplace, some-one gazed at him too long.

The shadow turned, headed back through the trees.

Something familiar now. Impossible, but familiar.

"Wait!" Renzo called. He started after the figure, hastening through the wet grass between the graves.

"Lorenzo!" Mama's voice was sharp. "Renzo, stop! Stop right now."

Reluctantly he did. The shadow vanished among the trees.

Mama caught up to him, her face tight with anger. "What were you thinking?" she demanded. "Have you gone mad? You mustn't go seeking trouble—not ever." She took him by the shoulders, shook him. "Lorenzo, look at me. Do you hear?"

He pried his gaze from where the figure had disappeared. He blinked at her. "Yes, Mama," he said. But he turned toward the far side of the churchyard wall, where in a moment the figure reappeared. It climbed over the low wall, crossed the path, and slipped into a dark alley between two houses.

Renzo had not seen his face. Only his gait.

Familiar.

Was it only because Renzo had been thinking of him?

But surely, even if he had managed to escape the assassins, he wouldn't return now, bringing danger to the family. No. As reckless as he was, he still wouldn't do that.

Still, it struck Renzo with such force of recognition, that gait. The gait of one who in time past had been a great, tall stallion, laughing all the way to China.

8.

Letta

Renzo thrust the stick of alder wood into the fire and was just reaching for another when he stopped, straightened, stepped away from the heat.

She was here.

Some disturbance in the air had alerted him, or maybe the sound of breathing, masked by the roar of the fire. He could not have said what told him, only that the back of his neck began to prickle, and he knew.

A shadow glided across the floor, and halted. Renzo sought along the flickering darkness to the root of the shadow, and there she stood—the girl—the little kestrel on her shoulder.

"Did you bring food?" she asked.

"Yes."

"Show me."

Renzo led her to a cool, dark corner of the glassworks, away from the heat of the fire. The napkin lay on the small shelf where he always kept his dinner. He opened it to show her the hunks of sausage and cheese, the small loaf of bread.

He had told Mama that he grew hungry in the small hours before the others came; she'd been giving him more food than before. He'd felt a pang of guilt; Mama would likely eat less herself to compensate.

But he would make it up to her, he told himself. If this girl would help him. If he could pass the test.

"I'll be needing more," the girl said.

"It's all we can spare!"

"I need more, for true!" The girl picked up the ends of the handkerchief, knotted them together, then set the food on a shelf by the door. With a quick flick of her eyes, or perhaps some signal unseen by him, she sent her kestrel fluttering up to perch on a high rafter.

He would have thought that a hungry girl would eagerly snatch at the food, gobble it down. But she didn't eat a crumb.

"Well?" she said. "What now?"

He breathed out a silent sigh. He hadn't been sure until that moment if she was going to run off with the food or if she'd come to work.

"What's your name?" he asked.

"What's yours?"

"Renzo." He took off his gloves. Held them out to her.

She hesitated. Then, taking the gloves, said, "Letta."

He waited while she pulled on the gloves, which were way too big for her hands. He gave her a few sticks of wood and walked beside her to the furnace. She had watched him feed it before, but she'd never gone in close. Now she would feel the heat licking at her in waves so ferocious, it would seem as if flesh were melting off her bones. She would feel the moisture being sucked from her eyes, feel her eyeballs grow granular and hot. He was accustomed to it, but she . . .

Her eyes set to blinking; the sticks wobbled in her hands. She thrust them into the opening and quickly backed away.

She turned to him, her face set, determined. "More?" she asked.

He nodded. "Until the fire is hot enough."

Renzo watched at first, but after a while left her to her work. He cut up more wood. Added it to the pile.

When there was sufficient wood to last, and the fire well stoked, Renzo began to school her in the proper role of the assistant. He wanted her to affix the end of the long, iron *pontello* to the bottom of a glowing-hot glass vessel he had shaped with his breath. He wanted her to hold the *pontello* until he took it from her, so he could shape the vessel. He wanted her to bring him new molten glass to attach, so he could make handles, or a stem, or a base.

Though Renzo had practiced with his father, there were many skills he'd never mastered. He made a point to study the *padrone* at work whenever he could. But it was one thing to watch others create and another thing entirely to create on one's own. The mind may grasp the work, but the body must know it too, know it without thinking—in the memory of the hands, in the wisdom of the eyes to judge from the color of the glass when it's time to blow it, to spin it, to warm it again in the furnace.

He looked at Letta—ragged, skinny, dirty. She did not

demurely avert her eyes like a good Venetian signorina but glared back at him, as if to say, *What are you staring at?* Could he train this contrarious girl so that she would be of use to him? Or was that too much to hope for?

"Listen," he said. "When I tell you to do a thing, you have to do it at once. No questions. Just do as I say."

She shot him a skeptical glance.

"There's no time for explanations when the glass is hot. You've got to watch me closely, be alert to whatever I need."

"Be your slave, you mean," she muttered.

"The glass gets hotter than you can imagine! You have no idea how dangerous it is!"

She shrugged and turned away.

Clenching his jaw, Renzo laid out the tools he would need to make an urn with handles. He told Letta their names and functions. At last he picked up the blowpipe. "Are you ready?" he asked.

She nodded.

Renzo gathered the molten glass on the end of the pipe, and began.

But she did not stand where he told her to stand, not even when he reminded her, not even when he shouted. She knew a better place to stand, she said. He bumped into her; she trod on his heels and toes. She did not hold the *pontello* as he told her to, nor affix it to the bowl in the instant he asked. "I do it in my own time," she said. "It can wait."

"No. It *can't!* That's what you don't understand!"

Again and again she ignored him — when he told her to

hand him the *pontello*, when he told her to affix the molten glass just *here*, when he told her to step away pronto so he could rewarm the vessel above the fire.

And so it went — six times, seven times, eight.

After the twelfth time, Renzo set down the pipe, slumped onto a bench, and buried his face in his hands. She was willful, stubborn, unmanageable. He should just send her away.

A tapping sound. He sat up, looked at Letta. She was drumming the *pontello* against the floor, lips pinched in impatience. "What now?" she said.

Renzo shrugged.

"You're just going to quit?"

"If you won't listen, you're worse than useless to me. You might as well take your food and go."

The tapping stopped. "Don't be shouting at me. I'm not deaf. I hate when people shout."

"I'm not shouting!"

"You are!"

"Because you refuse to hear me!"

"You confuse 'hear' with 'obey.' Maybe I heard but had a better idea. Did you think of that?"

"A better . . ." Renzo stared, stunned at her ignorance, at her audacity. "What do you know of glass that you could even dream of having a better idea than the masters, after they've poured their very lives into the glass for centuries!"

"What d'*you* know of it?" she retorted. "You're a drudge. A wood chopper. A fire feeder. If you knew anything howsoever, you wouldn't be playing with glass in the middle of the night. They'd let you help them in the daylight, for true."

Rage struck him mute. What did *he* know? Well, he'd show her.

He picked up the blowpipe, thrust it into the crucible, and gathered an orange-hot blob of molten glass. He rolled it on the *malmoro*, then huffed gently into the pipe. The glass bellied out, just so. He leaned again toward the furnace, into the wall of blistering heat, and spun the glass above the fire, feeling it grow more fluid. He brought the glass out, wheeling away from the heat, and filled it with his breath. He spun it in the cool air to shape it, spun it in the furnace to make it supple, breathed into it, spun it in the air again.

Now he reached for the familiar tools to shape it — *magiosso, tagianti, borsella, supieto* — all the while spinning, spinning, spinning. His hands and arms and feet all had the dance of the glass inside them. His eyes knew from long practice when the glass desired the softening of heat, or the firming of cool air. Knew when it was ripe to be pinched, or pierced, or stretched.

And now the glass, spinning overhead at the end of the pipe, had turned into a bowl, small and smooth and curving. Renzo stilled it. Cracked it off the end of the pipe. Smoothed its base and mouth, and set it on the marble shelf.

It was a simple thing. No handles or stems to connect. Easy enough to make without an assistant. Renzo had made such bowls for years. Yet still . . .

It shimmered in the light of the fire, the bowl — a lovely, gleaming, graceful thing. Like a poem. Like a song.

Letta gazed at it for a long, silent moment. She turned to Renzo.

"Don't be shouting at me," she said.

"I won't."

"I'll do as you say."

And she did.

9.

Poor, Crippled Things

Even so, the dance went badly. They were forever in each other's way—treading on toes and heels, bumping shoulders and elbows. Once, Letta grazed Renzo's cheek with the cool end of the blowpipe; another time she singed his arm with a mass of molten glass. She warped bowls in the furnace; she spilled hot glass all over the floor; she caved in the sides of urns by jabbing them with the *pontello*.

And it wasn't just she who erred. Renzo's hands seemed to have forgotten all they'd ever known. They spun too slowly and pulled too fast, they attached things in the wrong places, they misjudged angles and distances. Glass burst and shattered on the floor; slivers lodged in their clothes, their hair. Once, a shard nicked Renzo's temple and made it bleed; another time Letta stepped on splintered glass and pierced her feet.

Still, no one tripped and fell, as he had seen happen with some new teams of master and apprentice. Nor did they burn themselves, nor clout nor pierce the other with the *pontello*. And the finished vessels themselves—poor, crippled things — were not quite so ill-formed as they might have been.

Renzo set down their latest effort — gouged, scratched, precariously atilt on its stem — and studied it to see what errors he must learn to avoid. He plucked at his damp shirt, plastered to his body. He wiped a drop of sweat from his eyes.

It was a relatively simple form, a footed bowl. There were many more difficult forms that he would have to perfect to show the *padrone*. And still so much to learn!

Less than two months!

Impossible.

A sudden weakness seeped into his limbs; he stiffened his knees to prevent them from buckling. If he couldn't do better than this, he would never pass the test. Never be a glassblower. He would disgrace his father's memory and condemn his family to poverty.

"'Tis far from perfect," Letta admitted, studying the bowl. She shrugged. "But parts of it are nice. See how it curves, bells out at the lip — "

"It's an abomination." Renzo picked up the blowpipe and swept the bowl into the pail, where it shattered with a crash.

Letta gasped. She kept her gaze fixed on the pail of broken glass, as if mourning the death of the maimed little vessel they had birthed.

•   •   •

By the end of the fourth night's work, they had produced two workmanlike bowls upright on their bases, and a large jug with handles that was not nearly so drunken and listing as the ones that had preceded it. They would attempt another bowl the following night and, Renzo thought, if they succeeded at that, maybe it would be time for a stemmed goblet. He was still impossibly behind, but if they progressed at this rate, perhaps he would not humiliate himself so completely when it came time for the test.

Though, surely he would fail.

Unless the *padrone* saw enough improvement to satisfy him . . .

But in two months Renzo could never learn all that was required.

Unless the *padrone* took pity on him . . .

But he was not a pitying man.

And so Renzo reeled from fear to hope to fear again. The glass, he reminded himself. Just think about the glass.

Still, things had grown easier between him and Letta.

Since beginning his nighttime work, he had come to love the long stretches of solitude in the glassworks. When he could feel Papà's silent presence beside him, helping him. When he could design, in imagination, the exquisite vessels he might make one day. When he could try one thing and another, unobserved — just play.

But now he found there could be comfort in company, too — the presence of another quietly working there beside him, the companionable melodic *clink* of the iron tools above the ever-present roar of the furnace. Letta was not the chattersome type. She knew the art of silence. But she brought in a breath of the outside world: the smell of birds and the sea and the wind above the marsh. Her presence made him feel less cloistered, less alone.

Most nights her kestrel came with her. It perched up in the rafters, away from where they worked the glass. Usually it drowsed, fluffing out its feathers and tucking its head beneath a wing. At the end of every night's work, Letta scoured the floor for feathers and pellets and droppings.

A cage would prevent *that*, Renzo thought. But he sensed that she would not welcome this idea, so he forbore speaking about the kestrel at all, until the first night she arrived without it. When he asked where it was, she gave him a hard, steady glare that told him that he mustn't inquire about her bird—not ever.

Very well, he thought. He didn't truly care. He didn't care if she ever ate the food he gave her—which he never once saw her do. He didn't care if she never ate at all. He didn't care what she did—so long as she came to help him work.

On Letta's fifth night in the glassworks, Renzo was stooping to pick up another log to split when he heard a sound—a sharp rasping noise. A cough?

He stood. Listened.

Rain, drumming on the roof. The roar of the furnace. His bloodbeat pounding in his ears.

He scanned the room, peered deep into the far, dim corners. Fear reared up inside him, twisted into the shape of an assassin, of a spy, of the *padrone* standing in the shadows, preparing to cast him out. Or . . . He remembered the shadow in the trees at the churchyard. Might it be . . . ?

"Did you hear that?" he asked Letta.

"Hear what?" she said. Head down. Tossing a stick into the fire.

The sound again. Clearer now. Definitely a cough — from the storage room.

"There. Did you hear?"

"Hear what?" she said again. Not looking at him.

She knew. Whatever it was, she knew.

A bright flash of rage engulfed him, burned away his fears. If she had betrayed him, he wanted to know how. He took up a torch from a cresset, thrust it into the fire.

"Sounds like a cat," Letta said. "I must've left the shutters open. Stay here; I'll see to it."

"No."

"Don't," she said. She ran to him, took hold of his sleeve. He shook her off, made for the storage room.

"Stay," she pleaded. "You don't have t' know — you don't want to. If you see, you'll have to . . ." She caught his sleeve again. "Please."

He'd never thought to hear her beg. He tore away from her and flung open the storage room door.

A fluttering noise. Something moving on the shelves above; Renzo held up the torch and found them one by one: a crow, a magpie, a sparrow, a marsh hawk.

Something smelled different. A smell of sweat, of loam, of dampness — damp linen, damp wool.

The cough sounded again. Renzo turned his gaze to the welter of lumps on the floor, a floor that should have been bare.

They huddled together—sitting, squatting, lying. Children.

They gazed up at him. He brought the torch down, bathed them each by each in light. Seven children. A long-legged wading bird. A finch.

The children's eyes were green. Bright green.

Every single one.

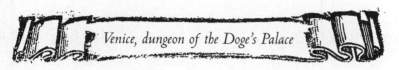

10.

Beware

The old woman felt it long before she saw it. Or rather, she felt her owl, who had been slumbering on her shoulder, rouse and fluff his wings. She kenned with him. Sensed curiosity. Excitement. Recognition.

Welcoming.

She rose painfully to her feet, hips popping, knees creaking as if rusted deep within the joint. The hard stone floor of the dungeon had cramped her muscles into knots; the damp cold crept numbingly into her bones and never left. She paced the perimeter of her tiny cell, stretching out the kinks in her spine.

She felt hope rising warm within her.

The woman stopped. Listened.

Nothing but dungeon sounds. The faint drip of water. The scuttling of a rat nearby. The distant human moans and cries that echoed about the stone walls.

Likely the other bird was still out over the lagoon, for her owl could hear far and sense farther.

The woman's own hearing had dimmed over the years.

Voices had grown thinner, often blurring at the edges, bleeding indecipherably into other sounds. Noises that used to be small and crisp now eluded her altogether. She seldom heard, for instance, the death squeals before her owl returned with some unlucky mouse or vole for his dinner. But her ears themselves now produced a music of their own—a faint, high ringing that robbed her of the peace of silence.

Her sight had faded as well. Yet her sense of smell, perversely, had hung on. In this place losing *that* would have been a blessing. She would not miss the reek of the dungeon, nor the stench of the food they brought her. Crawling with maggots. Encrusted with mold.

Her owl roused again. He flew from her shoulder and perched—shot through with alertness—between the bars in the window of her cell door.

The woman drew in breath. She stood still, eyes fixed on the barred window. Waiting. Remembering.

As the present world had grown dimmer to her, the past had grown strangely bright. Sometimes when she closed her eyes the dead came to her. Her sister and her brothers, her very first owl. Her father's rumbling laughter. Her mother's touch, smoothing her hair, resting warm on the crown of her head. Matteo . . .

Sometimes she felt the pain of their absence—sharp and convulsive, a seizing of the heart. Other times she felt that they were with her still, watching over her. That they had never truly gone.

She had felt so safe back in the far country of her youth,

in the mountains near Grenoble. But then the mobs came, and her people had been forced to flee and scatter.

For her people, nowhere was safe for long.

She'd known that they'd have to leave this place. She just hadn't realized how quickly the noose would cinch tight.

The owl stirred, let out a soft, eager trill. Now the woman could hear a beating of wings. The new bird swooped between the bars and circled in the gloom of the cell, shedding drops of water. It landed at last on the woman's wrist.

It was the one she'd most hoped for. And, tied to its leg, a message.

With practiced fingers she untied the capsule. It was wet. The new bird fluttered up to the sill, beside the owl. The woman unrolled the thin strip of parchment and squatted by the little oil lamp the guards had given her — a lamp that stank vilely and produced more smoke than light. She cursed her old eyes as she strained to decipher the tiny script. Fortunately, the rain had not penetrated to the ink; it had not smeared.

She read it twice.

Well. Her granddaughter had ever had her own ideas. Not biddable, that one. But she herself had never been biddable, even as a girl. She read the message a third time, to be sure she had understood it aright. Then she tore it into bits and strewed them among the heaps of dust and grime that collected in the corners of her cell.

"Take care, Letta," she whispered. "Beware."

11.

Blot Out the Sun

The children watched him, their faces standing out dimly in the gloom. Faces empty of hope or fear, but only waiting. As you would wait for a far-off storm to cross the sky. As you would wait for it to blot out the sun.

Rain drummed on the roof, rattled at the shutters. The wading bird with long, red legs fluttered up to perch on a shelf near the others. It tucked up one foot, then turned to regard Renzo with a quick, hard, pitiless eye.

Renzo turned to Letta. "What's this?"

"They're cold," she said. "They've nowhere t' shelter come nighttime."

"You let them *in*?"

She stared back at him. Didn't reply.

He glanced at the children. The weight of their gazes dragged at him. And those birds! He had seen the falcon and the wading bird without thinking too much about them. True, it was odd, keeping the birds about, uncaged. Especially the way Letta seemed to send her bird thither and yon without whistle, gesture, or word. But now, seeing all these birds together . . .

Wild birds.

Somehow, when he'd heard about a troop of children who performed with birds, he'd thought of doves, or maybe pigeons. But these wild birds, and the children's green eyes . . .

He shivered. They were more than odd. They were spooky.

"Make them go. They can't stay here. They'll ruin everything."

"Ruin?" A note of anger crept into her voice. "What d'you know of ruin? Ruin's nothing to do with your precious glass. It's three days with nil to eat, it's every night wet and shivering in a marsh, it's disappearing and nobody hears of you ever again."

"You know nothing of me," he said. "Or of my family, or of what we've endured."

"I know you're feverous t' prove yourself. I know you're to be tested. I know you're needing my help."

"I'll find someone else, then!" Though, where else, he wondered, could he find someone so quick to learn? Someone who required no pay? He sighed. "Be reasonable," he said. "If I let them stay, they'll be discovered. You could hide easily enough alone, but with all of *them* . . ." He'd lose his position. He'd have to give up the glass, forever. And Mama and Pia . . . "My family will starve; they'll be put out in the cold."

"And what of *my* family?" She gazed at him, a flat, dead stare — as cold as the wading bird's eye — and he heard the echo of his own words. As if it would be unthinkable for his own family to starve or be left out in the cold, but tolerable for these children. He felt a stab of embarrassment, of shame.

"These are . . . your brothers and sisters?"

She hesitated. "They're *family*."

He wasn't sure what she meant. Not, he suspected, what *he* meant by the word. But in any case these children were nomads. This was the life they were accustomed to. It was none of Renzo's doing.

"There must be somewhere else they can shelter," he said.

"There isn't."

"There must be."

"There's only the marsh, and it's colder by the day! Things're happening now. Things that you, in your cozy little world, can't imagine."

"You know nothing of my world! You're so full of your own righteousness, you think you're so smart, but it's *you* who know nothing."

A long, hacking spasm sounded from the storage room. Renzo peered through the doorway, lifted his torch to see. It was the boy, the one from the marsh. He was shivering. None of them had shoes, Renzo saw — just rags, like the marsh boy and Letta. Some few cloaks there were, but most of the children wore nothing over their tunics, patched and worn and tattered. Their limbs looked nearly as thin and bony as the legs of the birds perched on the shelves above. Tangled hair hung across the children's eyes; grime splotched their faces; their noses dripped.

The shutter flew open in a sudden gust of wind, banged against the casement. The torch guttered, sending black shadows flickering across the room. Needles of rain slanted in, tapping on the casement, on the floor. Renzo felt the chill creep inside, felt it thread in invisible currents across his body.

"They'll take sick in the marsh," Letta said. "They'll catch the lung fever and die."

He breathed in, filling his chest with a sinking heaviness. Bad enough that he was sheltering the girl, but if anyone caught the children here, the children and their birds . . .

"Only in the storage room," he said. "Only when you're here. And they'll have to cage their birds—"

"No."

"They must."

"We never cage our birds. Not ever."

"Well, then you'll have to clean up after them—every single feather and dropping."

She nodded.

"Promise," he insisted.

"I promise," she said. "For true."

But Renzo had a dark foreboding that he'd started down a path he'd soon regret.

◆　　◆　　◆

For a while they honored his wishes. Sometime after midnight Letta would watch for Taddeo to leave. Then she opened the unlatched shutters and helped the children crawl in through the window to the storeroom. She settled them in and then went to work with Renzo. Every morning, before she left, she and a few of the older ones cleaned up droppings and feathers.

Still, it distracted him—frightened him—knowing they were there. Knowing he could be interrupted at any moment. Imagining what would happen if someone came into the glassworks and found the children.

Sometimes, just when he was on the verge of attaching a stem to a base, or perfecting the lip of an urn, a small voice would call out, "Letta?"

She would say, "Wait!" and help Renzo finish what he was doing. But the rhythm had been broken; he could never quite get it back. Even after Letta returned from whatever crisis had required her attention—a bloody nose, a full bladder, another coughing spell—he seethed inwardly at the interruption. She always explained to him what had happened, but he didn't want to know their troubles, nor even their names. Didn't want to be *responsible*.

But the work went on, faring better than Renzo had dared hope. Letta seemed to have a natural grasp of what the glass wanted. Or perhaps it was that she could read Renzo in the eerie way that she and her kestrel seemed to read each other.

He quashed his curiosity. He didn't want to know.

In any case, over several days they went from molded bowls with ribs to fluted drinking cups to long-stemmed goblets. Moving in and out of the wall of pulsating heat, the bright orange glow of molten glass before them, the roar of the furnace in their ears. Learning the wordless dance of master and apprentice—shuffle and pivot and dip. Soon Letta knew exactly where to place the tools so that his hands could easily find them. She knew to bear the cooling glass to the furnace to make it pliable again whenever he took a drink of water. She knew when to breathe into the blowpipe while, with the *borsella*, he coaxed the glass into a pleasing shape.

But early one morning a week after the children had first appeared, Renzo heard a different sound from the storeroom. Another cough—but hollow and deep and long. A frightening cough. Letta, holding the *pontello* while he worked the lip of a bowl, looked away from the glass and turned her head, listening.

It came again, the cough. Again. And again—this time longer, so long that Renzo looked up too and waited for it to end, the glass cooling on the end of the *pontello*.

"Letta?" A girl, maybe nine years old, poked her head through the storeroom doorway.

Letta handed Renzo the *pontello*. He cracked the cooled glass into the bucket, lit a torch and, for the first time since the children had come, followed her to the storeroom.

It was the boy Renzo had seen in the marsh. Letta squatted beside him as he lay cradled in the lap of another girl who looked exactly like the one who had summoned them. Sandy-haired, snub-nosed. Twins, no doubt. The girl with the marsh boy looked frightened. Behind her the heap of huddled children shivered. A cold draft leaked in through the shutters; clouds of frozen breath rose up and vanished among them. The marsh boy coughed again, one long, racking spasm after another. Renzo held his breath, waiting for the cough to end. His eyes were drawn, absurdly, to the sick boy's feet. One was swaddled in rags but the other was bare—a tiny, dirty foot—its toes curled up as if to shrink itself smaller still, as if it wanted to disappear.

Without a word Letta scooped up the marsh boy in her arms, pushed past Renzo, and carried the boy to the warm space near the furnace. The wading bird fluttered after.

Renzo followed. "What are you doing?"

Letta ignored him. She turned round to the others, who stood watching, crowded in the doorway. "Come here," she said.

One of them, the girl who'd been caring for the marsh boy, stepped out of the storeroom. Two or three others crowded behind.

"No," Renzo said. "Tell them to stay."

"Come here," Letta said to them. "It's warm."

Slowly they tiptoed out of the storeroom. They stood in an unkempt huddle at the edge of the glassworks floor. Birds perched on their shoulders, their wrists, on the tops of their heads: a crow, a finch, a sparrow, a magpie, a hawk.

Wild birds.

Wild children.

"No," Renzo said. "You promised! Make them go back."

Letta didn't deign to respond but motioned impatiently to the others. "Come!" she said.

Renzo wanted to shake her. How dare she defy him! If it weren't for him, they'd all be out in the cold.

The marsh boy coughed again—heart-stoppingly long.

And now the others were coming, a tattered, grimy, shivering procession of them, padding silently across the floor.

There was the girl who had held the marsh boy, with her twin sister close behind. Then came a dark-haired boy, maybe seven years old, holding the hand of a boy who looked about four. A light-haired girl, maybe two or three years old, tripped along behind them. Catching sight of Renzo, she fastened herself to the leg of the boy who came last—maybe a year or so older than the twins?—and rode on one of his feet.

They all eyed Renzo warily as they passed, then gathered around Letta and the marsh boy. There, blinking at the furnace as at the blazing summer sun, their expressions were nearly identical. Of incredulity. Of bliss.

"D'you want to toss us out, then?" Letta asked. "You're bigger than any of us. You could try."

Renzo imagined himself picking up one ragged urchin after another, dragging them across the wide floor of the glassworks, thrusting them into the frigid storeroom and shutting the door behind them.

The marsh boy coughed, hollow and long.

Renzo sighed.

A fragment of Sunday's mass echoed in his ears: *Suffer the little children.* All at once he felt ashamed that he had denied them this wasted pocket of warmth. Warmth that meant so much to them, yet cost the *padrone* nothing.

But still . . .

"I can't have birds flying all over the glassworks, knocking things over, strewing feathers and droppings. If you refuse to cage them, at least tie them down. With jesses or something. Like falconers do."

"No need for jesses. The birds'll stay put."

"Stay put where?"

"On their shoulders."

"You're saying these children have trained wild birds to sit still on their shoulders for hours at a time?"

She shrugged. "Not *trained*, exactly, but . . ."

He didn't want to know. Events were moving, taking on a life of their own, despite his best efforts to control them.

And so it was especially unfortunate that in the small hours of the following morning, a little after Taddeo had left for home, the glassworks door opened and he came shuffling back inside. He retrieved his forgotten scarf from the hook near the door and was turning to go, when his glance swept across the wide floor near the furnace. He pulled up short, eyes wide.

If the situation had not been so dire, Renzo might have laughed. Taddeo scuffed a little way toward the children. The birds surged all at once toward the rafters in a burst of fluttering wings. Feathers rocked down from above. Taddeo turned to Renzo as if he could not believe what he was seeing and wanted to confirm that it was not a mirage. He twisted back toward the birds, then the children, who sat silent, staring. Taddeo blinked, astonishment spreading across his face.

"Renzo," he said. "What is *this*?"

12.

Nonno

No one moved. The fire roared and popped. Then Taddeo sucked in a deep breath and screwed his face into the expression Renzo knew so well: deeply aggrieved, working up to a dire complaint.

Renzo knew he ought to say something, cut him off now, come up with a credible lie. He cast about for the right words, but they escaped him. He could only stand there, waiting, sick with dread.

"Nonno!"

Renzo twisted round to see who had spoken. It was the light-haired girl who had clamped onto the boy's leg. She jumped to her feet and began to lurch through the welter of children. When she reached Taddeo, she threw her arms about one of his legs and stuck there like a burr.

Taddeo swallowed his complaint; his mouth hung slack. He blinked down at her, bewildered.

Letta flicked a glance at Renzo, then stood, held out a hand. "Grandfather, come sit here by the fire." She whispered something to the tallest boy, who hastened to Taddeo, pried the little girl off his leg, tucked her under an arm, and led Taddeo to the *padrone*'s bench.

"Sit, Grandfather," Letta implored. "Rest."

Abruptly Taddeo sat.

Grandfather? Renzo was confused. Was he the little one's *nonno*? But how was that possible?

The light-haired girl held out her arms to Taddeo. The boy set her down on Taddeo's skinny legs. The girl leaned into Taddeo, nestled against him. She thrust her thumb into her mouth and began to suck. Taddeo's arm, seemingly of its own accord, gently curved itself about her, supporting her.

Letta motioned for the other children to come, murmuring to them as they passed. Slowly they gathered about Taddeo. She motioned for them to sit at his feet. Taddeo gazed in wonderment.

Renzo caught Letta's eye. "Do you know him?" he whispered.

She shook her head, biting her upper lip. "The little one *thinks* she does. As for the others . . . He's very like someone they once knew. Someone who died in . . . Well, where we were before. And," she added, "they do as I say!"

When Taddeo recovered from his surprise, he would begin to ask questions. For which Renzo still had no acceptable answers. If Taddeo told the *padrone* . . .

The marsh boy coughed again, not so frighteningly as before. Letta watched him a moment, then turned to Taddeo. "Is there aught we can do for you, Grandfather? Fetch you a cup of water? Rub your feet?"

Taddeo's eyebrows shot up in astonishment. But he quickly recovered himself; his face crumpled into its habitual cast of grievance and pain. "My shoulders," he whined. "My old shoulders, they pain me." He looked down at the children, to gauge the impact of his words.

The twin girls came around behind him and began to rub his shoulders. Taddeo closed his eyes and leaned into their hands, moaning. But one eye opened and slewed toward Renzo, as if to make sure he saw. As if to reproach Renzo that *he* had never treated Taddeo with the kindness and deference he so richly deserved.

Renzo let out a deep breath, releasing the fear that had seized him.

For now it seemed that Taddeo would not tell.

But it was only a matter of time.

◆　　◆　　◆

"Gabriella?"

Renzo heard his mother's name as he stepped out of the church and into the cold winter sun. Pia slipped over the threshold to join him; he took her hand and peered back inside, whence had come the voice. The darkness was a balm to his eyes, which had been blinded by the dazzle of sunlight flashing off stone and water. Beside him Mama stopped and turned back too. Renzo breathed in the lingering scents of incense and candle wax, waiting for the man who had said Mama's name.

"Gabriella, it *is* you." A man approached them through the sea of departing worshippers. His face—long and thin and homely—was unfamiliar to Renzo.

The man fell in beside Mama, on the side opposite from Renzo and Pia. He was tall—the top of Mama's head reached only to his chin—and walked with a slight stoop, as if he preferred not to tower above others. He shuffled beside her down the steps, leaning into her, speaking so softly that Renzo could not make out his words among the voices of the other churchgoers. Mama smiled, replied. The man was touching Mama's elbow, Renzo saw. A light touch, well within the bounds of courtesy, but there was something about it that Renzo didn't like. As if, were Mama to stumble, it was this man instead of Renzo who should rightfully check her fall. And the way he called her Gabriella, instead of Signora Doro. . . . It was disrespectful. He had no right.

"Lorenzo," Mama said, when they reached the path, "do you remember Signore Averlino?"

Renzo shook his head.

The man's face creased into a smile. "It's good to see you again, Lorenzo." A sweet smell clung to him—a pleasant smell, and familiar, but Renzo couldn't quite place it. He did not return the smile.

"You met long ago," Mama said, "when you were Pia's age, I think. Marcello—Signore Averlino's parents were friends of my parents in Venice, when we were children."

"Why is he *here?*" Renzo said. The question sounded ruder than he had intended, but Signore Averlino didn't seem to notice.

"For my niece's wedding," he said. "She's to live on Murano; I may come here more often now."

"And here is my daughter, Pia," Mama said.

"Pia." Signore Averlino said, bowing to her. "So pleased to meet you."

Pia curtsied gravely.

"Signore Averlino is *padrone* of a carpentry shop in Venice," Mama said.

So that was the smell. Sawdust.

"Carpentry must seem dull work to you, Renzo," Signore Averlino said. "Compared with the splendid art of glass."

Renzo shrugged. Chests, tables, chairs, paneling . . . they were all the same to him. Heavy. Earthbound. Lightless. He felt sorry for men who worked in wood. It was a slow and tedious and pedestrian art. Nothing about it of quickness, of grace. Nothing to test a man's courage. Nothing to fire his soul.

The path narrowed; Mama and Signore Averlino edged ahead of Renzo and Pia, as there wasn't room for them all in a row. Renzo noticed, for the first time in a long while, how pretty Mama was. Graceful and lithe, with hair the color of honey. She laughed now, a warm, low rumble. How long since he had heard that laugh?

A sudden wind gust stirred up sand at his feet and flung it into his face. Renzo blinked and rubbed his eyes. Who was this Signore Averlino to come sniffing around, speaking so familiarly with Mama, taking her elbow, replacing Renzo at her side? Renzo was head of the family now. He could take care of them.

But could he? Things were going slowly in the glassworks.

Far too slowly, no matter how fast Letta learned. The children lurched from one crisis to the next. There were scrapes and cuts and bruises, there were toothaches and stomachaches and earaches, there were tears to kiss away and noses to wipe. And though Taddeo seemed to have taken to the children, perhaps he doted *too* fondly. He no longer went home early. He brought food—more food, Renzo feared, than he could possibly afford to buy. Renzo had heard rumors of pies vanishing from windowsills, of bread disappearing from the communal oven. If Taddeo had stolen them, and if he were caught, and if it were to come out why he'd stolen . . .

"Lorenzo!"

He lifted his eyes from the paving stones and looked up at Mama. "Where is Pia?" she said. "I thought you were watching her."

Renzo felt the heat of shame creep up his face, made all the more humiliating by the patient, concerned gaze of Signore Averlino. *He was but a boy. Couldn't even take care of his little sister. Must be reprimanded by his mother.*

Renzo turned to scan the path behind him. The churchgoers had mostly dispersed by now, though a few black-clad matrons still stood about talking. And there she was, all the way back at the church, holding out her hand to a beggar, perhaps the selfsame one she had given to the week before.

Renzo hurried along the path, skirting the matrons. Above him gulls cried, reaching to touch the sky with their feathertips, teetering in the air. Light glinted off the water, diamond hard. The wind, smelling of salt and fish, buffeted his ears, making them ache with cold. "Pia!" he called, hearing the sharpness in his voice.

She turned to him as the beggar's knotted fingers closed about her coin, the blue-black shadow of the wall veiling his face.

Renzo took Pia's hand and dragged her away. "Didn't you hear Mama last week? You're to put the coin in the alms box. We have none to spare for beggars."

"But he's hungry," Pia protested.

Renzo hauled her back down the path, remembering the night this past week when he had risen to go to the glassworks and had found Mama in the kitchen bent over the accounts, moving stacks of coins around the table.

How much longer could they survive on the dwindling supply of coins and the pittance Renzo made? Even if he became an apprentice, it would be years before he could truly support his family. And what if he didn't pass the test? How could they keep their house, feed themselves?

He glanced back to where the beggar had sat crouched against the wall. But he was gone.

Still, Renzo knew the silent, creeping dread that Mama must have been feeling.

There but for the grace of God went they.

13.

The Shape of Fear

It is possible, Renzo found, to work through fear. You can push it down, hoard it deep inside you, and breathe it into the glass. You can watch the glass swell, grow bubble-thin and gossamer, and know that fear is making it lovely, fear is giving it shape.

With glass, joy is the preferable medium. But fear is powerful, and it will do, when joy cannot be found.

He and Letta worked on through the night, though Renzo knew there was far too little time and far too much to learn. The footed bowl, the long-stemmed goblet, the crested wine flask, the eared jug . . . You could spend years coming to know them. You *must*—to master them. But Renzo did not have years. He had five weeks.

That first night, when the children had come out into the open, their green eyes had followed whatever he'd done, hardly changing in expression whether the glass shattered at the end of the blowpipe, or slumped to the floor, or formed itself into a perfect, symmetrical bowl.

They made him clumsy, the children's eyes. They made

him think too much. Especially with the birds watching too—though, true to Letta's word, they stayed perched on the children's shoulders as if fastened there.

By the next night, he had managed mostly to forget them. He breathed his fear into the glass, and when he looked up, he saw the children curled in a heap together, sleeping like kittens. The cough had swept through them, erupting here and there. But the new coughs didn't sound so dire as the old ones. Even the marsh boy's cough had abated, though he still seemed listless, his cheeks aflame.

The marsh boy. That was how Renzo thought of him. He didn't want to know the boy's true name. He didn't want to know any of their names. He didn't want to care about them.

After a few more nights, as the children grew accustomed to warmth and food, they began to stir and move about. The two older boys handed off their birds and began performing acrobatic tricks to amuse the others—cartwheeling across the floor, or somersaulting one over the other, or the younger one standing on the older one's shoulders and summoning his crow. Renzo cast a worried eye toward the crates and racks of finished glass; Letta barked out an order, and the two boys moved away. Still, there were stubbed toes and bloody feet, pricked by stray bits of shattered glass. There were skinned knees and barked shins. Once, the little light-haired girl shot out of the group and was nearly to the furnace before Taddeo's long arm reached out to snag her and pull her back.

Where you find children, Renzo observed, you will also find mud and mucus, vomit and blood. They wet themselves;

they poke their fingers where they don't belong; they babble; they shriek; they cry.

And through it all the birds stayed close — though they sometimes strayed from shoulders to perch on heads, on wrists, on knees. Birds pecked at cheeks and at strands of hair, they stretched their wings, they scratched their heads, they fluffed out their feathers and napped. Truly, they didn't seem forced to stay put but seemed somehow, mysteriously, *willing*.

Only once did a bird interfere with Renzo's work — when the magpie fluttered overhead and let fly a dropping that sizzled on the hot glass and burst into flame. Renzo cracked the vessel off the blowpipe, flung it into the pail. "Where are these children's parents?" he demanded. Then bit his tongue. Did he really want to know?

"Gone," Letta replied.

He scowled at her, feeling dismissed.

He breathed *that* into the glass too, along with the fear.

Soon some of the older children began to help. The tallest boy, with eyes that drooped at the corners. The twin girls. The sleek-haired boy with the crow. They hunted down stray feathers and pellets and droppings; they chopped wood; they swept shards of glass from the floor.

This eased Renzo's fear a little, but it never ended. Fear sent him vivid waking dreams of shattered cups and bowls, of the *padrone's* angry face, of pulling Pia through the marketplace, begging for scraps.

Renzo breathed . . . breathed it all into the glass.

Late one night, as he hastened through a dark alley on his way to the glassworks, Renzo heard a noise.

He stopped. Held up his lantern. Peered deep into the narrow cave of the alley.

Light shivered across the pavement at his feet and bloomed on the walls beside him. But beyond, darkness clotted thick.

He heard the plash and ripple of waves against the sides of the canal nearby. The creak of straining boat lines. The soft, hollow *thunk* of one boat drifting into another. A scuttling sounded somewhere up ahead — a rat, no doubt — and the soft wing beat of a bat or a night bird. He breathed in the smells of tar, of fish, of salt, of smoke.

Nothing uncommon. No cause for alarm.

He set off again, a little faster.

Renzo never relished his midnight walk to work. As he hunched against the chill, his lantern throwing long shadows before him, he couldn't stop fear from conjuring phantasms of lurking robbers and assassins. Now his heart began to beat faster; he longed to see the glassworks door before him and know he would soon be safe.

In a moment, though, he heard the sound again. No doubt this time — a footfall.

He took off running — but a voice hailed him, a voice he knew: "Renzo!"

He stopped. Turned round, ready to flee at any moment. Above, a corner of moon peeked through tattered clouds, but the alley was dark. He held up his lantern. Light seeped across the stone walls, into niches and corners—across a heap of rocky debris where one of the walls had begun to crumble, over a pile of fish bones, up to a window grille. And then down again, just below the window, not ten paces away:

The shape of a man.

The face of a ghost.

He was thinner than he used to be, and a matted beard hid half his face. But Renzo had no doubt who stood before him now, breathing puffs of frozen steam.

His uncle Vittorio.

Who was supposed to be dead.

"You!" Renzo whispered. He felt tears prickling his eyes, surprising him. He blinked them back; he *wouldn't* let Vittorio see.

Vittorio advanced, seeming to drink in the sight of him. "How is Gabriella?" he asked. "How is Pia?"

"Not well. Because of you!"

"I never thought . . . They've never been so harsh before. Never killed family."

"*You* killed him, as surely as if you'd snapped his neck yourself!"

Vittorio flinched but didn't look away. "I had ideas for the glass, things I wanted to try. He wouldn't let me. Everything had to be *his* way."

"He was *padrone*. Of course it had to be his way."

"He was my *brother*." Vittorio pursed his lips together, shaking his head. "And there was this . . . rage," he said.

"By the time it loosed its grip, I was halfway across the Mediterranean and it was too late. I wanted to go home, but I knew they'd be coming for me."

Renzo felt the fire in him cool and shrink and darken. No, surely Vittorio hadn't intended what had happened. He had acted first and thought later, as was his wont. "But what are you doing here now? You're endangering the rest of us! Can't you see that?"

"I thought I could hide from them—and I did! But I was all alone, Renzo. When you're a stranger, when you can't even speak the language . . . When you don't dare to ply your craft . . . I kept my ears tuned for news from home, and I heard about Antonio. I can't understand it, Renzo."

"They found that letter you sent him," Renzo said. "Where you asked him for help. It was with him when we found him. It was affixed to the wall with a knife."

Renzo saw it now—the tipped-over benches, the shattered glass, the spattered blood on the tiles. And Papà, lying on the floor as if sleeping.

Vittorio turned away. *"Maria santissima."*

"Go. Tonight. Stay away from us."

"But I want to be useful. To Gabriella and Pia and you. There's no place for my mind to rest; every thought is like a knife to the flesh—too painful to abide. If I could but help, I could find peace."

Peace? *He* wanted peace? "What about us? What about the danger you put us in? *You* want peace?"

Papà used to rail at Vittorio for his carelessness, and

Mama had defended Vittorio. Said that there were worse sins. Said that Vittorio's heart was good.

But after Vittorio had left them—left the republic—she too had seen the evils of carelessness. Of doing what one liked, not heeding one's duty to one's family. Papà—though he'd raged at Vittorio, though he'd said things that in the end could not be unsaid—had loved his brother all the while. But Mama had closed her heart against Vittorio forever.

Even if Renzo could have forgiven Vittorio, Mama would not. But now . . . He would put the family in danger because he wanted *peace*?

"Renzo, please—"

"You've come," Renzo said. "You've seen what you have done. Isn't that enough? Now go. You're dead to us. We never want to see you again."

14.

Small, Wet Boy

The glass was balky that night. Renzo couldn't concentrate, haunted by his encounter with Vittorio.

One vessel after another went clattering into the broken-glass pail, until Letta held out a hand and offered to wield the blowpipe herself. "Or maybe Federigo should try," she said, indicating one of the larger boys. "Or Sofia." She nodded at the leg-clinging girl.

It was a jest, Renzo knew. But he did not laugh.

His uneasiness infected the whole of the glassworks. The children, calm and drowsy at first, began to quarrel. Taddeo's pains grew worse, his complaints louder and more plaintive. Even the birds began to flutter and twitch and pluck at their own feathers.

Still, it looked to be no worse than the waste of several hours, though a waste that Renzo could ill afford. Until the marsh boy—who had recovered from all but the last remnant of his cough—broke out of the circle of children and turned the night into a calamity. Renzo heard a thump, a cry, an ominous rattle. He whirled round to see a crate teetering dangerously. He dropped the blowpipe and ran, but too late.

The crate tumbled to his feet with a thumping crash. The wooden lid flew off, and shattered glass spewed all across the floor.

Disaster!

Bits of blue glass glinted in the firelight. He could make out fragments of the goblets' molded bases, tiny ribbed ovals that had adorned the stems, and jagged pieces of what had once been lovely, rounded bowls.

These were the lidded goblets the *padrone* had made the day before. Exquisite things, far beyond the ability of anyone else in the glassworks.

How many had been in that crate?

Renzo counted the knobs for the lids—the only parts that hadn't shattered. Only three, *grazie a Dio*.

But still . . . How could he explain this?

What would the *padrone* do?

A little cough. He looked up to see the marsh boy gazing down at the splintered glass. Renzo took him by the shoulders, shook him. "Don't you ever—" he said. "Don't ever, ever touch anything here again! Do you hear me? Don't—"

The boy broke free and ran sobbing to Letta, who clasped him in her arms and glared at Renzo. They were all watching him now. Wide-eyed. Afraid.

Renzo bowed his head, cradled it in his hands. In a single night he had cut his uncle off from his family and had begun frightening little children. When had he become this person?

He picked up a broom and began to sweep the glass, feeling their eyes following his every move. One of the boys stepped out of the circle and offered to help, but, "No," Renzo snapped. "Stay there. I'll do it myself."

"Oh, you're in for it now," Taddeo told him. "The *padrone* . . ." He shook his head. "He'll be mightily displeased."

There was an understatement. What could Renzo tell him? *It wasn't my fault. It was one of the homeless children I've been secretly sheltering in the glassworks.*

No. He would have to say that *he* had broken the goblets.

He wielded the broom with hard, angry strokes, but his belly felt queasy, leaden. Would the *padrone* banish him from the glassworks at night? Would he dismiss him on the spot?

When at last Renzo took up the blowpipe again, his hands were nearly useless. He told himself to concentrate, that all might not yet be lost. The *padrone* had forgiven an honest mistake before.

But never such exquisite goblets!

And so, when a little while later it was discovered that the marsh boy and his bird had disappeared, Renzo set down the blowpipe, slumped onto a bench, and gave up all pretense of work.

"Federigo! Georgio!" Letta called, turning to the oldest two boys. "Find Paolo. Search the marsh first, then the town."

Renzo rose from the bench. Letta rounded on him. "It's 'cause of you Paolo left. If you hadn't shouted at him . . ."

"Yes," Taddeo put in, shaking a finger at Renzo. "It's all your fault."

"But he broke the *padrone*'s goblets!"

"All you care about's your precious glass," Letta said. "For us, you wouldn't give the skin of an onion. We're just hands and feet t' you, aren't we then, Renzo? Something to hold the glass, something to move it here t' there. "

Taddeo nodded. "Just here to there."

"He was just getting well," Letta said. "And now, a night out in the rain . . ." She turned away from him suddenly, wiped something from her cheek.

Was she crying? He'd never seen her cry. He didn't know she *could*.

He felt a strange, quick pain inside his chest. "Listen," he said.

She made a shooing gesture behind her back. "Just . . . go back t' your stupid glass."

Renzo watched her, wanting to say something but not knowing what. Waiting for her to turn round. He'd forgotten how small she was—willow-slim. He might have said "fragile," if he didn't know better. Her hair, a mass of tangled curls, hung halfway down her back; raveling threads trailed down from her sleeves and the hem of her gown.

He heard the door creak open as Federigo and Georgio slipped out. He heard rain pelting the stones of the walkway and splashing into the canal. He felt the weight of the other children's eyes on him; he heard the echo of Letta's words.

We're just hands and feet t' you, something to hold the glass, something to move it here t' there.

Was that what she thought of him?

And why did he suddenly care?

Uncomfortable, he realized that, except for Letta's, he hadn't known any of the children's names before tonight. He'd never asked where they had come from, or how they were related to one another. He hadn't wanted to know.

He set his blowpipe on the rack, shrugged into his cloak, and made for the door.

The marsh boy—Paolo—hadn't meant harm. He was just being a boy. Taddeo was right: This *was* Renzo's fault. Not for scolding the boy, for letting them in the glassworks at all.

•　　•　　•

It was a cold rain, the kind that gathers itself into fat, heavy droplets that strike your head and shoulders like a hail of tiny stones.

Federigo and Georgio had vanished into a narrow alley, leaving Renzo alone. He walked along the edge of the canal, uncertain where to begin searching.

If not the marsh, where might the boy have gone?

Traces of daylight leaked over the horizon to the east; the streets were not so black and fearsome as before. But darkness still inhabited doorways and niches and corners, any one of which might secretly harbor a small, wet little boy.

A hollow *thump* from the canal. A boat, tethered there. Covered with a canvas tarp. Hmm.

Renzo knelt, unlaced a corner of the tarp. He peered inside.

Oars. A heap of netting.

Nothing more.

He replaced the tarp and stood, surveying the boats. They lined the canal for as far as he could see. Many more, he knew, lay beyond. Still more on the other canals.

Impossible. He couldn't look under every tarp of every boat in Murano!

He let his gaze slide beyond the boats, to the rain-dimpled waters of the canal. Dark. Opaque.

The boy might have tried to hide in a boat, but . . . The image came to Renzo, unbidden: the slip of a foot. A small child falling, swallowed up with a splash. Dark water closing over a cap of dark hair, until the body fetched up later, bloated and white.

"Paolo!" Renzo cried. His voice, panicky and sharp, echoed in his ears until the rattle of rain drowned it out.

He wiped water from his eyes, feeling foolish. The boy wasn't likely to come to his call. Not after the way he'd chastised him. He'd have to start searching, that was all.

But where?

He moved along the canal, looking for a tarp that wasn't wholly fastened, peering into dim alleys as he passed. The rain was relentless. His cloak no longer repelled water but hoarded it, weighed on him as if it were woven of lead. The chill seeped into him, lodged deep in his bones. His feet, benumbed by cold, felt like hard wooden blocks inside his boots.

Once, he thought he saw the boy, but it was only two old beggars huddled in a doorway. Another time he heard a splash on the pavement behind him, but when he looked back, nothing. He wondered if Vittorio was stalking him. Or some other ghost.

After a while, when he looked up, something caught his eye—a square tower, so tall, it split the sky. The campanile by Santi Maria e Donato.

A church. If you were a small, wet boy, you might well take refuge in a church.

Renzo sloshed through the puddles in the *campo*. He pushed open the heavy oaken door and stepped inside. The sound of the rain dimmed at once. It was darker here. Renzo waited to let his eyes adjust, waited until he could make out the dim colonnades to either side, the ancient mosaic floor, the rows of benches before him.

He trod forward, feet squishing loudly in his boots. He scanned the benches.

It was the bird that he saw first—a fluttering motion, a small, gray-brown blur atop long, spindly legs. And beside the bird, a boy-size lump.

Renzo edged along the bench, toward the boy. The bird hopped a short distance away. The boy was sleeping, Renzo saw. His wet hair clung to his scalp. His skinny wrists and arms stuck out too far from his sleeves; his skinny legs and ankles stuck out too far from his trousers. One of his foot wrappings had come loose and dangled toward the floor in tatters. A puddle of water had formed beneath him.

The boy coughed, then buried his head deeper within his arms.

Renzo hesitated. The boy might fear him, might bolt. He leaned over the boy so he could stop him if he tried to flee. Renzo cleared his throat.

Nothing.

He shook the boy gently.

Nothing.

"Paolo," Renzo said.

The boy sat bolt upright, startling the bird. With a harsh *kyip-kyip-kyip* it flew into the air and circled above. Renzo braced himself to prevent the boy's escape — but the boy lunged *for* him instead. Clasped onto him, sobbing. "Sorry," he said. "I didn't mean t' break them. Sorry, sorry, sorry!" He had an odd lisp; his *s*'s sounded like *th*. He seemed to have lost his two front teeth.

Renzo eased himself onto the bench. He let the boy climb onto his lap, cling to him. He put his arms about the thin little body to warm it. The bird fluttered down and alit on the boy's shoulder. It pecked at the hair on his head.

He was so light, this boy, just bones and air. Renzo felt the ragged breathing, next to his own. "Don't fret . . . Paolo," he said. "There's little enough harm done. I'll put all to rights."

There are some lies, Renzo thought, for which you might be forgiven. Surely God would forgive him for this one.

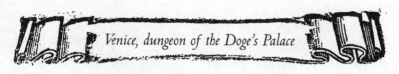

15.

Assassin

He swept into the dungeon like a large, dark bird, the shape of Guido's nightmares: sharp beak, gnarled talons, black cloak flapping behind.

"Where is she?" he asked.

Five women, Guido knew, were currently housed in the dungeon. Five "shes." He did not need to ask which one, nor did he dare. He pointed down the dim corridor and told how to find the bird woman in her cell.

The man did not thank him nor acknowledge him in any way. He glided swiftly down the corridor, pausing only to pluck a lighted torch from its cresset before he rounded a bend and vanished in a haze of smoke and scattered sparks.

Guido let out his breath. So that's how it was to be.

Usually they came at night. They would glide past him, black-caped and granite-eyed. He would never see the body, but by morning the prisoner would have vanished. Sometimes there were signs of a scuffle—a tipped-over waste pail, a broken bench. Sometimes blood spattered the floor. But most of the time, no. Most of the time no trace remained to show that the prisoner had ever existed.

Now he heard Claudio's footfalls, heavy and slow, approaching from the eastern wing. "Was that . . ."

Guido nodded. Even alone they did not like to say it, did not let the word pass, hissing, between their lips:

Assassin.

"Who?" Claudio asked.

"The bird woman."

"Good," Claudio said. "She was trouble. If they caught that bird of hers with a message, the blame would have fallen on us."

This was true. Who knew where the bird went or what it did on its nightly forays? Though the woman couldn't send messages — she had nothing to write with — she could likely receive them. And sometimes Guido had seen another bird in there with her as well. A little falcon.

Yes. She was definitely trouble. And yet . . .

Just the other day, on his rounds through the dungeon, he had peered through the bars in her door. He had seen them sleeping, the woman and her owl. She had sat slumped on the bench, leaning against the wall — head tipped back, mouth half-open, defenseless. Now that she wasn't skewering him with those strange eyes of hers, she hadn't seemed so much like a witch. Even in the faint glow of her lamp, Guido had seen how thin she was, how wrinkled, how frail. The owl, perched on her shoulder, had leaned into her neck, its ear tufts tickling her chin. It was downy, speckled, and tiny. You could hold it cupped in one hand if you wanted to.

Guido blinked, struck by a sudden thought. What would happen to the owl? When the woman . . .

"He won't kill her owl, too, will he?" he asked Claudio.

Claudio shrugged gloomily. "Who knows?"

"But a little bird like that . . ." Guido swallowed.

Surely he would not!

◆   ◆   ◆

In his neat, orderly mind he sorted things into compartments. Family was separate from work was separate from wenching was separate from politics. A place for everything; everything in its place.

Which might be why, he reflected, rounding another bend in the dark corridor, he felt so oddly comfortable in dungeons—despite the clamminess and the moaning and the stench. So many problems here, but each stayed locked in its own separate cell. Things didn't leak into other things. Didn't overlap.

Outside, though, something had overlapped, and it disturbed him. One problem had bled into another unrelated problem, and he needed to know the source of it, needed to know why.

Early that morning, a while before dawn, he had observed the nephew of the missing defector at some distance from his home and the place where he worked. The assassin had followed the boy, hoping he might lead him to the defector, who had been sighted on the island. Instead the boy had met up with one of the bird children who had been chased out of San Marco.

Ordinarily the assassin would have had no interest in the bird children. The Ten had charged him to deal with the defector, that was all. He had dealt with them before — glassworkers who had left Murano, taking their secrets with them. Now he had been given this one particular assignment, and that was all he cared about. Keep it in the box. But the coincidence had pricked his interest. Two entirely separate problems had come together, and one of the two problems was *his*.

He had followed the nephew back to the glassworks. He had seen exactly eight children climbing out a back window — with their birds.

A puzzle indeed.

He had tracked the bird children to the marsh, but they had divided up, and the muck was oozing into his boots. . . .

Children were unreliable, in his experience, at providing accurate information. Even with the application of pain — though, some would disagree with him on that point. But he had neither desired nor needed to go tramping about in the marsh. He knew another way.

Now, just past the threshold to the women's prisons, he peered through the bars of a door and found her. He set the torch in an empty cresset and rubbed his aching hands. Every year they grew more painful. He couldn't keep this up forever.

He opened the leather purse that hung from his belt. Reached inside. Drew out the key.

Officially he was not allowed to have a key of his own. He was supposed to request one from a guard. But one does not always have time to argue with a guard when one requires a key. It was an open secret that those of his profession had their own master keys made; now he did not even bother to ask.

* * *

The woman lay perfectly still until she heard the click of the lock behind her, heard the footfalls fade away down the hall. Cold wicked up through the stone floor and spread into her flesh, into her bones. She could feel that her owl wanted to return to the cell, but she kenned him to stay hidden.

She sat up slowly, painfully. She tipped her head back, pinched her nose to stop the bleeding. The echoing sounds of the dungeon drifted in, nothing out of the ordinary: somebody pacing, somebody babbling, somebody sobbing.

When at last the bleeding ceased, she clambered to her feet. Still shaking, she made her way to the bench and lowered herself, knees creaking, to sit. She leaned back against the stone wall and let out a great, deep sigh.

Everything hurt.

Time was, she could have been knocked to the floor a couple of times and felt only flesh pains. But now her bones pained her too, and all the sinews in between them, and all the organs underneath.

She spit into her hand, thinking to scrub the blood from her face. But her spit was bloody too.

Still, it could have been worse.

Much worse.

Gingerly she touched her nose, explored the shape of it. Likely not broken. He would know precisely how to break a nose, and had chosen not to.

He would know precisely how to snap a neck.

He hadn't asked any of the questions she'd expected when she'd heard the footfalls cease before her door and had glimpsed him through the bars. Questions about spying and witchcraft. Questions about the birds. Questions about where the others were hiding, and where they planned to go next.

No. He'd asked only about a boy, a glassmaker's drudge: How much did the children know about this boy? Why would a glassmaker's drudge be willing to risk sheltering the children and their birds?

She had lied to the man, told him she'd never heard of the boy. Though, in truth, she knew little enough. Only what might be scrawled on a scrap of parchment small enough for a kestrel or a pygmy owl to carry.

He had not believed her. Not quite.

Though, for some reason, he did not yet want her dead.

She summoned her owl from wherever he had hidden himself. Soon he swooped between the bars. Alit on her shoulder. Pecked at a strand of her hair.

She stroked his back with a finger and gave him a comforting ken.

Then she rose from the bench and, with a popping of hip joints and knees, knelt to pull the loose stone from the wall. Some previous guest of the Ten had hollowed out a small hiding place behind the stone; the guards had not yet discovered it. She drew out the quill, the tiny ink pot, and the scraps of parchment. She had smuggled them inside in secret pockets sewn in her clothing—under the knot of her sash, inside the hem of her shift. It was good, though, that she'd found the loose stone. Otherwise the ink pot might have broken when she'd hit the floor. The assassin would surely have found it.

She dipped quill in ink and began to write.

16.

Miracles

"You say you tripped, and fell against the crates?"

The *padrone*, rolling one of the glass knobs between his fingers, shook his head as if baffled. As if Renzo had told him that elves had come into the glassworks and destroyed the goblets. Which, Renzo reflected, wasn't so far from the truth.

"On what, pray tell, did you trip?"

"I just . . . The tip of my boot caught, and . . ." Renzo could feel the lie burning its way up inside him, warming his face. He could feel the heat of the others' gazes upon him—the two other masters, the assistants. He wanted to apologize again, but in the face of the loss of those magnificent goblets, his "I'm sorry" had sounded so feeble, it had almost been insulting. He wanted to say, "I'll pay for them," but that would be another lie. He couldn't begin to pay.

The *padrone* peered down at Renzo's boots, as if the answer to the mystery lay there. From near the furnace came muffled laughter and Sergio's voice: " . . . tripped on air." Renzo clenched his jaw. He watched the *padrone's* face—cold and masked. Papà would have been shouting, waving his arms.

Taddeo plucked at the *padrone's* sleeve. "I saw him do it!" he said. "It was Renzo—none other!"

The *padrone* jerked his arm away. "There's nothing amiss with your boots," he said. "Perhaps you were overweary? Or perhaps . . ." He squinted at Renzo, studying him.

Renzo shifted, uncomfortable. The *padrone* smelled the lie.

"But he did it!" Taddeo said. "No one else! I saw it with these very eyes." He pointed to his eyes, as if their existence proved his point.

"The air got in his way," Sergio said, and chuckled.

Something flashed behind the *padrone's* eyes. He turned his gaze from Renzo and fastened it on Sergio. "You find this amusing, do you? The loss of an afternoon's work?" His voice was neutral. Dangerous.

Sergio reddened. He shook his head.

"You'd best attend to your own work, which has been a disappointment to me. I wonder, Sergio, will you ever be *padrone* here? I do not know."

The air shuddered, a silent thunderclap. Renzo couldn't look at Sergio. The shame was too painful.

The *padrone* turned back to Renzo. Rolling the knob between his fingertips. Calculating.

Words rattled around in Renzo's head; the lie burst out before he could stop it. "I'll pay for them. No matter how long it takes. You can garnish my wages. I—"

The *padrone* cut him off. "No. You cannot. You're a drudge. I tolerate you here only out of pity for your mother, but now I'm done. One week. Take your test, and then . . ."

The *padrone* flung the glass knob hard into the broken-glass pail. He spun round, picked up his blowpipe, and headed for the furnace.

◆   ◆   ◆

One week. Seven days.

Impossible.

Barring a miracle, Renzo would humiliate himself so thoroughly and so publicly that he would never be allowed to work the glass again.

But he had to keep up the pretense. What else could he do?

Could he confess to Mama that he knew without a doubt that he would fail?

No. Not yet. He couldn't.

He told no one.

He arose after midnight, he trudged through the dark streets to the glassworks, he took up the gather on the end of the blowpipe, he worked the glass. Exactly the same as before. Trying to hide the fact that he was a sleepwalker, a ghost. That he was halfway gone already.

Letta seemed softer after he'd found Paolo in the church. She wasn't so quick to take offense, and her eyes, when she looked at him, seemed to have lost their mocking glint. Sometimes she even smiled. But this night, after a while, she began to question him. "You've made three like this

already; whyn't you move on t' the next thing on your list?"
Before long she began to nag: He should not take so long to
rest, he should attend more closely to the work, he should
rescue this cup or that bowl before it was hopelessly lost.

He let the blowpipe slip from his hands. It clattered on
the stone floor, rolled a little way, and came to rest against
the base of the *padrone*'s bench. "It's no use," he said.

Letta frowned at him. "What d'you mean, 'no use'?"

"I mean, I can't do this. I'll never pass."

"So you give up? Just like that?"

He slumped down onto the *padrone*'s bench, head in
hands. "You don't understand."

"I understand you're a coward."

He snapped upright. "I'm not afraid! It's—"

"I know fear when I see it. And I know fear's useless.
Worse 'n useless."

"Listen, Letta. I don't have as long as I thought. I have
one week."

Letta blinked, seemed confused. "But . . ."

"The *padrone*. After the . . ." He flicked a glance toward
the welter of sleeping children, and lowered his voice. "After
the goblets. He changed the deadline for the test."

"When were you going to tell me this?" she demanded.

He shrugged.

"And when the week's done?"

"I fail the test. I'm forbidden from working the glass
after hours. No one will take me as an apprentice. I'll be a
drudge for the rest of my life . . . if I'm lucky."

"And what of us? What of *them*?" Letta stabbed an angry finger in the direction of the children.

Renzo picked out Paolo, curled up among the others. The wading bird had perched on one of his grimy, swaddled little feet. The bird ruffled its feathers, then folded up one long red leg beneath it and tucked its head beneath a wing. The crow turned its head to preen its feathers; a few of the children stirred.

"Taddeo will let you in," Renzo said. "Long after I'm banished, you'll all still be here, warm and cozy by the fire."

Letta snorted. She picked up the blowpipe from the floor and held it out to him.

Renzo looked away.

"I've no respect for people who give up." She thrust the blowpipe at him, reminding him of that first night, when she'd wielded it as a weapon.

"You don't know what you're talking about," he said. "It's impossible."

She fixed him with a searing look. "I know people who've refused to give up in far worse straits 'n yours. There's others counting on them, so they keep on trying. No matter what."

It came to him, then, that the fate of these children rested on her shoulders, just as his family's fate rested on his.

Out of the corner of one eye, Renzo caught a fluttering of wings. The children were waking, watching.

Letta stepped nearer, touched the end of the blowpipe to his chest. "Take it," she said.

Her eyes — so intensely green — reached down into a

deep place within him, and made everything go still.

"Take it," she whispered.

And this time, reluctantly, he did.

.   .   .

Over the next couple of days and nights, a strange thing began to happen. Renzo's life, which had felt like an unending struggle, began to open up to moments of peace, moments when the ordinary events of his days seemed piercingly fragile and dear. He drank in the look of Mama working in the kitchen, her hands deep in flour. He drank in Pia's lively stories about the events of her day. He drank in the glass, all the lovely ways of it. He tried to etch into memory the feel of the waves of heat on his arms and chest and face, the weight of the glass on the end of the blowpipe, the taste of iron on his lips.

He no longer strove to master the glass but only to know it, to play.

More often than before, his gaze strayed to the children and their birds. He drank in the sight of Paolo drowsing peacefully, still coughing a little but not much the worse for his night in the rain. He watched the sparrow and the finch flitting back and forth from one twin girl to the other—Marina, he reminded himself, and Ottavia. He listened to a conversation between Federigo and his marsh hawk, where they *queck-eck-ecked* back and forth at each other, seeming to share a joke. He saw the crow pushing its head against Georgio, begging to be stroked with a finger. He smiled at the magpie, who surveyed the world from its perch atop the littlest boy's head, like a preposterous black-and-white hat.

This bond they shared, the children and their birds . . . it began to seem a bit miraculous. Renzo almost longed for a bird himself.

Once, as Sofia hitched a ride on Federigo's leg, Renzo recalled a pair of tiny, fur-lined boots he'd seen in the alms sack. Pia's boots — she had outgrown them. They might be a little large for Sofia, but she would grow too.

How easy it would have been to take those boots out of the sack and bring them here. And the moth-eaten leggings he had put into the sack, and maybe an old shirt or pair of breeches from Mama's rag basket.

Why hadn't he thought of that before?

Letta he watched as well. The way she pursed her lips in concentration as she affixed the bowl of a drinking cup to the *pontello*. The way she glanced over her shoulder at the children, her eyebrows pulled together in worry. The way she spoke to them — sternly at times, and yet never far from leaping into battle on their behalf.

Tentatively he began to ask her questions. Where had they come from? What had happened to their parents? How had they all come to have birds?

She told him little. They were not a family, or at least not *family* as Renzo understood it. True, each one had those striking green eyes. But not all were related by blood and, with some who were, it was a distant kinship, as with members of a tribe. A few of their parents had died in a plague; she wouldn't tell him what had become of the others. In any case, the children had come to Venice with Letta's grandmother.

What had happened to *her*, Letta wouldn't say. Nor would she tell him much about their bond with the birds. "It's who we are," she said. "Since time before memory. Nobody knows why, for true. It's just"—she shrugged—"who we are."

"But Sofia doesn't have one."

"She's too young. When the time's right, she'll know."

They had no one, no one at all. Letta wouldn't tell where they spent their days, but Renzo thought it must be in the streets and in the marsh. Who would look after them after he failed the test? Once, Renzo had found them shivering outside, crouched beneath the locked shutters—and Taddeo fast asleep and drooling on the *padrone's* bench.

No, they couldn't stay forever. But maybe until the nights were not so cold.

Now he turned to watch Letta take a small gather from the furnace. She swiped a hand across her face, and the copper light of the furnace flickered across the high, broad planes of her cheekbones and the bowed curve of her lips. He'd never noticed them before. Distracted by her strange eyes and disheveled hair, he'd never seen that she was . . . quite pleasant to behold.

She looked up suddenly, caught him staring.

He quickly turned away.

As he was about to consign his next failure to the broken-glass pail, Letta set a hand on his arm. "Wait," she said. "See that." She pointed to the malformed globe at the end of the blowpipe.

Renzo frowned, examined it. "It looks sort of like a bird," he said.

"Like a falcon. Like my kestrel."

He eyed the kestrel, perched on Letta's shoulder, then turned back to the glass.

Yes. He could see the resemblance — a blunt, squarish head set securely on an upright oval body. The hint of a wing and a tail.

"Could you make wings for it?" Letta asked.

Renzo considered. "I think so. If you'll bring me some molten glass and set it just here . . ."

It seemed an idle game, the wings. Renzo worked the glass and Letta watched, advising him on the shape of a falcon's wings, how they tapered at the base and at the tips, how they crooked and arched and tilted. Many falcons and twice as many wings later, Renzo cracked off the end of the blowpipe a glass creature the size of his hand. They studied it a moment together.

Renzo could hardly breathe.

It was quick and light and joyful — poised as if it had just sailed out of the sky to alight on a branch.

A little miracle of a bird.

"Should I — " Letta began.

"Yes! Take it to the annealing oven! Before it shatters!"

Renzo had seen birds wrought in stone and clay. He'd seen painted birds and birds made of tiles. He'd seen birds wrought of glass as well, but they'd been lumpish, earth-bound, lifeless things.

Nothing like *this*.

He shivered, as a new idea struck him.

What if . . .

He stood, filled with a surge of restless energy, and began to pace before the fire.

What if, come time for the test, he created something so new, so striking, so astonishing, that he could vault right past the usual trials of skill? What if the *padrone* couldn't bear to give up someone who could do *this*, and would give him more time to learn the other skills?

If the *padrone* had hoped that Renzo could bring him some of his father's secrets . . . Well, Renzo wouldn't have to say where this bird came from, but the *padrone* could think what he liked.

It wouldn't do to show him a finished bird beforehand. He would have to create it alone, before the *padrone's* very eyes. And the *padrone* would have no patience with mistakes; it would have to be perfect on the first try.

To learn this in three nights?

Impossible.

And yet it was just a single thing to master. With a bit of luck . . .

He felt something stirring deep inside. Something lift-ing, like a feather wafting upward in a draft, in a slanting shaft of light:

Hope.

17.

Witches and Ghosts

The next night, on his way to the glassworks, Renzo again heard footsteps behind him. His breath caught; he whirled round and beheld a cloaked figure standing in the gloom.

Vittorio.

"You!" Renzo said. "I told you: Stay away."

Vittorio set a finger to his lips. "Hush, Renzo. Hear me out. Please."

Renzo hesitated. His heart still went molten with rage when he thought about Vittorio's carelessness, about what he had done. And yet sometimes, when the memory of their last meeting blinked suddenly into Renzo's mind, a burst of astonished gladness swept through him, and swarms of unwelcome tears stung his eyes.

Vittorio. Alive!

But he was still careless, still putting all of their lives in danger, even now.

"I need to speak to you," Vittorio said. "You're in danger."

"Yes—because of you!"

"There's something else. But we can't talk here."

Motioning for Renzo to follow, he slipped into an alley and vanished around a corner.

Renzo followed, looking round lest anyone should see them, and begrudging every moment spent away from the glass. But Vittorio seemed so certain. *Danger.* And despite everything, Renzo didn't think Vittorio had ever intended him ill.

Vittorio motioned him to a small boat tethered to the edge of a canal. "Where——" Renzo began.

"Shh. Get in."

Vittorio rowed them quickly through the narrow canal, merging into a wider one in a district of great *palazzi.* Many were deserted for the winter. Soon Vittorio made for one of them, a tall, narrow confection three stories high, with tiers of high-arched windows one atop another, like a frosted layer cake. The lower windows had been shuttered. The windows in the upper stories, crosshatched with iron bars, stood lifeless and dark.

Vittorio guided the little boat to the water door, a large, padlocked gate of iron filigree. They edged up beside it.

"Hold the boat steady," Vittorio said.

Renzo took hold of the gate. "Do you know these people?" he asked.

Vittorio didn't answer but drew two slender iron implements from his purse. He fiddled with the padlock; with a soft *snick* it snapped open.

Renzo stared at Vittorio. When had he learned to pick locks? And why?

Was he a thief?

Uneasy, Renzo looked about. No other boats nearby.

"*Presto, presto!* Open it!" Vittorio said.

Renzo pushed on the iron bars. The boat slipped into the dim, cavernous space beneath the living quarters; Renzo closed the gate behind.

It smelled of seaweed and mildew and damp. They moored the boat to a stone pier, then Renzo followed Vittorio to a wooden bench near the foot of the stairs that led to the house.

"Well?" Renzo said. "What danger?"

"The bird children."

The bird children. Vittorio knew about them? But how?

Moonlight trickled in through the iron door and glimmered across the water, swirling like wrinkled silk. Shadows rippled in waves across Vittorio's face.

"I listen," he said. "I watch. I know, for example, that eight children climb through a window into the glassworks late each night and climb out again just before sunrise. I know that each child but the smallest has a bird. I know that the children used to go in after you arrived, but of late they've been coming earlier. I know all of this but can only guess at why."

"How are they more dangerous than you? The assassins are searching for you!"

"And the Ten are searching for *them.* Listen. The Ten arrested the matriarch of the bird children's tribe, and Venice is churning with rumors of witchcraft. Last week the doge's daughter saw two magpies on her balustrade before she miscarried. A flock of pigeons knocked down a pediment, which struck a gondolier on the head and killed him. And an assassin was seen entering the bird woman's cell . . . but failed to kill her."

"That's not witchcraft. It's just coincidence."

Vittorio shrugged. "Are you sure?"

Renzo nodded, uneasy. True, the children had that uncanny bond with their birds. At first he'd told himself that it was just training, but he'd known for quite some time that it was more than that. Something deeply sweet and wondrous, but not entirely natural. And those eyes . . . He was accustomed to them now. He'd forgotten how strange they'd seemed at first.

"It doesn't matter one way or the other," Vittorio said. "It matters what people think. It matters what the Ten will do. And here you are, sheltering a whole flock of them. If I've seen them, it won't be long before someone else does too."

"How *would* they, unless they were lurking about every night, stalking me? We're careful. We pick up every feather, every dropping."

"Why do you do it? Why take such a risk?"

Renzo's fingers reached to touch the smooth surface of Papà's pin on his cloak. The boat bumped against the dock with a hollow *clunk*. Moonlight rippled across the walls, the stairs. He felt unbalanced, as if the world had shifted and he now lived in some dim, watery realm, a realm apart from ordinary people, a realm populated by witches and ghosts.

"They're helping me," he said. "With the glass. There's a test—"

"I've heard about that. If I could help you, I would, but—"

"No! You stay away." Besides, it was too late.

"But if the *padrone* finds out about you and the children—"

"He won't," Renzo said, with more confidence than he felt.

"He might."

"He won't."

"What of the carpenter?" Vittorio asked. "Your mother's friend. Surely he could procure you an apprenticeship."

"In *wood*?" Renzo heard the shrillness in his voice. His failure hung in the air between them. He couldn't support his family. His only hope was to go groveling before another man for help—a man outside the family, a man he hardly knew.

"It's a respectable trade—"

"But it's wood! It's dark and heavy and lightless. There's no fire to it, no glow. Woodworkers don't dance. They hunch over, pound at things, hack at them."

In the cold, gray, undulating light, Renzo could see that Vittorio understood. He knew the pull of the glass. He had left the republic for the sake of the glass, so he could work with it however he liked, unfettered by Papà's strictures.

Suddenly Renzo ached to tell Vittorio everything. About the broken goblets, about Letta, about the falcon in the glass.

But no.

Vittorio shifted on the bench. "Listen, Renzo. I have to leave the island."

The sharp pang of loneliness surprised Renzo. "Where will you go?"

"That I will not tell. Although . . ." He gazed at him long and hard. "I won't go far, for now. But I'll be near Antonio's grave every Monday at midnight."

Renzo shook his head. "I won't——"

Vittorio interrupted. "I won't expect you, but I'll be there." He opened his mouth as if to say something else, then swallowed, seeming to think better of it. "You may well need me, after all. I suspect you're all in greater danger than you know."

18.

Falcon in the Glass

That night, with just three days remaining before the test, Renzo embarked on the last frenzy of work — gambling, not even trying to master the skills the *padrone* had mapped out for him, but bending all his efforts toward one end only: to craft a falcon in the glass.

At first Letta helped, adding molten glass for the wings, affixing the *pontello* to the body of the bird and holding it still, so that Renzo could concentrate on shaping the beak and wings and tail. She pointed out when the head was too tall or too flat, the beak too long or too squat, the crook of the wing misplaced.

The children, who had paid little heed to cups and jugs and bowls, now gathered round to watch. When one of Renzo's birds cracked early, they groaned in sympathy. When a bird came out well, they cheered. Some of the live birds chattered and fluttered their wings; Georgio's crow stretched up and *caw-caw-cawed* as if in approval. Even Taddeo watched, offering criticism from the sidelines. "You blew too long, Renzo," he said after the body of one bird grew bloated and misshapen. "You didn't affix it right," he said after a wing fell off and shattered on the floor. "You let it go cold," he said when the glass grew hard and dark before Renzo had finished shaping it.

"*Grazie*," Renzo muttered. "I wouldn't have known."

After yet another failure Letta said, "Wait. Stand here. Hold out your arm." Puzzled, he did so. At once he heard a fluttering noise; the kestrel swept down from the rafters and alit on his wrist. Renzo turned to Letta, alarmed. She smiled, half-mocking, half-reassuring. Though the little bird was very light, Renzo was conscious of the weight of it on his wrist — the weight of aliveness, of blood and breath and bone. The bird fluffed its feathers and turned to regard him with a large, round eye — serious and alert. Its heart trembled in its chest.

Hardly daring to breathe, Renzo studied the precise arch of the kestrel's breast, the hunch of its shoulders, the curve of its talons on his wrist.

"Turn your arm," Letta said. When he did, the bird thrust out its wings for balance, the ends of its feathers, like fingertips, seeming to reach out to stroke the air.

After that, Renzo made a kestrel or two that satisfied her. But he wanted to create a bird without any help at all. If during the test he added molten glass to the body of the bird to form the wings, someone else would have to bring it to him. Would the *padrone* allow that? He didn't know. So he tried to pull the wings out of the excess glass on the sides of the falcon, but there was never enough glass, and the birds came out malformed. At last he concluded that it was impossible to make a lifelike kestrel without adding more glass for the wings. If the *padrone* wouldn't allow it . . .

But he must.

He *would*.

Still, even with the added glass, bird after bird after bird went crashing into the pail. Renzo's arms and back began to ache, his hands to cramp. When he produced an especially unfortunate-looking specimen — one that resembled, according to Taddeo, a loon on stilts — Renzo threw down the blowpipe and slumped onto the bench. Paolo patted his arm. "It didn't look *so* bad," he lisped. One of the twins, Marina, said, "The wings were nice." And little Sofia toddled across the floor, flung herself at his legs, and clung to them like a second pair of leggings.

Witches? That was absurd. Yet he told Letta to tie the broken shutters together with string after they entered, and to clean up the stray feathers and droppings right away. That night the children practiced fleeing into the storeroom and out the window, in case someone showed up unexpectedly.

In the dark of the second to last night before the test, Renzo raided the alms sack. He pulled out Pia's too-small fur-lined boots and one of his own stained and moth-eaten shirts that Mama had declared unfit to wear.

Would Mama miss them?

Maybe not. He'd offer to carry the sack to church on Sunday, and no one would be the wiser.

Then, from Mama's mending basket he took two pairs

of woolen stockings and, after a moment, Mama's third-best mantle, with a tear she hadn't got round to mending. These, he knew, would be missed in time.

How would he explain their absence to Mama?

He didn't know.

At the glassworks Letta received his offerings with a somber nod. Before long Sofia was clumping proudly across the floor in tiny boots that were yet too big for her. Federigo, in possession of one of Renzo's castoff shirts, stripped off his own and gave it to Georgio, who stripped off his and gave it to Paolo, who stripped off his and gave it to the youngest boy, Ugo, the one with the magpie. Letta gave the stockings to Marina and Ottavia. They sat on the floor together, exclaiming over them, rubbing the soft wool against their cheeks.

Renzo hesitated, then reached into the sack and held out Mama's mantle to Letta. "For you," he said.

She took the mantle. Ran it through her hands. Peered at the lattice of roses embroidered at the hem. She looked up at him, and Renzo saw color rise in her face. She blinked.

Oh, no. She wasn't going to cry again, was she?

But she didn't. She held out the mantle to the twins. "Here," she said briskly. "You can take turns with it."

"It's for *you*," Renzo insisted.

The twins glanced at Letta, then back at each other. They giggled, covering their mouths with their hands.

Renzo felt his face grow warm.

Letta shook her head. "Take it," she told the twins.

" 'Tis for you," Marina said, and Ottavia echoed, "For you." They cut their eyes at Renzo and giggled again.

Slowly Letta took back the mantle. She wrapped it about herself. It enveloped her in a cloud of thick rust-colored wool. She traced the faded roses with her fingers; she smoothed the fringes. She flicked up her eyes at Renzo, then gazed down at the mantle again.

Renzo's heart swelled into an odd, aching mass that pressed against the hard shell of his ribs. He had wanted to . . . what? Make her grateful to him? Be a hero in her eyes? But instead he felt a queasy twinge of shame. Why hadn't he done this before?

And the children . . . All this time, he had seen them shivering in their threadbare rags and had done nothing to help them.

And yet . . .

It was his own family he ought to be protecting! If he failed the test, which was all but certain, they'd have need of every pair of stockings, every moth-eaten bit of wool. A man's duty was to his family. He had no business taking from them — stealing! His mother's mantle, especially.

And yet . . .

What would befall Letta if he failed? And the children, what would become of them? How long would Taddeo be able to protect them?

Renzo sighed. All he had ever wanted was to work at the furnace making beautiful objects of glass. But now it seemed he was responsible for the welfare of not only his own family but also this second one — a family of complete strangers to him until just a few scant weeks before. The weight of it pressed down on him. He imagined that he knew exactly how the doge must feel.

And yet the doge could take care of his people. Whereas those who depended on Renzo . . .

A single word echoed in his thoughts, like the toll of a great, iron bell:

Doom.

The next night, he dreamed of a great, gleaming sculpture — a lovely, fragile city made of glass. It slipped sideways, splintering, throwing off tiny, sparkling fragments . . . then tumbled down, down, and down through the air.

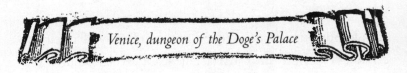

19.

The Owl

If it weren't for the owl, Guido might have thought the woman was dead.

True, most of the food and water he left for her had disappeared. But rats ate the prisoners' food and drank their water. Guido had seen them at it many times, if a prisoner was too sick to eat or drink.

If a prisoner was dead.

Still, rats seldom came into this woman's cell — because of the owl.

It was such a tiny owl. You wouldn't think it could kill a rat. But he'd actually seen it happen. Granted, it was a small rat. Likely young and inexperienced. One evening Guido had been doing his rounds, and something had shot past him, just over his shoulder, softly brushing his cheek. It was lighter than the darkness, and winged, and utterly silent — until it hit its prey. The rat had let out a squeal that sent a shiver through Guido's bones, it truly had. High and terrified and piercing. An eerie, ratty death squeal.

Surely rats wouldn't dare slink into the woman's cell and steal her food — not with the bird sitting right there on her chest. So she must have eaten it herself.

And anyway, if you stood there long enough, at the window of the cell, sometimes in the dim lamplight you could see the owl rising and falling the slightest bit, riding the waves of the woman's breath.

He liked to watch them, the woman and the bird. Sometimes he stayed for quite a while. The woman seldom opened her eyes anymore. She curled up into herself, wrinkled and frail. She seemed to have shrunk.

But the little owl always swiveled its head and saw him right away.

After the assassin had left the woman's cell, Guido and Claudio had found her: bleeding, propped against the wall. They'd been amazed she was alive.

In Guido's experience no prisoner had ever survived an assassin's visit before.

But since then she seemed to sleep all the time. Maybe she was dying.

If she died, what would happen to the owl? Who would take care of it?

How would it be, Guido wondered now, to have an owl of his own? One that would keep him company, be loyal to him, do his bidding? It was a wild little thing. Dangerous. He could train it to fly in the face of anybody who threatened him. Maybe pluck out an enemy's eyes.

He put his face right up to the bars. The bird blinked

at him with its spooky yellow eyes. He reached his hand through, stretched out a finger.

"Here, birdy, birdy."

The woman's eyes flew open. Guido snatched back his hand.

She moaned and sat up slowly. Guido stepped back and was about to steal away, when she turned to him and spoke.

"Would you like t' hold my owl?"

Guido stopped. He couldn't recall having heard her speak before. She talked funny — a little foreign, like.

They said she was a witch. True, he himself might have started the rumor. He had told his sister and her friends about the assassin; he had told his aunt and his uncle and the neighbors who lived below. He'd told them too about the little owl — how it seemed to obey the woman, to come to her bidding, to know her thoughts.

Witch! they had whispered.

"Well?" the woman asked.

He eyed her warily. She rubbed her back, squinting in pain. "Will it bite me?" he asked.

"Not if I tell him not to."

He knew he shouldn't do it. He should walk away, right now.

"Will you tell it not to bite?"

"'Course. If you'll fetch me some of that water."

Guido put his key into the lock. The door opened with a rusty *creak*. He set the torch in the wall cresset, then dipped the ladle into the water bucket, poured water into the cup, and took it to the woman.

She drank. When she was done, she turned to him and said, "Hold out your finger, like so."

She held out hers to show him.

Guido did the same. "It won't bite?" he asked. "Certain sure?"

"He won't. I promise."

She flicked her eyes to the bird, and something passed between them: quick and light, but with a sizzle to it, like the tingling blue flash when you touch metal on a cold, dry day.

The bird jumped onto his finger.

He felt the weight of it, impossibly light. Through the wiry, clutching talons he could sense its aliveness—the beating of its heart. Its feet were warm. Its feathers tickled his fingers. Soft. So soft. The owl's breast was speckled with gray; its wings and back were a tawny brown. Its eyes, which had looked so fierce from across the room, now seemed thoughtful and sad.

"Little thing," Guido breathed.

It fluffed its feathers, settling down. It squirted out a chalky dropping and closed its eyes.

Guido glanced at the woman.

She smiled.

Looking kindly and pleased, like somebody's grandmother. Not like a witch at all.

20.

The Test

O n the night before the test, Renzo crept through the dark alleys, his conscience pricking him. He had meant to tell Mama that the test had been moved up, but . . .

How to explain *why* the test had been moved? How to explain that he'd given up on the *padrone's* list of skills and risked all on the falcon in the glass?

Reckless!

Foolish!

Childish!

He couldn't tell her. Couldn't face her disappointment.

Not yet.

At the glassworks with the children, his hands didn't work as they should. He broke six birds in a row, and completed none.

Doom.

As he was gathering the glass for a seventh, he heard a key grate in the front door lock. His eyes, of their own accord, sought Letta's. They gazed at each other for a stunned moment, then — "Go!" he said.

The children bolted for the storeroom as the outer door creaked open; their birds fluttered after them. Renzo took his blowpipe from the furnace and held it before him, advancing toward the intruder as the glass cooled. It must be someone from the glassworks, else he wouldn't have a key.

Behind him he heard footsteps and murmurs — the children. "Who's there?" he called, hoping to drown out the noise — but then Sergio materialized out of the dark before him, running hard, heading for the storeroom.

Renzo tried to block him, but Sergio feinted one way and dodged past him on the other side. Renzo dropped the blowpipe with a crash of shattering glass, and followed.

Just as Sergio reached the storeroom doorway, Taddeo burst out of it; they collided in a heap.

"Umph!" Taddeo grunted. "Oh, my hip!"

Sergio leaped to his feet and disappeared inside.

Renzo arrived a moment later. He leaped over Taddeo and found Sergio leaning out the storeroom window.

Moonlight slipped in through the space between the shutters. In the storeroom there were only the shallow, cluttered shelves; there were only the sacks and crates and baskets on the floor.

Sergio turned. "I saw them," he said.

"Who?"

"You know who. What were you doing with them?"

Behind him Taddeo moaned. "Oh, my elbow! My leg!"

"You saw shadows," Renzo said.

"I saw witches — and their birds."

Sergio bent down, picked up something from the floor, then held it up before Renzo's face, twirling it, the accusation plain in his eyes.

A tail feather. Long and gray, with a black stripe at its tip. Probably from the kestrel.

Renzo reached for it; Sergio jerked it away. A wind gust rattled at the shutters. They flew open, banged against the casement — one straight and true, the other askew on its hinges.

Sergio tucked the feather inside his doublet. He brushed past Renzo, stopped at Taddeo. "And *you* were in on it too."

Taddeo looked up at him for a long moment, and Renzo feared he was going to tattle. "Oh," Taddeo whimpered at last, "my neck!"

Sergio stepped over Taddeo and disappeared into the glassworks.

For a moment Renzo couldn't force his feet to move. Was it over now? Would the *padrone* refuse to let him take the test? And why had Sergio come in so early, anyway? To spy on him?

No telling. One thing for certain, though. The children couldn't come here anymore, ever. No matter what happened with the test, Renzo would have to stay up late tonight and warn Letta, send them away.

◆   ◆   ◆

The *padrone* wanted to be done with it, and quickly. He hung up his cloak, strode to the furnace, and called to Renzo. Sergio tried to intervene, but the *padrone* waved him away.

"*Basta*," he said. "I'm through with waiting. We decide this now."

"But——" Sergio protested. He murmured something into the *padrone's* ear; the *padrone* cocked an eye toward Renzo but pushed Sergio away.

"Forget Renzo. He's nothing to do with you. Look to your own skills, which have much need of your attention." The *padrone* raised his voice. "All of you, attend to your work."

An odd sense of calm came over Renzo as he assembled his tools. There was nothing more he could do to prepare. The *padrone* would allow someone to bring him extra glass for the wings—or he wouldn't. The bird would come out well—or not. He would pass—or he would fail.

For a moment as he stood before the furnace with the blowpipe in his hands, Renzo thought he could feel Papà's presence filling the air around him: *You have the eye and the hand and the heart for greatness. You will bring honor to the family.* Suddenly Renzo felt steady on his feet. A surge of strength flowed down through his arms into his fingers.

"Well?" the *padrone* demanded.

Renzo began. The banded bowl came out well, and the one-eared jug. The long-stemmed goblet listed a bit to one side, but the *padrone* did not stop the test. He grunted and motioned for Renzo to continue. The large platter. The mold-blown bowl.

After a while, he came to the end of the skills he knew with confidence. His back was beginning to tire, and his arms felt heavy. Sweat dripped into his eyes and plastered his shirt to his chest; his eyes were gritty and dry. He didn't know how long he'd been working—only that it must have been hours.

It was time.

He gulped down a glass of water, then gathered a mass of glass from the crucible, trying not to think too much, trying to feel Papà there beside him. Quickly, quickly. The *padrone* would soon see that Renzo was making something he'd never asked for. The sooner he got to the wings, the better.

The body of the bird came fairly easily, considering the weariness in Renzo's arms. They were beginning to get shaky. The head came out well enough, and the little rounded base. He shaped the curve of the beak, expecting at any moment to hear the *padrone* command him to halt. Instead, he heard Letta's voice, in imagination, urging him to *see*. The barbed hook at the end of the beak. The rounded convexity of the falcon's wild eyes. He coaxed out the tail from the body of the bird, tugging gently, for the illusion of feathers.

Now, for the wings.

Renzo's throat felt rough and dry. "Could somebody," he asked, "fetch me a bit of glass?"

Silence. Renzo moved to the furnace, warmed up the little falcon. If the *padrone* took too long to decide, the bird would be ruined.

Behind him came Sergio's voice, sharp with anger. "What's he doing? This isn't what he agreed to. Why don't you end this? Tell him he's failed!"

"What *are* you doing?" the *padrone* asked.

Renzo removed the bird from the furnace. He lifted his gaze to the *padrone*. "I need more glass," he said.

A bead of sweat dripped into his eyes. The glowing glass began to dim.

The *padrone* moved. He picked up a *speo* rod and glided to the furnace, then touched a pendulant drop of glass to the place on the bird where Renzo indicated. Renzo snipped off the excess, then teased out feathers, straining to control his trembling arms. He took the bird back to the furnace to warm it for a moment, and, "Once more," he said.

Behind him Sergio was protesting, but the *padrone* fetched more glass. Renzo tried to shut out Sergio's voice, but his hand slipped, and to his horror he saw that he'd distorted the shape of the second wing. He'd have to warm it up again and try to repair it. He wiped the sweat from his brow and returned the falcon to the furnace, praying that the wing wasn't too far gone. He removed the bird from the heat and began to rework the wing. The *padrone* moved in close. Again Renzo feared that he'd stop him, but the *padrone* merely circled the glass bird, examining it from one side, then the other, and before Renzo knew it, the second wing was coming true — the wing tips stretched long, seeking to row on the air.

The glass was hardening now. Darkening. Renzo tweaked the wing one last time, then cracked the falcon off the blow-pipe and laid it on its back on the marble tabletop.

Suddenly he was aware of the silence. No voices. No sounds of clinking tools. Renzo dared not look up, but he could feel all eyes upon him. He counted to ten, then set the bird upright—a light and feathered thing, caught in the last moment of flight.

Joyful.

Alive.

Renzo's knees went weak. He turned to face the *padrone*.

The *padrone* gazed at the bird. Then "Anzoleto!" he called. "Take this to the annealing oven. And heaven help you if it cracks!"

The *padrone* watched as Anzoleto bore the bird away; then he turned to Renzo. "Did your father teach you how to do that?"

"Yes," he said. Only a half lie. Papà had taught him the skills that had made the bird possible. And if the *padrone* craved Papà's secrets, why disappoint him?

"Why did he never show it? I've seen his work. But never anything like this."

Renzo shrugged. "It . . . wasn't ready."

"Show me how to make it."

Renzo swallowed. Stood firm. "I will if I'm to be a glassmaker. If you decree that I've passed the test."

"But he hasn't finished!" Sergio said.

The *padrone* shot Sergio a warning glance. To Renzo he said, "You haven't yet completed my list. Can you?"

Renzo hesitated. Shook his head.

"Then he fails!" Sergio said. "Tell him, Father. It's over. He's a drudge now, once and for all."

The *padrone* wheeled on him. "Shut your stupid yawp! Do

you hear me? I don't want to hear another bleat from you."

Sergio threw down his blowpipe, stalked away. And Renzo felt a small, mean gladness in his heart, that the *padrone* might be embarrassed and disappointed by Sergio. That he might, in this one thing, put Renzo above his own son.

"You will have to learn those skills, Renzo," the *padrone* said sharply, "and learn them soon. Ettore will teach you. You'll trade off, working with him and with me."

But Renzo wanted to get the *padrone*'s word, wanted the other men to hear it. "So I've passed the test? I'm an apprentice now?"

The *padrone* nodded curtly. "You've passed."

◆   ◆   ◆

It was not as Renzo had imagined, passing the test. He had thought to feel a flame of triumph burning. He had thought to comport himself with quiet dignity while singing and dancing inside. But the way it had happened — almost wresting it from the *padrone* without having mastered all the skills . . . Almost tricking him to think he was giving him Papà's secrets . . . It made an odd, heavy queasiness in Renzo's belly. Which grew worse as he watched the argument between Sergio and his father. Sergio drew out the feather, pointed to Renzo. But the *padrone* flung the feather to the floor and slapped the back of Sergio's head.

Ettore was the second-best glassworker in the shop, and he kept up a grueling pace. Renzo's hands slipped; he maimed things; he dropped them. Still, he ached to know all the many secret ways of the glass. Ettore was matter-of-fact and brisk—neither scolding nor sympathetic. By the time for the midday meal, Renzo's mind felt addled, and every muscle ached.

But for him there was no respite. The *padrone* dismissed everyone else, but motioned for Renzo to stay. Together they fumbled their way toward another falcon in the glass, retracing the steps Renzo had taken—first with the *padrone* watching Renzo, and then with Renzo assisting, manning the *pontello*. The bird did not come easily or well; Renzo's hands were clumsier now than they had been before. He had been fortunate during the test; perhaps fear or hope had guided his hands. Perhaps Papà *had* been there, looking over him. In any case only labor and sweat and patience could bring them a second falcon as fine as the first.

The *padrone*, on the other hand, moved gracefully, without a flicker of wasted motion. He learned quickly. Renzo feared that once the *padrone* had mastered the falcon, he might demote Renzo to drudge again, despite what he had said earlier. Still, it was the small details about the bird that were hardest to grasp. How to capture its lightness, its fierceness, its eager anticipation of flight.

When the *padrone*'s daughter arrived with food, they still had not produced a bird nearly as fine as the one Renzo had made by himself, but the *padrone* seemed well enough satisfied.

"We will do this again tomorrow," he said. "And tomorrow and tomorrow again, until it is mine."

As they ate—bread and cheese and sausage—there

came a timid knock at the door. Renzo went to get it, and there stood Pia, with his dinner wrapped in a napkin. "You didn't come home," she said. "Mama is worried."

Renzo ached to pick her up and embrace her; he wanted to dance with her, shout, "I've done it! I passed!"

"Who is there?" the *padrone* called.

"It's my sister, with dinner."

"Tell her you'll be late tonight. Some of us are meeting at the tavern after work; I want you to come."

Renzo took the napkin. He bent down close to Pia. "Tell Mama not to worry," he said softly. "Tell her I have very good news."

And, he thought, there were others who would be glad to hear what he had done. Letta . . . Would she be happy for him? Would she be proud?

•   •   •

The tavern was dark and warm, filled with the smells of sweat and wet wool and cooking meats. Renzo joined the *padrone*, Sergio, Ettore, and the third master, Luca, at a table near the fire. The *padrone* ordered a flagon of wine, a dish of stuffed capons, and a platter of steaming beef. Luca told Renzo that he had worked for a short time with Papà ten years or so ago. "He was a wizard with the glass," he said. The others nodded, all save Sergio, who sat sulking. And then they were congratulating Renzo on his apprenticeship, and commenting on the glass falcon—although carefully, not dropping any useful information for prying ears to hear. "I'll wager your father had many secrets," Luca said.

The *padrone* raised his glass. "To the first of many!"

Ettore and Luca raised their glasses as well. "To the apprentice!" Ettore said.

Belatedly Sergio lifted his glass and cocked an ironic eye at Renzo. "To secrets!"

Renzo gulped his wine, uneasy. The children. He mustn't forget to warn Letta about Sergio.

And yet the platters of food kept coming; the wine flowed. Soon Renzo felt as stuffed as one of the capons he had consumed. There was no more talk of secrets; he ate and drank in a pleasant haze. The twin warmths of wine and fire seeped into his sore muscles, easing the pain. Twice he stashed bits of meat in a napkin on his lap to take home to Mama and Pia. But the long-legged, mangy dogs that roamed the tavern quickly nosed out the treats and gobbled them up.

And all the while the glassblowers spoke with him as one of themselves: joking and swearing, boasting and complaining. Spoke with him as a man. Renzo drank deeply, swimming in the glow of their companionship. He contemplated his future, which stretched out bright before him.

But a small peck, peck, peck of worry niggled at the back of his mind. Something he should remember; something he ought to do . . .

"Renzo, hold out your cup!" The *padrone* motioned to a serving maid to pour him more. Renzo drank.

In a while Sergio rose from the table and made the rounds, laughing with young men at other tables, teasing the serving maids. And soon Ettore rose as well. Renzo made to do the same—but when he did, he discovered that the room was spinning. The rich food, which had felt so good going down, now churned in his belly—hot and bubbly and sour. He lurched into the table, making the drinking cups teeter. Luca took his arm to help him balance. "Shall I fetch a boy to help you home?"

Only women, invalids, and children would need such help. A man could walk home by himself. Renzo shook his head, thanked Luca, and staggered out the door.

Again something pricked at his mind, something troublesome. But the difficulty of setting one foot squarely before the other on the narrow path beside the canal pushed every other worry aside. What an irony it would be, Renzo thought, if the future legendary glassmaker were to fall into the dark water and drown on the very day when his career had begun!

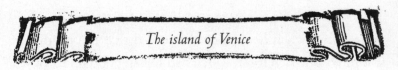

21.

Lion's Mouth

By the time Sergio reached the island of Venice, the bitter-cold wind had sliced through the layers of linen and wool in which he'd wrapped himself. He had no sensation whatsoever in his ears and nose; likewise, his toes had gone numb.

And yet the chill did not penetrate to his heart. The rage still smoldered there.

Renzo!

Sergio nosed his little boat into the mouth of the dark canal. At once the wind died down. The water grew smooth, almost glassy. He unbent his shoulders and stood up straight, glad to find respite from the squalls and lurching waves of the open lagoon.

For the thousandth time he wondered where Renzo had picked up that little trick, the trick with the falcon. From his father, as he had claimed?

Doubtful.

For that morning Sergio had seen the very bird. Or a real one exactly like it, a little kestrel. He had caught sight of the children who had tamed it—or enchanted it. Slipping through the glassworks. Disappearing down the alley behind the storeroom, with four or five birds flying behind.

He had come to watch Renzo, to see if he was likely to pass the test—and had found more than he could have hoped for.

Now Sergio nudged his boat into a canal to his right, paddled a little way, then turned left into another. He knew his way through the labyrinth; he had come here many times. Though glassworkers were not supposed to leave Murano, he and his friends often visited the city of Venice after dark.

For pleasure.

Not like tonight.

Tonight was for revenge.

Ripples splashed against the stone walls. High above, candlelight glimmered from a row of tall Moorish windows, lending the black water an iridescent sheen, like the feathers of a raven.

Yes, those children must have had something to do with Renzo's glass falcon. Though, whether they were truly witches—as rumor had it—Sergio did not know. He had watched Renzo carefully and seen nothing of conjury about the crafting of the falcon. It was a trick, that was all—a series of fairly easy steps done quickly and put together in an unlikely way. But it came out so birdlike, so like that kestrel. The children must have helped, someway.

As Sergio neared the Grand Canal, the houses flowed close to either side, looming larger, more ornate, more perforated with light. Sergio rowed through their rippling reflections, stewing.

He had told his father about Renzo and the children. He had shown him the feather as proof, but his father hadn't cared. He had humiliated Sergio before the others; he had advanced Renzo despite his ignorance of the craft; he had taken Renzo under his wing as if *he* were his son.

If his father didn't object to Renzo's associating with witches . . . Well, others would.

Sergio tied up his boat and carefully stepped up onto the dock. Ragged clouds blew across the full moon. The bell of the campanile tolled the hour past midnight, a great, deep, booming *bong*.

Sergio rolled his aching shoulders, then set off down a narrow street.

How many times, he wondered, had he been forced to lift his cup?

To the apprentice!

To the first of many!

Pah!

Sergio turned a corner, nearing his destination:

Bocca di Leone — the Lion's Mouth.

Because surely the doge would like to know what Renzo was up to. Surely he would like to know where the bird children might be found.

And dropping a note into the slot in the Lion's Mouth was like whispering into the doge's ear.

There it was now, a light stone plaque on a dark stone

wall. He could see the carved face of a man, the furry eyebrows, the ears like those of a lion. He could see the dark slot that formed an open mouth.

Many Lion's Mouths decorated the walls of Venice, but this was the one for denunciations of heretics and witches.

Sergio pulled the note from his doublet. He hesitated. What they would do to Renzo and those children . . .

Shut your stupid yawp!

Sour bile rose into his throat. Sergio slipped the note between the lion's jaws, and with a hushed *swish* of parchment on stone, it was done.

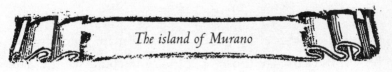
22.

Cold Fire

He had thought that Mama would be asleep. It was well past midnight now; surely she wouldn't wait up this long. But a rustling of cloth caught his ear as he shut the door. He turned and saw her in the light of the glowing embers. Sitting on a bench, perfectly still, her mending in her lap. Looking up at him expectantly.

"It's done," he told her. "I passed."

She made a little sound then, something between a gasp and a sob. She dropped to her knees, her mending falling to the floor, and clasped her hands in silent prayer.

He waited awkwardly, feeling that he should go and pray beside her but not knowing if he could accomplish the feat of kneeling without stumbling or tipping over.

Mama rose, walked to him. She set her hands on his shoulders, kissed him on both cheeks. Then she held him at arm's length, seeming to search for something in his eyes. "I'm proud of you, Son," she said at last. "And your father would be too."

◆   ◆   ◆

It was Taddeo who reminded Renzo what he'd forgotten. He was shuffling out the glassworks door just as Renzo came in to work the next morning. At the sight of him Renzo halted in his tracks.

Letta.

Taddeo scowled at Renzo, leaning in as he passed, to whisper: "We were all waiting for the news. And you never came, then, did you?"

But it was worse than that. Renzo was supposed to warn her. "Listen, Taddeo. They can't—"

But Ettore called to Renzo and motioned for him to come inside.

He searched for Sergio and the *padrone* and found them together by the furnace. In their faces he saw nothing that seemed amiss. It was true that the *padrone* hadn't seemed to care about the feather when Sergio had shown it to him. So maybe there was no need to worry.

And yet . . . Sergio knew about the children. Or at least he suspected.

Dangerous.

Well. Renzo would warn them tonight.

◆ ◆ ◆

And so it began, his new life in the glassworks. That day Renzo slipped easily into his role with Ettore, eager to learn the skills he'd missed. Ettore worked steadily and hard. He was quick and exacting, and expected Renzo to keep up. Renzo pushed through fatigue and headache, willing his mind to stay alert. He cocooned himself in glasswork and allowed nothing else to penetrate. When at last they broke for the midday meal, Ettore nodded and said, "Well done."

Renzo's entire body ached; his arms shook; his head throbbed. And yet he felt happier than he had in a long time.

This was what he was meant to do. This was what he'd been made for.

Again he did not go home for the midday meal but worked with the *padrone*, who could soon make the falcon as well as Renzo, and more consistently. But there was something of clockwork about the *padrone*'s methods: *Now let it cool to the count of ten. Now blow three quick huffs into the pipe. Now place the* borsella *at precisely this angle.*

And each bird looked exactly like the last.

Renzo recalled how with Letta the bird had seemed a little like magic, and it had changed and grown more *itself* each time.

Ah, well. To be profitable, the *padrone* said, the birds had to be made quickly, with no wasted effort.

That evening Renzo celebrated with Mama and Pia. Mama had roasted an entire rabbit, and Pia had made a little brown cake studded with nuts and dried fruit.

It should have been one of the happiest, proudest days of his life. And yet, he thought later, lying awake on his bed that night, why was he so unsettled? Was it the hint the *padrone* had dropped that perhaps Renzo could show him more of Papà's secrets? Was it Sergio's hostile glances? Was it knowing that he hadn't truly earned his apprenticeship by mastering the list of skills?

Was it Letta?

But he'd had no time to warn her. The celebration at the tavern had gone on far into the night. With all the wine that had been thrust upon him, he'd just barely managed to stagger home. And then he'd had to tell Mama, and . . .

A picture blinked into his mind, of the children all waiting for him, waiting to find out if he'd passed the test. Of Letta, with that look she'd had when he'd given her the mantle, when the color had risen in her face.

Renzo groaned, turned over onto his side. She had come to rely on him. And who else was there to help her?

So he would go there tonight, in the small hours. He would warn them.

But what would they do then? Where could they go to get warm? Where could they hide?

◆   ◆   ◆

The outer door to the glassworks stood wide open.

Renzo stopped before it. Peered inside.

Dark.

A wind gust picked up the hem of his cloak and flapped it against his legs. He shivered, suddenly afraid.

What combination of events, he wondered, would lead to this door standing wide and unattended in the middle of the night?

Nothing good — that was certain.

He moved into the doorway. "Hello?"

He listened for an answer, straining his ears against the dark. Behind him: water splashing against the sides of the canal, and the hollow *thump* of one boat jostling another. Ahead: the dull, throbbing roar of the furnace.

It sounded wrong somehow. Not loud enough?

Renzo edged forward until he could see an opening in the furnace. Usually the fire was a dazzling white-gold, so bright, you had to squint to look into it. But now it had dimmed to a dullish copper.

Cold fire.

That should never happen. Never.

"Letta!" he called, and when there was no answer, "Taddeo!"

Quiet.

Renzo crept into the glassworks, alert for movement, for sounds. Something odd ahead — an overturned bench. And now he made out the shapes of tools, strewn about the floor, and feathers — far too many feathers. Something glittered ahead. A plume of glass shards, winking in the light of the furnace. Renzo scanned along the trail of broken glass until he found the pail, tipped over onto its side.

He crossed the wide interior floor, his lungs filling up with a thick, choking dread. He burst into the storage room.

The shutters stood open. A band of moonlight striped the floor and laddered across the tiers of shelves.

Empty. No one here.

But wait. There, in a dark corner, something . . .

An arrow?

Renzo moved forward. He stooped, grasped the wooden shaft. Its tip was embedded in something dark and small. Renzo took it into the moonlight.

It was a bird. A little wading bird with long, red legs. Paolo's bird.

PART II

FLIGHT

◆ ◆ ◆

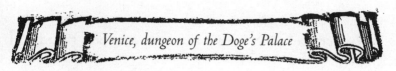

23.

The Message

The old woman cleared her throat. "He will abandon us," she said.

But Letta did not look up from her writing. The woman watched the pen scratch across the strip of parchment, leaving a trail of tiny script. She squatted on the stone floor in the corner beside Letta. This far from the lamp, the message was no more legible to her old eyes than a line of sugar ants. "You know he will," she said. "They all do."

"What of *Nonno*?" Letta said, still not looking up. "He didn't."

Matteo? She would compare this boy to Matteo?

"So there's no other like him in all the world?" Letta persisted. "Only one, and he fell in love with you?"

The woman sat perfectly still. What's this? she thought. What has happened between them? What have they done? "Letta . . ."

"Don't!" Letta looked up at her, eyes sharp but hurting. And young. Though not so very much younger than she herself had been when Matteo . . . Those days in the hills above Verona . . . Not two words in common they'd had, and yet . . .

Someone called out in sleep—Sofia. Earlier she had had a nightmare. The woman listened as Sofia muttered something unintelligible, then settled back into silence.

She brushed her memories away. She must attend to *now*. To her youngest grandchild, to her grandnieces and grandnephew, to the children more distantly related. Who had been caught, arrested, terrorized, knocked about and bruised . . . Who had been bound, gagged, hooded, separated from their birds, dragged through the marsh, shipped across the lagoon . . . Who had been flung, sobbing, into this dank, foul-smelling hellhole to await whatever fate the Ten had in store.

The one mercy was that they had put all the children in here with her.

Letta's pen had begun to move again. "'Tisn't like you and *Nonno*," she said. Though the woman hadn't asked. "He doesn't even know that I . . ."

Love him? the woman wondered.

". . . think of him at all. But I believe he's . . . honorable."

Honorable? Perhaps. Honor was not yet entirely dead in this world, however often it seemed so. But it was a concept the woman seldom dwelled on anymore. Survival, that came first.

She leaned back against the cold wall, watching Letta write.

Back in the early days with Matteo, there had been time

for falling in love, time for building a snug cottage in the hills, time for having many children.

But then the plague had come, with the mob on its heels, crying witchcraft.

How could they have thought that *we* had brought the plague, the woman wondered, when it had taken so many of our own?

But it was the birds, she knew. Her people's bond with them. This bond was too alien for outsiders to countenance for long; it was mysterious even to those who possessed it. Their green eyes might have been tolerated, but their birds—only for a while. Nevertheless, the bond was immutable; it was precious. It was part of who they were, no less than the hair on their heads, the noses on their faces, the lines on the palms of their hands.

It had been decided that the old woman should take the children to Venice, while the children's parents—those still alive—should seek far and wide for a place more hospitable to strangers. At first the scattered groups had sent messages back and forth, but after a while the messages had ceased. The old woman had sent her owl to find them, but he always returned with the selfsame messages she had sent.

Somewhere to her left Paolo moaned. The woman stood, feeling the familiar creaking rasp in her knees and hips. She picked her way through the welter of sleeping children until she came to Paolo. She sat again and took him onto her lap. His breath was easy. The smell of the marsh still clung to him, though it was fading, overcome by the sour reek of sickness and piss and sweat. He had ceased with the vomiting at last, the vomiting that went on and on until she'd thought he must be hollow, just breath and bones. To lose your bird that way, so young. To see it slain . . .

Miraculously, the other birds had survived. The woman had found each one by kenning; she had overridden the children's kens and told the birds to wait hidden on the roof with her owl until after dark. She felt them now, pressing against her thoughts: *quick, tremulous, twitchy, hungry, eager, fretful.*

She kenned them to be still, be calm.

She wondered how long the jailers would keep her and the children here together.

She wondered how long the littlest ones could survive.

She wondered if they would hang her as a witch, and if the children would share her fate.

Letta blew on the ink, rolled up the strip of parchment.

Don't pin your hopes on this, the woman wanted to say. *He will be loyal to his own people, and there is honor in that. Us he will have to abandon.*

Letta turned to her, scanned her face. The woman did not smile or make her countenance go blank to hide her doubt.

Letta pursed her lips. "I'll send it," she said. "We'll see."

24.

Wading Bird

It had gone cold, the bird. Renzo cupped it in one hand—its spindly red legs limp between his fingers—half-hoping to feel the beating of a tiny heart.

But no.

It was still.

He felt along the shaft where the arrow entered the little body. It penetrated deep, too deep to leave space for life. He stroked the bird's speckled neck and back, as he had seen Paolo do. So smooth and silky. He had never actually touched a wild bird before. He set it down carefully, though he knew nothing could hurt it now.

He scooted a crate beneath the window, stepped up, peered out into the dark. Nothing moved. But a little way down the alley, a familiar shape . . . He scrambled over the casement, thumped down onto the packed dirt outside. Just a few steps, and he held it in his hands.

A boot.

A tiny fur-lined boot.

Sofia's boot.

Something cracked apart deep within him. His knees buckled; he knelt there on the ground, hugging the boot to his chest.

Letta . . .

What had happened to her—to them?

Was it a gang of witch-hunters? The constabulary? A band of thieves?

An assassin?

He rubbed his cheek against the soft fur at the top of the boot, then rose slowly to his feet and looked about. To the east, low on the horizon, the sky gleamed pearly gray. Morning would come soon. Though the alley was dark, he could see a churning of footprints in the dirt leading away from the glassworks; he could see feathers.

He jogged a few steps down the alley, then stopped, seized with indecision.

But by now they must be long gone. Long enough for the furnace to have cooled. And even if he did find them, what could he do? Fight off the constables, or a gang of thieves? No use, either, to go for help. Who would come to the rescue of a band of homeless, foreign children, deemed by many to be witches?

On the other hand he'd never heard of an assassin going after a band of children. And Taddeo . . . surely no one would see him as a threat. Whoever had taken the children would probably banish them, that was all. And the children had been banished before. They knew how to be banished.

Warmer days were coming. Letta was canny and fearless; she'd keep them safe.

Meanwhile, in the glassworks . . .

The overturned benches, the scattered trail of broken glass, the tools strewn across the floor. The feathers. The droppings.

An image of Sergio blinked into his mind. Twirling the feather. Showing it to the *padrone*.

The *padrone* began work every day not long after dawn. He would be here soon. If he saw signs of many birds, he'd likely give credit to Sergio's accusations. And then, for Renzo, there'd be no more of spinning and shaping the hot glass. No more stemmed goblets, footed bowls. His days in the glassworks would be over.

He made for the window, chucked the boot inside. He jumped up, climbed over the casement, dropped into the storeroom. Then he set to work. He swept the floor, seeking out every feather, every dropping, every shard of broken glass — scouring the glassworks of every trace that the children had ever been there, every trace that they had ever lived. He fed stick after stick of wood into the furnace, stoking the flames until they were roaring, until sweat rolled down his forehead, down his back.

Memories of Letta kept rising before him. Leading the children across the floor to the furnace, brooking no resistance from *him*. Thrusting the blowpipe at him, refusing to let him give up. Tracing the embroidered roses on Mama's mantle.

Where was she now?

At last, reluctantly, he threw the little boot into the furnace; it vanished in a burst of flame and a whiff of burning leather. He knew he should destroy the wading bird as well—but it didn't seem right that it should be bound together in death with the instrument that had slain it. He cradled the bird in one hand—soft, gray-brown, speckled—and carefully worked the arrowhead from its breast. He flung the arrow into the furnace first and watched the fire consume it. He brought the bird up near his face, breathing in the dusty smell of feathers, remembering how it had perched on Paolo's shoulder and pecked at the top of his head. A heaviness settled on his heart; for a moment it was hard to breathe.

He tossed the bird lightly, gave it to the flames.

Above him now light sifted in through the glass roof panels. He walked to the main door and peered out.

The sky glowed pink, the color of the inside of a polished shell. A soft breeze blew in from the west, bringing the smells of salt and tar and fish. Pink tipped the choppy gray wakes of the boats that plied the canal. The fishermen had long been up and gone, but the water teemed with boats—boats bringing in grain and spices, bricks and sand, kegs of wine.

And here came the glassworkers: Ettore, tying up his boat at the side of the canal. Anzoleto, with his little dog trotting beside him. The *padrone* and Sergio, walking up the path, the *padrone* with his chin thrust out, and Sergio trailing sullenly behind.

Nothing out of the ordinary.

Nothing that seemed amiss.

Renzo slipped back inside, unseen.

He was stirring the batch as they entered. He kept his head down, minding his work, but tuned his ears to their conversations.

A new commission for *Carnevale*. Somebody's wedding, somebody's saint's-day feast. A tiff over breakfast that morning. The *padrone* announced that there would be clients in the glassworks on Monday, merchants who wanted to see the latest innovations and might well commission much work based upon what they saw.

The glassworkers must not know, then, what had happened here last night. Not yet.

Very soon he would have to tell the *padrone* that Taddeo had been gone when he'd arrived. But that was all.

Of course, Taddeo might turn up at any moment, telling a tale of bloody abduction. Or a constable could come knocking. Could tell about the bird children, and that Renzo had been sheltering them.

But for the space of this brief moment, it seemed that he was safe.

◆　　◆　　◆

After Renzo told of Taddeo's absence, the *padrone* sent Anzoleto to search. When he returned, the news was ill. He had not found Taddeo, nor had any of his neighbors seen him. "Should I keep looking?" Anzoleto asked.

The *padrone* frowned. "No. Go back to work. Maybe

he'll turn up later. If not, I'll ask around, see what I can find out."

And it was back again, to the glass. To the heat and roar of the furnace, the sun-bright glow of the gather. Renzo tried to close himself up inside his work and shut out all else, but his hands were stupid, weary, clumsy. Things slipped away from them, stretched out of shape, shattered. Ettore barked at him, "Think, Renzo!" "Move!" But something dragged down inside him, fathoms deep.

There would have been men, Renzo thought, three or four of them at least. Shouting, surging through the glass-works doorway. Snatching up the children, hauling Taddeo to his feet. The children would have cried; the birds would have flapped and called; Letta would have fought. There would have been fists to pummel, and maybe knives to draw blood—

"Not there, boy! Over here!" Ettore snapped. "What are you doing? Pay attention!"

Renzo managed to recover his focus with the *padrone* later on. But the heaviness returned to sit upon his heart, and the mere act of breathing made him ache.

◆　　◆　　◆

Late that day, while lifting a white-hot gather from the furnace, Renzo became aware of a commotion somewhere in the glassworks. A clapping of hands. Shouting: "Go! Begone!"

Renzo blinked, turned away from the glass. Dazzled, as if waking from a dream. It was Sergio who had called out;

now he pointed up toward the ceiling. Renzo blinked again, waited for the afterglow of molten glass to fade from before his eyes and allow him to see into the gloom.

It was a bird. A little kestrel, winging above the glassworks.

Letta's bird?

Sergio and Ettore waved their blowpipes at the bird. It circled the glassworks, dipping low toward Renzo, then circled away again. But in the moment when it came nearest, he saw something affixed to its leg.

A message capsule.

For him?

That would mean . . . she was alive.

He wanted to leap into the air, to call to the kestrel, to hold out an arm for it to land on.

"It's just like the one *he* made," Sergio said. Accusingly. Pointing at Renzo now.

Anzoleto burst through the door and began hurling pebbles at the bird. It swooped toward Renzo again.

"Renzo," the *padrone* said, "have you seen this bird before?"

Renzo ached to untie the capsule, to unroll the message, to find out where she was.

He glanced back at the *padrone*, whose eyes were curious. Probing.

"No," Renzo said. He clapped his hands, shouted up at the kestrel. "Shoo!" he said. "Begone!"

25.

Ill Tidings

Signore Averlino was droning on about wood.

He had approached Mama after mass again, had taken Renzo's place at her side, had walked with her down the aisle in the slow procession of jostling parishioners. Mama had proudly told him that Renzo had passed his test, and Signore Averlino's long, homely face had crinkled into a smile. He had grasped Renzo's hand in his — large, sinewy, rough with calluses.

"Excellent, Renzo. Well done."

Renzo had shrugged, not meeting his eyes. He itched to be out of the cloying air, heavy with the smells of candle wax, incense, and sweat. He wished Mama would tell Signore Averlino to leave them alone. Renzo was the man of the family. *He* would support Mama and Pia, would bring them honor. Though it would be years before he graduated to glassmaker, now their future was secure. At least, if no one found out that he'd protected the bird children. But two days had passed with no news . . .

Now Mama was encouraging Signore Averlino, asking

about his work. At first he had tried to deflect the questions about himself — affecting modesty, Renzo thought. Still Mama had insisted, and now, as they approached the door, he spoke of miters, of joists, of crowns. Of dull and heavy matters, of interest to no one.

They stepped into the sunlight, turned the corner toward home. A cool breeze swept in across the lagoon; clouds sailed across the sky like fleets of galleons. Pigeons rose up before them in the *campo*, flapping and creaking, shadowing the sky. Renzo searched for the shape of a kestrel, halfway hopeful, halfway afraid. As the birds crossed the dazzling face of the sun, he narrowed his eyes to a squint, but he did not shut them. Because every time he shut his eyes, her face swam in. Lips pursed in concentration, regarding the glass. Holding out the blowpipe to him — *Take it*. Color rising in her face as she held Mama's mantle for the first time.

Behind him Pia said, "You look sad today."

Renzo turned to answer, but she hadn't spoken to him. She had found her beggar again, squatting beside the churchyard wall in his accustomed place after several Sundays away. He was swaddled in rags, his face hidden, but his cupped and outstretched hand, with its gnarled fingers, was clear to view. Pia bent forward to hand him the coin, seeming to peer into his eyes. He tipped his head toward her, and a wedge of sunlight slashed his face, its gaunt lines suffused with something like longing.

Renzo took Pia's hand, suddenly uneasy. "Come, Pia,"

he said. "Let's go." He pulled her away. "You're to put the coin in the alms box, not give it to the beggar!"

Mama stood beside Signore Averlino. She looked back at Pia and Renzo, shading her eyes against the glaring light. Her face was glowing, pink. Her eyes shone. She used to look like this when Papà—

A bright flash of anger shot through him.

She should be attending to Pia!

And Signore Averlino . . . Who did he think he was, this tall, stooped, balding, soft-spoken, dreary man? This *carpenter!*

Renzo remembered how Papà had sung to Mama, how he had danced her around the table, whispering in her ear and making her laugh. He had been a man of gusto, hungry for life. He had eaten and drunk overmuch, but the weight sat well on him, gave him substance. True, he had a temper, but his storms soon blew over, and afterward no one could be more tender. He flirted with every pretty woman who crossed his path, but Mama was the only one he loved.

And he was an artist with the glass, a great master.

This man could never compare to Papà. Not ever.

"Signore Averlino has an important commission, Renzo."

"Only doors," Signore Averlino murmured.

"*Palace* doors, Marcello," Mama said. "I remember when you opened your shop, all those years ago. Did you ever imagine . . . the Doge's Palace!"

Signore Averlino shook his head. "It was a complete surprise. We put in a bid, but—"

"Doors!" Mama said, turning to Renzo and Pia. "The doge wants to leave his mark on the palace. He's commissioned new and handsome doors, each carved with the winged lion of San Marco. Every exterior door of the palace."

Doors. Nothing of beauty there. Nothing of art. Renzo snorted in contempt.

Signore Averlino inclined his head slightly. But Mama turned to look at Renzo—hard. Not with her usual affectionate reproof but with something different. Something cold. The way she might look at a stranger. She took Pia's hand, then turned to Signore Averlino and said something Renzo could not hear. Then they set off, the three of them, across the *campo*, leaving Renzo behind.

◆　　◆　　◆

By the next day, Monday, the *padrone* still had no tidings of Taddeo. It was, he said, as if Taddeo had fallen into a canal, never to reappear.

Renzo pushed aside his worries—for Letta, for the children, for Taddeo, for himself. He tried to lose himself in work.

But later that morning a tiny owl flew into the glassworks. It circled about them, *whooting* in high, flutelike notes, and would not leave until chased out with blowpipes and stones. It might have had a message capsule; Renzo couldn't see for certain. But none of the children had owls. Still, it was odd to see an owl in daylight, and this one so persistent.

Soon clients converged upon the glassworks, and Renzo's thoughts were taken up with the making and selling

of glass—except for a thin hum of worry that wormed its way in, unsettling him as he worked.

The first client was a merchant from the main island, a proud-looking man, richly garbed, with an aquiline nose and sleepy eyes. The *padrone* and Renzo made a glass kestrel for him, the two of them performing a graceful dance before the furnace. When it was done, the *padrone* held the bird out before the merchant, bowing deeply. As Anzoleto bore the bird to the annealing oven, the *padrone* and the merchant sealed an order for forty more, the largest single commission of the year.

After that there were more merchants, and some noble-men, and the captain of a trading ship—a portly, bushy-haired man with a hearty air and a watchful eye. They wanted to stand in the heat of the great furnace; they wanted to watch the falcons emerge from the flowing glass as if by sorcery; they wanted to buy. Now Renzo made the birds alone, save for the addition of glass for the wings. The *padrone* stood beside him, telling a story in his booming voice, a story of fire and soda and sand, a story of transformation, of magic.

The clients all admired the birds, though with the restraint typical of merchants who don't wish to seem over-eager and thereby raise the price. The captain, though, upon gazing at the finished bird, made a disturbing leap.

"All the talk is of birds of late. Have you heard the tidings of the bird children, the ones the Ten are holding in the dungeon?"

Renzo started, nearly dropping the blowpipe.

Sergio was staring at him. Renzo turned away, and was caught by the *padrone's* gaze.

"Bird children?" the *padrone* asked, his voice carefully level.

"I heard tell they were taken in Murano. I thought I saw them once, though I could be mistaken." He shook his great curly head as if to banish the image.

The dungeon. Renzo's knees turned to water beneath him. Quickly he finished the bird and cracked it off the end of the blowpipe. Then he sank to the floor and made a pretense of lacing up a boot.

He'd heard tales of the dungeon. Though it occupied a wing of the Doge's Palace, there was nothing grand about it. People said it was dank and foul and reeking.

It could have been worse, he told himself. If they'd been kidnapped by ruffians, they might all have been slain. And surely the Ten would just deport them.

But still. If only he'd warned them.

The dungeon.

He shivered. Well, at least now he knew for certain they were alive.

◆　　◆　　◆

Late that afternoon two men came into the glassworks. They were garbed as government officials, in velvet caps and long, dark woolen robes. The *padrone* set aside his work and went to greet them; they stood talking in a knot by the doors.

It was over. Someone must have told; they must know what Renzo had done.

He glanced at them from time to time while assisting

Ettore, but the roar of the furnace drowned out all sound of what was said. In a while, though, the *padrone* turned from the men. "Renzo," he called. "Come here."

Renzo handed the blowpipe to Ettore. He crossed the floor, his heart thundering in his chest, looking straight ahead but feeling the weight of every eye in the glassworks upon him.

The *padrone* didn't bother to introduce the men but launched right into a question. "When you came here every night," he asked, "was Taddeo always alone?"

Renzo nodded.

"You never saw anyone with him?"

Renzo shook his head.

"Speak up, boy! You're saying you never saw anyone else in the glassworks with Taddeo? Anyone who didn't belong?"

"No," Renzo said. "I did not."

The words tasted sour in his mouth. He felt his face grow hot with the brazenness of his lie, with the shame of his betrayal.

The *padrone* nodded, shifted his eyes away. Renzo wasn't sure if the *padrone* truly believed him or if it was merely convenient to believe, because of the glass birds.

"It was Taddeo, then," the *padrone* said.

One of the officials raised his brows. "It's a pity he's not alive to defend himself. We'd been searching for those children, and then —"

Renzo gasped. "Not . . . alive?"

"Dead," the *padrone* said gruffly. "Not slain — or at any

pass, it seems not. He was likely affrighted; his old heart probably seized and gave out." He dismissed Renzo, turned again to the men.

Renzo stumbled back toward the furnace.

Dead. Taddeo, dead.

All at once Renzo recalled the look on Mama's face the day before, as if she'd been regarding a stranger. Someone she'd thought she'd known but did not.

Who are you, Renzo? What have you become?

26.

Visit with a Ghost

Renzo couldn't sleep.

He lay in bed, gazing up at the dark rafters, listening to the rain tapping on the roof. His thoughts refused to settle. They leaped about, kicking up visions — of feathers; of blood; of birds; of stern-faced officials in long, dark robes; of mounds of sleeping, ragged children in the depths of the dungeon of the Ten.

Of Letta.

And Taddeo!

In his mind's eye Renzo saw him, dozing on the *padrone*'s chair, drooling contentedly, with Sofia snuggled on his lap.

Dead?

How could that be?

Not five days past he had been fully alive in all his prickly cantankerousness — pointing a sharp, accusing finger at Renzo, upbraiding him in his high, querulous voice.

Taddeo had never seemed to care much for Renzo. And, truth be told, Renzo had not been overly fond of *him*, though he had never wished him ill.

Still, if it weren't for Renzo, Taddeo would be alive today.

But no, Renzo told himself. No one had forced Taddeo to let the children into the glassworks when Renzo was gone. No one had forced him to stay all night. And besides, it was Taddeo's old heart that had killed him—not an assassin's blade or a hangman's rope.

So why the sick guilt that weighed on Renzo's chest?

You didn't need a knife or a rope in order to kill. You could kill with heedlessness, with neglect. People said the dungeon was always chilly and dank. If Paolo's cough returned . . .

It's not my fault!

Renzo threw the blanket aside, leaped to his feet, followed the glow of the dying embers to the hearth, and began to pace before it.

How had *their* problems become *his*?

Surely the Ten wouldn't hold the children long. They were just vagrants, like gypsies. A year ago, when a band of gypsies had come to Venice, they'd been held briefly and then herded onto a boat and let off down the coast, near Ravenna. Likely that was what the Ten would do now.

Vittorio's words echoed in his ears. *Rumors of witchcraft.*

But no.

They'd be banished. Spring was coming. They'd find somewhere warm to shelter, maybe farther south.

But with the gypsies, hadn't they been flogged? Hadn't some of them died?

His knees buckled; he dropped to the floor and lowered his face into his hands.

What could he do?

You may well need me, after all.

The voice echoed in memory. Slowly Renzo raised his head.

He'd never wanted to see Vittorio again. He was dead to them. A ghost. And yet . . .

Who else could Renzo go to?

No one.

And only a ghost could be trusted to keep a secret.

Every Monday at midnight.

Maybe he wouldn't be there. But if he was, he might know something. Maybe he could assure Renzo that the children were well and that they'd only be banished.

And then, maybe he could sleep.

◆　　◆　　◆

At first Renzo didn't see him. The lantern hollowed out a small circle of light, pierced by slanting needles of rain. Beyond, in the darkness, the headstones bristled so thickly that the seated figure seemed but another stone. Yet when the stone unfolded, and stood, and spoke, Renzo knew the voice of his uncle Vittorio.

"Renzo. It's you?"

Renzo edged nearer. Vittorio looked thin and hunched and sodden. How long had he been waiting? Had he been coming every Monday night since he'd made his promise? Had he refused to believe Renzo when he'd told him he would never come to meet him, not ever?

Renzo moved through the thicket of headstones until

Vittorio stood before him. "I want to know about the bird children," Renzo said. "Do you know what's become of them?"

Slowly Vittorio nodded. His eyes had sunk deep into shadowy hollows. His face, in the darkness, seemed to be waiting, seemed to be wanting something else.

Renzo realized he'd spoken abruptly. It would have been kinder to greet Vittorio first, to ask him how he fared.

But Renzo didn't want to be kind.

He pressed on. "I heard they're being held in the dungeon."

"I . . . heard the same."

"It's like those gypsies last year," Renzo said. "They kept them for a couple of days, then transported them down the coast." He waited. Vittorio said nothing.

"*Will* they banish them?" Renzo asked. "Do you know?"

Water oozed into his boots, chilling his feet. He lifted his lantern to his uncle's face. It was gaunt and grave and still. "Vittorio?" he asked, suddenly afraid.

"No," Vittorio said. "They won't banish them, like the gypsies. They're going to put them all on trial . . . as witches."

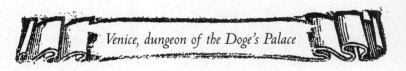

27.

Turtledove

After dark the birds came swooping in. They dipped down from the rooftops and, brushing cold iron bars with their wings, glided from the living, breathing darkness to a place where the air lay still and dead.

They followed the faint kenning-threads toward the nest of their companions, so deep in the belly of the dungeon that the scents of sea and fish and grub scarcely penetrated. Feathers brushed iron again—and then the bliss of reunion.

Only three of the companions remained apart—the youngest one, the hawk's child, and the severed one, whose bird was gone forever.

•   •   •

This bird, Guido thought, had only ever bitten him. It had bloodied the finger he'd poked between the bars of its cage in the marketplace; it had attacked his thumb when, after the bird seller had bound its feet with twine, Guido had thrust it into the burlap sack; it had savagely struck at the back of his hand when he'd tried to stroke its head.

Blasted little bird.

But maybe the boy could tame it. Not the oldest boy, whose hawk, they said, couldn't fit between the bars. But the sick little boy, the one with the missing front teeth, the one whose bird had died.

Guido moved through the dark corridor toward the cells of the women prisoners. He held the torch in one hand and cupped the other on his shirt, over the bag that hung round his neck. He could feel the bird in there, feel its wings straining against the cloth, feel its quick, urgent heartbeat. He had feared that Claudio would notice the bulge there beneath his shirt, but he had not.

Guido set the torch in the cresset just outside the cell. His key grated in the lock; he pushed open the door. They all turned to stare at him — the bird eyes and the bright green human ones. "I brought something," he said, "for the little boy."

He shut the door behind him. He pulled the pouch up from under his shirt, slipped the leather thong from round his neck, and made his way carefully through the huddle of children and birds until he came to where the boy sat leaning against the old woman. He crouched beside them, undid the cord that tied the pouch. Carefully he took out the bird. It flapped and squawked and tried to bite him. The heavy twine crippled it; it couldn't walk; it couldn't stand; it couldn't fly.

"Untie it," the old woman said. "Let it be free."

Guido would have thought that she'd be grateful. He'd have thought she'd at least have smiled.

He bent, untied the bird. It attacked him savagely with its beak. Blast! He put his finger into his mouth, sucked off the blood.

The old woman cupped her hands; the bird jumped in. It settled itself there, as in a nest, as cozy as you please. "A turtledove," the woman said. Now she sounded pleased. She held out the bird to the boy, the poor little birdless boy, who was pale and looked bruised under his eyes.

The boy ducked his head and turned away.

"Paolo," the old woman said. "This young man has brought you a bird."

The boy coughed, long and deep. He waved his hand as if to shoo the bird away.

The old woman turned to Guido. "'Tis kind of you," she said. "But this . . . You can never tell."

The bird fluffed its feathers, stretched up. It hopped onto the little boy's shoulder. The boy tried to shrug it off, but the bird stuck fast. The bird made a cooing sound. Gently it pecked the boy's cheek.

It had only ever drawn blood with Guido. But this peck was like a kiss.

Slowly the boy turned to face it. The bird pecked at his nose, then cocked its head and regarded him with its small ringed eye. They sat there — boy and bird — each gazing at the other, unblinking. For a very long time they sat.

And then, at the selfsame moment, they blinked.

The bird fluffed its feathers; the boy coughed. Chills rippled across Guido's back; he crossed himself.

Witches?

Well, maybe they were, and maybe they weren't. But the old woman turned to smile at him now, and Guido was glad for what he'd done.

28.

House of Bones

Witches.

They hanged witches, Renzo knew.

Or burned them.

He wavered on his feet. He set down the lantern with a clank; the flame leaped. He put out a hand to brace himself on a tombstone — cold, and slick with rain. Vittorio reached toward him, as if to support him, but stayed his hand. He picked up the lantern, motioned to Renzo. "Come."

He set off through the forest of headstones, toward a row of small crypts on the north edge of the churchyard. Renzo followed the bobbing light, a little way behind. Soon Vittorio opened a small door in one of the crypts. He went down a few steps until his shoulders were on the level of the ground, then motioned for Renzo to follow.

Inside, Vittorio set the lantern on the packed earth floor. Renzo shut the door behind him and sat on the lowest step as Vittorio rounded up a motley collection of candle stubs and began lighting them from the lantern.

Stolen candles. Stolen from the dead.

All at once Renzo wondered how Vittorio managed to live day to day. Where did he go? What did he do? Haunting the shadows, breaking into abandoned houses. Stealing, picking up scraps of food and gossip.

Rain pelted at the door but did not reach them, snug in Vittorio's little house of bones. Something brushed against Renzo's hand. A spider. He flicked it off; it scuttled away in the dirt. Vittorio perched himself on a small raised platform between two coffins. His face, at the dim, flickering edge of the light, looked haggard and old.

"Was it those coincidences?" Renzo asked. "The doge's daughter and the magpies? The pigeons and the gondolier?"

Vittorio shrugged. "Rumors of witchcraft dogged them from the moment they set foot in Venice. But their tricks were amusing, and most people saw them as harmless. There was an old woman with them, but she stayed mostly out of sight."

The old woman. Letta had mentioned a grandmother. "But then winter came," Renzo prompted.

"Yes. And suddenly they were a nuisance. The old woman was arrested; the children somehow escaped and came here. Then came those coincidences, and now . . ." Vittorio shook his head. "Who knows why these rumors take root when they do?"

"But they're not witches," Renzo protested. "They're not . . . evil. They're not practicing a craft."

"Maybe not," Vittorio said. "But those eyes of theirs aren't going to help them. Nor the birds."

Renzo sagged. Their eyes: too strange. Too green. And the birds . . . Other performers kept their animals in cages. Not these. And the bond between them, between the children and their birds . . .

Wild birds.

Renzo could almost envy it. But it was strange.

They might not be witches, but they were . . . something. Different. That was certain. And that could be all it took.

Damp soaked through his cloak and into his skin, into his bones. He breathed in candle smoke and the scent of wax, and the dark, rich musk of dirt and grubs. His belly felt sick and heavy.

"Well," Vittorio said, "it's possible the Ten will be sensible and just send them away. But be wary, Renzo. Keep your distance."

"But there must be something—"

"Your duty is to family. Family! I know this better than anyone. When you break with family, you have nothing."

"But I owe them . . . at least the eldest girl. Without her I would have failed the test."

"Look at me, Renzo! Do you want to end up like I am? I was stupid, headstrong, selfish—"

"*You* were selfish. But I want to help someone, someone who helped me."

"You want to help a stranger and risk your family in the process!"

"*I* won't be leaving Murano and setting the assassins on us. I could just . . ."

Just what? What could he possibly do?

A wind gust buffeted the door; the candle flames flickered, leaning all together. A dark weariness had massed behind Renzo's eyes. He lowered his head into his hands. What had he hoped for, following Vittorio to this place? Had he thought Vittorio would help him? Or had he truly hoped that Vittorio would say exactly what he had? That he mustn't bring danger to the family, or to himself.

Renzo lifted his head. "I can't sleep," he said miserably. "I want to be able to sleep."

"Just shut the door on them," Vittorio growled. "Shut the door."

"Can you sleep, Vittorio? Before, you said you couldn't, but can you now?"

Vittorio groaned. His hair hung down in wet strings, and his sodden cloak had shed so much moisture that he was sitting in a pool of water. "How could I sleep," he murmured, "after what happened to your father?"

Renzo reached to touch his silver cloak pin. All at once he longed so strongly for Papà, for his solid physical presence, for his confidence, for the certainty of his convictions. But he, too, would have urged Renzo to care for the family. To shut the door on mere strangers and pour every ounce of energy into the glass, into becoming the legend Papà had dreamed of.

And yet . . .

She came to him again, brandishing the blowpipe at him, instructing him in the curve of a falcon's wing, touching the embroidery of Mama's mantle.

He couldn't imagine never seeing her again in this life. That she and the children should be tried as witches . . .

Unthinkable.

He picked up a pebble from the floor of the tomb and flung it hard against a wall. It bounced off the stones, ricocheted off a coffin, and *thunked* against the door.

Door. *Shut the door.*

Renzo sat up straight, remembering.

External doors for the Doge's Palace.

And the dungeon was inside.

"What is it?" Vittorio asked.

"I have an idea."

"They're in the dungeon of the Ten, Renzo! There's nothing to be done!"

"Maybe. But it wouldn't be so dangerous to find out just this one thing."

If he could do nothing — which was likely — at least he would have tried. And then, and *then* . . .

Maybe he could sleep.

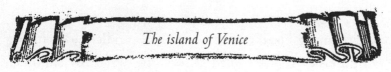

29.

Dagger and Noose

Venice shimmered before them, diamond-bright, a great glass chandelier of a city suspended between the starlit sky and the dark lagoon. Renzo had seen it often — the profile of its skyline on sunny days, the glimmer of lights above the water at night. But he'd never been this close before, well beyond the islands of San Cristoforo and San Michele.

The night was clear but cold. A chill breeze blew in from the Adriatic, numbing Renzo's ears and nose as he hunched in the bow of the little boat Vittorio had bought for himself.

For he had insisted on coming too. "If I can't keep you from this folly," he'd said, "I'll do my best to shield you from harm." Despite his disapproval Vittorio had somehow discovered the location of Signore Averlino's shop. Soon Vittorio deftly navigated the maze of canals to the north of the island until, when they came out on the Grand Canal, the wind had lost its sting and Renzo had forgotten he'd ever been cold.

He gaped at the length of the canal before them, at the fringe of *palazzi* looming to either side — vast and ornate, many blazing with lamps and candles, and ringing with music. Light spilled across the water in shimmering reflections—mirror images of the splendor to either side—broken only by torch-lit gondolas ferrying wealthy Venetians to and fro.

"You might wish to close your mouth, Nephew," Vittorio said. "A bat could fly in that cave."

They paddled along the canal, through the dark waters. When a gondola passed hard by, Renzo glimpsed the sparkle of jewels and a watery froth of bright silks. Smooth, pale shoulders. Half-moons of pink rounded breasts. The girl laughed, like a chiming of goblets of *cristallo*.

Renzo turned to stare as the gondola passed. He breathed in the fragrance of flowers and spice and musk that wafted on the air. Suddenly he was filled with longing for a life of beauty and grace and excitement. A life that was not out of reach for a first-rate glass master, if he stayed out of trouble.

"Watch where you're going!" Vittorio barked out. "And pull up your hood, shadow your face. If you're going to go gawping at every signorina on the canal, people will notice. And you never know who might be a spy."

◆　　◆　　◆

At last they came to the carpenter's shop. It was not on the Grand Canal, but on a smaller canal, a little way north. Two windows faced onto the water; both were securely shuttered. Vittorio glided past the shop and tied up a little way down.

They lay silent in the boat, covered in tarps up to their eyes, and watched. When after a time no night watchman appeared, Vittorio stirred. He pushed back the tarps, withdrew the picklocks from his purse, and motioned for Renzo to wait. He stole across the narrow pavement to the shop door and bent over the lock.

A wave slapped the boat, jostling it against the canal wall. Renzo looked about but saw no other boats save for a few empty ones moored to the sides of the canal. In the distance he could hear faint strains of music. All at once a dark feeling engulfed him, a feeling that he shouldn't be here, that this expedition was perilous as well as futile. The idea he'd had . . . it was beyond impossible; it was mad.

The door opened with a creak. Vittorio vanished inside. In a moment he reappeared and motioned to Renzo: *Come.*

Renzo forced himself to pick up Papà's measuring tools, a lantern Vittorio had brought, and a small, perforated tin box with a few warm coals from the hearth. He joined Vittorio and shut the door behind them.

Dark. Renzo breathed in the sweet scent of wood shavings, the sharp tang of turpentine, of paint. Vittorio took the candle from his lantern and lit it on a still-smoldering coal. By the lantern's flickering glow they made their way among trestles and workbenches, neat stacks of lumber, planed and sanded planks of many sizes, racks of tools, and barrels full of iron nails and wooden pegs. Despite himself Renzo was impressed by the size of the shop, by the fineness and condition of the tools, by the signs of orderly conduct of craft. Signore Averlino didn't dress richly or hold himself grandly; there was nothing about him to suggest that he was the *padrone* of such a place. Renzo had pictured a tiny, dark shop, cramped and cluttered, with maybe one other woodworker and a single, clumsy apprentice.

He drew his fingers across well-oiled, ornately carved panels, each with a winged lion at the center. He peered into crates of wide and narrow bands of iron, iron hasps and hinges, iron locks, iron studs, and pointed iron spikes.

But where were the doors?

"I know he's making doors," Renzo said, feeling foolish. "I heard him say it. And look at all the hinges, the hasps."

"Oh, he's making doors, all right." Vittorio set his lantern on a table. "But they're all in pieces. There's no way of knowing which parts go with which."

Renzo caught sight of something on the table before him. He moved the lantern, set it down beside a stack of paper.

They were neat sketches, with cross sections indicated, materials specified, and measurements marked. The working drawings. Renzo bent over, examining them. They put him in mind of clockwork, with each part fitting precisely into an adjacent part, and all of it gearing together. There was an elegance to this work that he had not appreciated before.

He flipped through the stack of drawings, then stopped. And there they were. Exterior doors. Thick wood; carved panels; iron straps and studs; high, barred windows. Two different doors marked *prisons*. One wide and tall. The other narrow and short.

Vittorio came up beside him. Together they pored over

the drawings. "I don't see any weakness in the design," Vittorio said. "I don't see how they could be jimmied, or the window bars pried loose."

Renzo scanned the drawing again. No. Impossible. "Have you seen the bars?" he asked.

"The window bars?"

Renzo nodded. "Have you seen them here in the shop?"

"No. They may not have been made yet. Look, Renzo, I've humored you long enough. Let's go."

Humored? Was that how Vittorio saw him? As a child, to be humored?

Renzo turned his back on Vittorio. He hunted through the workshop again, peering beneath tables and behind shelves, into open barrels and crates. At last he discovered them stacked against the far wall—two sets of heavy iron bars.

He picked them up, set by set, and laid them on a bench. Each set had a rectangular iron frame around the outside; the bars fit into holes in the frame. One set had bars the width of a grown man's thumbs; they were as long as the distance from Renzo's knee to his ankle. These matched the bars in the drawing of the larger door. The other bars were shorter, thicker. Renzo ran his fingers along the smooth surfaces of the bars and felt a little jolt of excitement.

They were flat black, which wouldn't be difficult to copy. And the frames for the bars were constructed without nail holes. Which meant that the frames would be set *into* the door, not nailed to it. Good! Because if someone were to hammer at the frames holding the bars Renzo was imagining, the bars might shatter.

For they would be made of glass.

◆　　　◆　　　◆

"It's crazy," Vittorio said.

"I know."

"You could get caught making them."

"So I'd break them."

"They wouldn't feel like iron, anyway. Whoever touched them would know."

"I can make them feel like iron."

"You can't make them cold like iron."

"If the room is cold, the glass will be cold enough. It wouldn't work in summer, but . . ." Renzo huffed out a breath of frozen air. "See? And it's not likely to get much warmer for a while."

"We'd have to come back here, and by then the iron ones might have been mounted in the doors."

"So we could . . . I don't know . . . pry the doors open and replace the bars?"

"And then somebody would have to go to the dungeon."

Renzo dipped his head in acknowledgment. That was the part he didn't want to think about. The impossible part.

"It's crazy, Renzo!"

"I *know*."

He picked up the thicker set of bars. His earlier

excitement had fled. Some cowardly part of him wished he hadn't found the bars, because in that case there'd have been nothing he could do.

But he had found them.

Surely the Ten would only banish Letta and the other children. But if it was worse than that . . .

Well. He had to try something.

If only so he could sleep.

◆　　◆　　◆

Vittorio studied the sketches while Renzo emptied the leather pouch he had inherited, filled with Papà's equipment — a sharpened quill, a vial of ink, a rolled-up piece of parchment, and three different kinds of calipers. He measured the lengths and diameters of the bars themselves and the lengths, widths, and depths of the rectangular iron frames that held the bars all together.

"Look at this bit of cleverness," Vittorio said, pointing to one of the drawings. "The door comes together like two hands praying, leaving tidy notches between the layers to hold the window bars in place."

Renzo looked at him. It seemed that the craftsman in Vittorio was intrigued.

"But when they nail the halves of the door together," Renzo said, "isn't it bound to jar the glass and break it?"

"It's all held together with iron straps and studs. Nothing is nailed; it's done with an auger."

Still, Renzo thought, you didn't need a hammer to crack a set of glass bars.

He was rolling up the parchment with his measurements when Vittorio laid a hand on his arm.

"Did you hear that?"

He shook his head.

"Outside, by the canal."

Vittorio blew out the candle. They stood motionless in the dark. Renzo heard the soft hiss of Vittorio's breathing. He thought he heard the splash of a wave against the seawall, and a little thumping scrape.

Vittorio crept toward the door.

Renzo stuffed Papà's tools into the bag—all except for the large, straight calipers with the pointed ends. He dropped the coal onto the floor and ground out the last remaining sparks, then put the tin box in the pouch, pulled it shut, and slung the looped pull-string over one shoulder. He felt for the lantern and took it in one hand; he felt for the calipers and gripped them in the other. Slowly he groped his way through the dark to the door, where Vittorio waited.

"What is it?" Renzo whispered.

"Shh." Vittorio unlatched the door and pushed it a little ajar. He was still hesitating when the latch sprang from his grasp, and the door was flung wide.

A dark, hooded cape. A white full–face mask hiding a face. The man came at Vittorio, pulling him through the doorway, twisting him to one side. A hand—large and twisted—rose above Vittorio, and by the starlight Renzo made out the shimmering outline of . . . What was it? A thin cord of some kind. It dropped over Vittorio's head and tightened around his neck.

Vittorio gasped, put his hands up to his throat, tried to pull the cord away. He sputtered, made a terrible gurgling noise.

The mask had turned away from Renzo, but he could clearly see one of the hands that held the cord. He stabbed it with the pointed tips of the calipers. Again. Again.

A grunt of pain. Vittorio stumbled backward. A flash of steel; the man lunged at Vittorio. Vittorio ducked, then howled. Renzo rushed at the attacker, dropping the lantern and flailing wildly with the calipers. His toes *thunked* against a paving stone; he toppled forward onto the man. He felt the ends of the calipers gain purchase, felt them pierce through some sinewy barrier. Then they sluiced on in, as if through soft pudding.

A groan. The man twisted out from beneath him, began to rise. Renzo felt the calipers start to lurch from his grip, but he held them tight, yanked them back.

They were slick with blood.

The man tottered to his feet. A *clang*; something metal hit the pavement. A dagger. The man bent as if straining to retrieve it, but Renzo was quicker; he scrabbled across the pavement and kicked the dagger into the canal.

The man cursed. He was bleeding. Blood on his hands, blood on his arm. His cloak had pulled away from one shoulder, and blood bloomed in a spreading stain across his shirt. He leaned over, coughed up something dark. He straightened, turned toward Renzo. The mask regarded him, pitiless and blank. Renzo rose to a crouch, his hand clenching the calipers tight.

The man turned from him and was seized with a spasm of coughing. He spat, and staggered away.

Renzo watched, transfixed, until the man disappeared into an alley. He let out his breath, loosened his grip on the calipers. He turned to his uncle, still lying on the pavement.

"Vittorio," he said, "let's go."

Vittorio moaned.

"Uncle?" Renzo went to kneel beside him. Blood everywhere. On his face, his throat, his cloak, his hands.

"I can't see," Vittorio said.

Renzo set down the calipers and pulled Vittorio's hands away from his face. Blood. So much blood. A wound to the head? Renzo wiped some of it away with a corner of his cloak. Now he could see the cut itself, slashing from Vittorio's temple and across one eye. Renzo daubed at the blood near the eyes. Then stopped and stared.

One of Vittorio's eyes looked up at him. But where the other eye should have been . . . was a mass of bloody pulp.

30.

Leaks

His first mistake, the assassin thought, had been pausing to look at the boy. It wasn't that he'd broken a rule. The boy was not his intended target, and so the rule he had made for himself — never look quarry in the eye — did not apply.

Still, he shouldn't have paused, shouldn't have looked. The look had penetrated, unexpectedly. It had broken his rhythm. Thrown him off. He'd made a similar mistake with the boy's father. He hadn't gone in intending to kill him — not for certain. As it had turned out, that death was not required. Except that the father had fought, fought hard and too well. In the end he'd had to die.

A waste.

The assassin hated waste.

Painfully he leaned forward in bed and wound the end of the bandage about his shoulder. The wound wouldn't kill him; he knew that now. Earlier he hadn't been sure. But the bleeding had slowed, and when he spit into the pail, it was pink — no longer the full, rich red of grapes on the vine.

Not leaking anymore, inside him. The calipers must have grazed his lung, but they hadn't pierced it, or at least hadn't torn it. He would live.

True, he'd have to rest awhile. But he must strike again, and soon. He couldn't afford to wait.

The calipers. That had been his second mistake. He'd had no reason to think the boy might have a weapon. But he should have looked; he should have checked.

He took a sip of wine from the cup on his night table. It hurt to move his arm. Hurt to swallow. Hurt to breathe. His fingers ached—his warped and untidy fingers. Which used to be so supple. Which didn't used to cause him any trouble at all.

Morning light had begun to ooze through his windows, leaking watery shadows onto the wall, striking light on the bent silver cloak pin on the table by the cup.

No, he thought, his first mistake had come much earlier. He had underestimated them. All his other mistakes—and there had been many—had flowed from that. He ought to have struck right away, on Murano, the moment he'd recognized the defector meeting his nephew at the boat. But he'd been curious; he'd continued to follow. And then, in Venice, he shouldn't have chosen the cord. It should have been a stiletto to the kidney, or a snap of the neck.

Had the cord seemed softer somehow? Less painful for the boy to witness?

He set down the wineglass, then gingerly lay back in

bed. Something heavy there, squatting on his chest. He closed his eyes.

The pain had been astonishing. Bright. So blazingly bright. That, too, had distracted him. It had been long since he'd felt that kind of pain.

He drifted back to his first time, when he was seventeen, and to another enemy of one sort or another. Had it been a spy? A conspirator? A defector? He couldn't recall. The man had seen him coming, had stabbed him in the side with a sword. He in return had slit the man's throat. Then dropped to his knees and heaved into the canal.

He drifted farther back, to the village where he was born — and to a time when he was not alone. The little brook that gurgled past their cottage. The sweet smell of apple blossoms in spring. The grape vines heavy with fruit. His mother's voice, and his little sister . . .

So like the other one, she was. Their faces overlapping . . .

He had thought he could lock up his sister in a tight little box in memory. Let her out only when he wished. But the boundaries were blurring, had sprung a multitude of leaks; the memories threatened to flood him. It would not be long before he made another mistake, one he could not hide, and then . . .

Carefully he sat up again. Took another sip of wine. Yes, the pain had ebbed, but he could still feel the weight there on his chest.

All at once it came to him how he would die — alone. Not now, but sometime in the not-too-distant future.

Perhaps in this squalid little room, perhaps in another like it. Or it could happen suddenly. There would be a quick, bright pain, and then . . .

Nothing. Oblivion.

Or maybe the fires of hell.

He wasn't ready for that. Not yet.

He would have to fulfill this commission. If he did not, they would seek him out, they would dispatch him.

Think. He must think. It would not be by strength or skill at arms that he would finish this. It would have to be by guile.

And after that, if he could manage to disappear completely, he might have a chance at life.

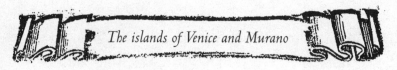

31.

To Snuff Out a Life

R enzo stared, unable to look away. Something heaved in his belly, like a fish flopping, heavy and deep. At first, he'd thought the eye itself was gone, but now he could see that it was still intact but bleeding profusely and oozing a pale, runny goo like raw egg whites.

A burst of laughter; Renzo ripped his gaze from the eye and looked about. A little way off, a cluster of bobbing lanterns—a group of partygoers threading away from them along the edge of the dark canal. Renzo leaped to his feet. "I'll get help."

"No," Vittorio said. "Stay. Don't draw their notice."

"But your eye . . ."

"Sit. Wait."

Renzo didn't want to wait. He wanted to do something, get away from the horrible, ruined eye. Fetch someone else to deal with it. But he moved toward Vittorio and squatted down beside him. He wiped the calipers on his shirt. He put them into the pouch. In a moment the revelers disappeared down an alley.

"Are they gone?" Vittorio asked.

"Yes."

"Are you hurt?"

Was *he* hurt? How could Vittorio think of him, when his eye . . .

"*Are* you?" Vittorio repeated.

"I don't think so." Renzo patted himself about his chest and sides. Sticky. His cloak was all-over wet and sticky. He reached underneath and touched his shirt. It felt sticky too.

Blood.

But he didn't hurt enough in any one place to have produced all that blood himself. It must be the blood of the man who had attacked them.

"You have to bandage my eye. Can you do that?"

The eye — a churn of gore.

Vittorio didn't wait for an answer but, groaning, rolled to a sitting position. "Tear a strip from the bottom of your shirt."

Renzo did. He wrapped the cloth twice about Vittorio's head, covering the bad eye and leaving the good one exposed. He tied the ends of the cloth together. It was easier to look at Vittorio now.

"Help me into the boat."

Renzo took his arm and tried to lift him to his feet, but Vittorio was too heavy; he cried out in pain. "It's my ankle," he said. "I'll have to crawl."

In the distance Renzo heard more voices. Coming this

way? But the boat wasn't far, no more than five or six steps. Still, it took Vittorio forever, pushing a knee up under himself, scooting forward, pushing and scooting, pushing and scooting. Renzo held the boat steady as Vittorio sat at the edge of the canal and toppled into the bottom of the boat with a *thud* and an echoing splash. Renzo started to get into the boat, but Vittorio rasped, "The lock."

"What?"

"Replace the padlock and snap it shut. I heard it fall."

But voices swelled, and a spray of lanterns appeared around a corner. A group of well-dressed young men and women, coming in their direction.

"Uncle, I think we should go now."

"Fasten it," Vittorio said. "Hurry."

Renzo bolted across the blood-slick pavement to the carpentry shop door. The hasp—empty. He dropped to his hands and knees and felt along the threshold, along the pavement, along the floor inside. His fingers flicked something hard; it skittered away from him. He groped for it; his fingers closed around cold iron. The padlock. Still open. He stood, shut the door, and threaded the shackle through the door's hasp. He snapped the lock shut.

The revelers were nearly upon him. Renzo scrambled back across the path, heading for the boat. One foot kicked something—Vittorio's lantern. It clattered away on the pavement. Renzo slipped, went crashing down, knocking a knee so hard against a paving stone that for a moment he couldn't breathe for the pain.

Don't cry, he told himself. Just don't cry.

He felt a strong hand grip his arm, pulling him to his feet. "So, what have we here?" Renzo looked up into the face of a grinning young nobleman. His breath reeked of spirits. Renzo whipped his arm away and ran for the boat.

Shouting, behind him. A woman laughed.

Renzo jumped in, slipped off the mooring lines, picked up the oars, and slid the boat down the dark canal.

He rowed as hard as he could, his bloodbeat thudding in his ears. He turned one corner and then another, glancing back from time to time, fearing there might be someone behind them, someone following. The canals wove through canyons of looming palazzi, churches, and warehouses. But soon he was deep in a maze of smaller, narrower canals. The noises had faded behind him; all he could hear was the swishing of his oars in water. The buildings squatted to either side, unbroken by flickers of torchlight or lamplight.

Where was he?

Where was the lagoon?

In Murano he knew every bend of every canal, day or night. But Venice had more canals—many, many more— each one unfamiliar.

"Uncle?"

A groan.

"Do you know where we are?"

Vittorio, lying on the bottom of the boat, didn't sit up to look. "Just go north," he said. And then, more softly, "San Cristoforo."

San Cristoforo. One of the two little islands on the way to Murano. Had Vittorio been staying there? That, at least, would be easy to locate . . . if Renzo ever found the lagoon.

Go north. Easier said than done. The canals wound this way and that; they paid no attention to *north*. But the stars at least were familiar. At last Renzo glimpsed the lagoon ahead, gleaming faintly in the moonlight. The wind freshened, and the close, suffocating canals of Venice dropped away behind.

◆   ◆   ◆

By the time they came abreast of San Cristoforo, Renzo had begun to worry. The wind blew hard against him, slowing him down, forcing him to strain at the oars. Whitecaps rose up on the water and hurled streams of icy spray against his face and chest. A bank of clouds bore down on them, blotting out most of the stars. Renzo's legs had begun to wobble, and he could feel his energy ebbing away.

He thought about the sets of iron bars, still sitting on the bench. What if someone noticed they'd been moved? But the carpenter must have at least a couple of helpers. Who could know who had moved what? In the glassworks no one would remark on such a thing.

Another worry assailed him: His cloak pin was gone. Papà's cloak pin. He'd lost it.

Well. Maybe it had fallen into the boat. He'd look later.

He gazed down at Vittorio, huddled near his feet. Shivering now, his breath loud and ragged. What did he do there, in San Cristoforo? How did he live?

He was not fit to take care of himself. Even if he could risk seeing a surgeon about the eye, something was amiss with his ankle; he couldn't walk.

The other island, San Michele, had a monastery. Might he leave Vittorio there for the monks to care for?

But no. Even monks could be dangerous for glassblowers who left Murano.

The assassin . . .

He must have been an assassin, the man who had attacked them.

But Renzo felt there was something familiar about him, something he couldn't place.

With a sick lurch Renzo recalled the feel of the calipers piercing sinew, ramming home. Was that what it felt like to kill? To snuff out a life? To send a soul flying from its body?

The man had staggered away. Had he survived?

Vittorio moaned. He opened his good eye and looked about dazedly. "Where are we?"

Renzo set down the oars, let them drag in the water. He rubbed his aching shoulders. "San Cristoforo."

Vittorio raised himself on one elbow. "There's a dock on the north side of the island. Let me out there."

"But, Uncle, who will take care of you?"

Vittorio shrugged. "I have no need of care."

But he did. His teeth were chattering now; he had a feverish look about him. His eye would likely fester; he couldn't walk.

Somewhere, in a far back corner of Renzo's mind, a bell was tolling a warning: Don't. Don't bring him home. He's a danger to us all. He's brought this on himself.

"Take me to the island, Renzo. I order you: Leave me."

Renzo knew he should. But . . .

To snuff out a life . . .

His traitorous hands, of their own accord, grasped the oars. They began to row for Murano.

Vittorio lunged for an oar, then recoiled, seized with a spasm of coughing. "I *order* you," he croaked out.

Renzo's arms kept on rowing. He did not reply.

◆   ◆   ◆

First light, the color of egg yolks, gathered beneath a low, black mantle of clouds to the east. Renzo guided the boat through the familiar canals of Murano. A haze of weariness pressed down upon him; pain rode his shoulders, his back, his legs. At last, when home appeared before him, relief coursed through Renzo's body so powerfully that his knees buckled and the oars nearly slipped from his grasp. He forced himself to row the last little way, then slipped the lines over the bollards at the edge of the canal. He stowed his oars and crouched beside Vittorio.

It had been a hard crossing. At times Vittorio had been taken with bouts of coughing; at times he'd writhed and moaned with pain; at times he'd seemed to doze for a while before the pain had woken him again. At times he'd muttered — foreign-sounding words, perhaps names of people or places Renzo had never heard of.

In the thin glaze of morning light, Renzo could see that Vittorio's good eye was closed, and that blood and puss had seeped clear through the bandage over the ruined one. He shivered. Renzo set his hand on Vittorio's forehead. Hot.

He pondered what to say to Mama, but couldn't find the words. She would do what she would do.

"Uncle," he said. He shook him.

Vittorio groaned. The good eye blinked open, looked blearily about.

"You have to stand now. Get out of the boat." Renzo took him by the hands, helped him to sit up. He put an arm about him. "Straighten your legs, Uncle. Stand up." Renzo strained to lift him, and had just begun to despair when Vittorio's legs suddenly stiffened, and before Renzo could shift himself to guide him, Vittorio stepped out of the boat and onto dry land.

Perhaps, Renzo thought, getting out of a boat is a thing that people of the lagoon never forget. Perhaps it is woven into our sinews, knit into our bones.

They went tottering toward the doorway, Renzo's arm clamped about Vittorio's waist.

Just as they reached the threshold, the door swung open. Mama gave out a cry. She moved toward Renzo, then looked at Vittorio, puzzled.

She didn't recognize him. Not yet. How could she? It wasn't just the filthy bandage, which covered a goodly portion of his face. Even without it he was not the laughing, reckless Vittorio she had known. This man was sober, gaunt, bearded, limping, bloody, ragged, stinking, soaked.

She turned back to Renzo, questioning. Then, as he watched, recognition flickered in her eyes and then flooded the planes of her face. "Vittorio," she whispered.

Renzo nodded. "He's hurt, Mama. It's bad."

32.

Amends

Mama stared, absolutely still. Renzo didn't know what she was going to do—whether slam the door in their faces or collapse in a faint or throw herself at Vittorio in a rage. He groped for words, but they all skittered away from him, leaving him blank. Mama made a little sound, a dry, hoarse, choking sound. Her hands flew to her mouth, and she seemed to break in the middle, as if someone had clouted her in the belly.

Vittorio whispered, "Gabriella," and then he was limping toward her across the threshold. He reached out a hand toward her cheek. "Oh, Gabriella," he said, "I'm sorry."

She was crying then, Mama was. Both of them wept, leaning into each other, seeming to prop each other up.

"Mama?" Pia appeared in the gloom behind them.

Renzo slipped into the house, skirting Mama and Vittorio. He took Pia's hand.

"Who is that?" Pia asked. "Why is Mama crying?"

"It's Uncle Vittorio," Renzo said.

Pia studied Vittorio, then turned back to Renzo. "But I

thought . . . ," Pia began. She lifted her face to Renzo. "We hate him, don't we?"

He shrugged. "Maybe not." They watched in silence. Anything could happen. Mama could spit on Vittorio, she could slap him, she could shove him out the door.

But in a moment Mama dried her eyes on her sleeve. She took Vittorio's hand, drew it across her shoulders, and put an arm about him. She led him into the house, and with a sigh of relief Renzo pulled the door shut behind.

◆　　◆　　◆

He would have liked to sleep — to fall into bed for the hour that remained before he had to leave for work — but Mama wouldn't let him. She drew an old blanket over his bed and directed him to help Vittorio onto it. Then she examined *Renzo* for wounds, despite his protestations. He was a man, or very nearly so. He didn't need his mother inspecting every scrape and bruise. *Vittorio* was gravely injured; she should attend to him right away.

She was deaf to his words. But in a moment, when she had satisfied herself that Renzo was not mortally wounded, she turned to examine Vittorio, bidding Renzo to strip out of his bloody clothes, wash himself, dress himself, chop wood, start a fire in the hearth, draw water from the well, and heat it in the cauldron.

She was on a rampage. She sent Pia to and fro, fetching honey and herbs and linens. She tore up rags and knotted them together. She set tea on to steep; she chopped things and boiled things and strained things. And in between she peppered Renzo with questions. "Why were you going to the glassworks at night? Aren't you done with that now?" she demanded, pounding the pestle into the mortar, releasing the sharp smell of poultice herbs.

"I, uh . . . Sometimes I'll have to—"

"And what of all that blood?" she asked, not giving him a chance to answer. "Both of you were soaked in it, but I don't see from your injuries where so much blood could have come from."

Renzo picked up a log and threw it onto the fire, buying time to think.

He didn't want to tell her about the assassin. He didn't want to tell her about the bird children, and he most certainly didn't want to tell her what he and Vittorio had planned to do at the carpentry shop. So he'd concocted a tale in which Vittorio had approached him on his way to the glassworks and they'd had a chance encounter with a thief. Ever since, Mama had been poking holes in his story.

"Well?" she demanded now.

"I think," Renzo said, "Vittorio may have cut the thief. With his, uh, knife. And so, much of the blood was the thief's. And then I was trying to lift Vittorio, so I got bloody too." A bead of sweat slid down his forehead; he wiped it off.

"Lorenzo, this doesn't make sense. He should never have come back, putting us in peril like this!" She thumped the pestle hard into the mortar. *Thump. Thump. Thump.*

If she only knew how perilous the situation was. Renzo had wounded the assassin, perhaps killed him, but how long would it take the Ten to send another one? The assassins had never killed women and children before, but . . . Renzo and his family could be put in prison for harboring Vittorio. They could lose everything.

"Why *did* he come back?" Mama demanded. "Did he say?"

"I think," Renzo said, "he wanted to make amends."

Mama went still for a moment, the pestle loose between her fingers. Then she set to grinding again.

"Never." The word was so soft, Renzo wasn't certain he had heard it. But then Mama faced him, eyes fierce. "I can't just let him die, but he can never make amends."

⋄ ⋄ ⋄

The morning passed, for Renzo, in a haze of fatigue. He made falcon after falcon for the commission of the sleepy-eyed merchant. Sergio wanted to make them too, but he couldn't seem to get the knack. His birds looked rigid, leaden, earthbound—like Renzo's early attempts, before Letta had taught him to truly see and appreciate the living falcon. Time and again the *padrone* held up some poor clumsy artifact of Sergio's, then flung it into the broken-glass pail. "Too stiff!" *Crash!* "A masterpiece of gracelessness." *Crash!* "When bullocks fly, this bird of yours will join them." *Crash!*

Despite himself Renzo pitied Sergio. His own father would never have humiliated him this way. The *padrone* had ever been harsh with Sergio, but after Renzo's promotion it seemed to have grown worse.

But there were birds to make — birds and birds and birds. The long, sleepless night weighed on Renzo, a heavy black fog that throbbed in his skull and penetrated to the outside corners of his eyes. He was proud to work as a man on this commission—as a full-fledged glassblower—but he began to grow weary of crafting the same falcon over and over. Once, when he made some small change—an improvement, Renzo thought—the *padrone* corrected him, told him that the merchant had paid to receive precisely the falcon he had been shown.

Renzo knew he ought to be grateful. He was an apprentice now, on the path Papà had set out for him. Already his work was admired by the powerful and the wealthy. Someday he would be able to support Mama and Pia in comfort. One day he might be famous, even legendary.

But still . . .

That first night, when he and Letta had made the falcon together, it had seemed a miracle, a thing of joy. But now, after so many . . . Something that had been glowing in him began to darken, grow brittle and hard. More and more as he worked that day—making the same wings, the same beak, the same head and belly and tail—more and more he thought fondly of those nights in the glassworks, interrupted by children who needed noses wiped and bruises kissed . . . of the way he and Letta had worked together on the bird, trying one thing and then another until, when it was done, he couldn't recall who had thought of what.

She had discovered the falcon in the glass. *She* had called down the kestrel to his wrist, had taught him how to see it. Everything he had now he owed to her.

How had he come to a place where the glassworks, a place for men to work, felt empty without this girl?

Were the children with her, all in one cell? Or had they been separated? Was the food sufficient? Were they warm enough? Did they have hope of getting out, or had they despaired of ever seeing daylight again?

This plan of his, it had been chancy from the start. Now, with Vittorio gravely wounded and the assassin on to him . . .

Impossible.

Surely the Ten wouldn't condemn the children as witches. Surely the children would be banished to some new place, where life would be difficult. But they would get by—as they had ever done before.

◆　　◆　　◆

A turmoil of restless dreams roused him in the wee hours of the following morning, and despite his weariness he couldn't get back to sleep. The dreams had dredged up a memory—that Papà had once experimented with making "unbreakable" glass. He had failed, but some of the glass he'd formulated had been surprisingly strong. Renzo lay awake trying to recall what the formula had been, and before he knew it, he found himself hurrying through the dark alleys to the glassworks, imagining assassins around every corner. He announced himself to the new nighttime fire tender—a tall, burly man who'd been charged with guarding the glassworks as well—and went straight to work.

It was good that the bars in Signore Averlino's shop hadn't been rusted. Making black glass that mimicked the patina of iron would not be too difficult. Well, iron was not as smooth as glass, but he could play with the surface texture. But the real challenge would be making them strong. Strong enough to survive being attached to the doors; strong enough to survive being dropped or kicked or jostled as the doors were transported and installed at the dungeon; strong enough to survive the multitude of ordinary slams and rattles of daily use. At least for a while.

Over the next few nights Renzo tested several batches, made many sets of window bars of the correct dimensions, texture, and hue.

Just to see if it could be done.

Likely they would never be used. The plan was crazy, even more so after what had happened to Vittorio.

Nevertheless, the strongest bars, he kept.

◆　　◆　　◆

For a while there was no opportunity to speak to Vittorio alone. Mama hovered nearby, tending to him at all hours of the day and night. Pia scurried back and forth, fetching bandage cloths and pots of ointment. Once, Renzo came home to find her sitting on the edge of Vittorio's cot, telling him a story. Another time she held his hand and steadied him as he walked.

Renzo searched for his silver cloak pin but couldn't find it. He replaced it with his old copper one, feeling sick. Mama hadn't noticed yet, but when she did . . . Papà's cloak pin! He didn't want to face her.

But on Sunday, Mama and Pia dressed for mass. If

they didn't go, Mama said, people would begin to wonder if something was amiss. People might come to visit. But Renzo should stay with Vittorio; Mama would make apologies for him, would say he had been working late at night.

Vittorio was dozing when they left. He looked much improved. A clean, white cloth lay over the gash in his brow and his ruined eye. His skin, which had been gray, had recovered its color, and his long, dark hair lay clean and combed about his head. His breath came easily, and the corners of his mouth turned up in a peaceful smile.

Vittorio should leave now — or very soon. Before they were caught sheltering him. Before he brought down disaster upon the family for a second time.

Renzo knelt beside him. "Uncle," he whispered.

The eye blinked open. It flicked toward the corners of the room, then came to rest on Renzo.

"Uncle, how are you?"

Vittorio groaned and struggled to sit up in bed. Renzo fluffed up a pillow and set it behind his back. "Did you make the window bars?" Vittorio asked.

"Yes."

"I was afraid of that."

"They're strong. I remembered one of Papà's formulas to strengthen the glass. The bars look like iron, and the surface texture —"

Vittorio made a swatting motion. "It's crazy!"

"Listen, Uncle. I can take them to the workshop and replace the iron ones. There's little enough danger in that."

"Little enough danger! Do you hear yourself? Look at me, Renzo." He leaned forward and jabbed a finger in the direction of the cloth that covered his eye. "And you say there's no danger?"

"But I . . . stabbed him with the calipers."

"Did he walk away?"

"Yes, but——"

"Was he limping? Bleeding?"

"Yes! More than limping. Staggering."

"You didn't see his face? His mask never slipped?"

"No."

"You swear it?"

"By almighty God."

Vittorio let out a long sigh. He eased himself back against the pillow. He seemed . . . weary. Not just body-weary but weary in his soul. "Well, then," he said, "you may be safe enough for now. So long as you can't identify him, I doubt he'll come for you. Antonio was punishment for me, because they couldn't find me. But the man has seen me now, knows I'm somewhere on the lagoon. It's me he wants." Vittorio leaned his head back and closed his eye.

Truth be told, Renzo had expected Vittorio to put up more of a fight. Truth be told, Renzo didn't want to row across the lagoon again, all alone, to the place where they'd been accosted. Didn't want to break into the carpentry shop, knowing he might be watched, knowing he might be caught. And what if the dungeon doors had been assembled already?

He could never pry them apart and reassemble them by himself.

But he had to try.

Yet after that . . .

Then what?

"Uncle?"

The eye opened. "You still have a problem, don't you?" Vittorio said. "Once the doors are installed in the dungeon."

"You must know people who can break into things, and . . ." Thieves, Renzo thought. Beggars. In Vittorio's twilight world there must be many desperate people. Renzo couldn't scrape up much to pay them, but . . .

Vittorio was frowning at him. "You're going to do this no matter what I say, aren't you?"

Renzo nodded. He'd do something. He didn't know what.

"Did something happen between you and the girl?"

"What?"

"With the oldest girl? The one with all that dark hair?"

"Happen?" Renzo's face grew warm as he realized what Vittorio was asking. "No!"

"Hmph." Vittorio was quiet for a moment. He tipped back his head; the lone eye gazed up at the ceiling, as if searching for something it had lost. "They none of them had shoes."

"What?"

"The children. They don't have shoes."

"No, just strips of cloth, wrapped around. I did give

one of them a pair of Pia's outgrown boots, but—" He stopped, remembering the tiny boot in the alley.

"The little boy . . . that terrible cough . . ."

"Paolo," Renzo said. "He was getting better, but—"

"Strangers," Vittorio murmured.

"What?" Renzo was having trouble following this conversation.

"They're strangers here. They're all alone."

Something Vittorio had said earlier came back to Renzo. *When you're a stranger . . . I was all alone.*

"Well, then," Vittorio said. "The Ten don't send assassins after people for breaking into carpentry shops. Just switch the bars. If you're about to get caught, throw them into the canal. If we're lucky, we may have a little time."

We. So Vittorio would help?

Renzo gazed at him, hope rising. But Vittorio yawned, shut his solitary eye, and turned to face the wall.

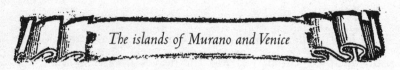
33·

Acqua Alta

At the stroke of midnight Renzo rose. He dressed quickly, tonged a hot coal into the tin box, drew on his cloak, and picked up the lantern. He slipped outside, closing the door softly behind him.

Inside Vittorio's little boat he checked the bundle he had stashed in the bow the night before: two sets of glass bars, wrapped in cloth, supported with boards on either side and bound together with twine.

He pulled up his hood against the light rain, undid the mooring lines, and paddled silently down the canal.

Something felt different tonight. It took a moment before he realized what it was. The wind. A warm wind, coming from the south.

A *scirocco* wind.

Renzo steered toward the side of the canal and eyed the water level.

Just as he'd feared. It was higher than usual. Not three fingers' breadth from the top of the wall.

Acqua alta. High water.

He stilled his hands on the oars, staring out across the rain-dimpled canal, hearing the waves splash against the stone walls. Soon, very likely, water would stream across the lanes and seep under doors. People would wake. They would rise from their beds to stuff rags beneath the doors of homes, of churches, of workshops, of warehouses. They would go stirring about the town at a time when they usually stayed abed.

When Renzo *wanted* them abed.

But now, because of the *acqua alta*, he might be missed. Mama would scold if he wasn't there to help.

Not an auspicious night.

But still, who knew when the carpenters would hang the new doors? After that it would be too late.

He dug his oars into the water and began to row.

At last, sodden and weary, he reached the island of Venice and guided his boat into the shelter of a canal. The wind abated, and even the rain seemed to ease. Lamplight flickered in the windows of some of the shops and houses. But unlike the last time, when masked and glamorous party-goers had glided past in torch-lit gondolas, now only dark figures bustled about, hunched against the rain. All around he heard the gurgling of water as it lipped over the edges of the canal and flowed into the streets.

What would he do if the carpenters were already there, come to set everything of value above the likely high-water mark and stuff rags between the door and the threshold?

But when at last Renzo turned a corner and rowed

within sight of the carpentry shop, no light leaked through the cracks at the edges of the shutters.

Had they already come and gone? Nearing, Renzo searched for rags. But no. Water lapped against the door, flowed unimpeded through the gaps.

He hesitated. They might come at any moment.

No time to lose.

He tied up a little way down from the shop, so his boat would not likely be noticed. He picked up the lantern and the tin box, then bent to lift the bars. Carefully he stepped out onto the paving stones, where water reached well above his ankles.

Something bumped against his boots. A stream of rats, swimming past. He jumped back sharply to avoid them, but felt a squirming bulge beneath one boot and heard a squeal. His feet slipped; he landed hard on the ground.

Splash!

Crack!

The glass.

Hands shaking, he unwrapped the bars and ran his fingers along them. The top set — the thicker ones — seemed fine. But the bottom set . . . had snapped.

He picked out the broken pieces, five of them. He rose gingerly to his feet, carried them to the canal. He dropped them into the dark water and felt the weight of them dragging him down, as if he were sinking too.

Gone.

There had been two dungeon doors in the carpenter's

sketches, but Renzo had only ever heard of one. If the thicker bars were for a door to some different part of the palace, they were no use to him. And the others had broken so easily! They'd been weak!

He groaned. Maybe he should just go home.

But still . . .

The shorter, thicker window bars had always seemed sturdier. And once fitted properly into their slots in the little door, they would be braced on all sides. They might hold fast.

Carefully he rewrapped the bars and clasped them to his chest. He gathered up the lantern and the tin box and waded across the slippery pavement to the door. He set down the bars, fished Vittorio's picks from his purse, and fumbled for the one he'd told him to use.

To his relief the padlock soon snapped open. He hung it on the hasp and collected the bars. He had to lean hard against the door to open it; the water resisted. But at last he let himself in and shut the door fast behind.

Dark. He stood there a moment, thinking about rats, thinking about water snakes, thinking about the last time he had come.

The assassin.

Voices now, outside. Light stretched across the room, shrank back, stretched again. Sloshing sounds. Renzo held his breath, stood perfectly still. In the moving light he made out a table just in front of him. He searched for the iron bars, realizing he had no idea where he might find them. They could be anywhere, even mounted in the doors.

The light passed. The voices faded. Renzo let out his breath. He swished through the water to the table and set down lantern, box, and bars. He opened the tin box.

The coal had gone dead.

He felt himself sag. What was he doing here, in Venice, in the middle of the night? He should be home, warm in bed.

A thin wash of gray leaked in through the shutters, but just a few paces away from them, the room was as black as a crow. Renzo tried to remember what the brighter light had shown a moment ago — the positions of benches and tables. He swished through the water. Was it higher now? It seemed so. Halfway to his knees. One leg bumped against something hard — a table. Reaching for the edge, his hand brushed against something hard and smooth and cold.

He ran his fingers along it.

Bars.

These were the longer ones. He knew the shape of them by heart. He moved along the edge of the table, groping blindly for the second set.

And there they were.

He felt them, learning their dimensions.

Yes.

He went back for the glass bars and switched the two sets, putting the iron ones on the floor. The glass bars felt naked, unprotected. How was it possible they wouldn't be jostled or hit or twisted? How was it possible they wouldn't break?

Voices.

He stilled, hoping they would pass.

They grew louder. A bright light flickered through the shutters. A rattling sounded at the door.

The padlock. Still open, hanging from the hasp.

He cast about for a place to hide. The door opened; a widening pool of light bled across the surface of the water. Renzo threw himself under the bench, shuddering at the shock of cold water.

"Fiorello? Are you here?"

Renzo recognized the voice—Signore Averlino.

"Look, he left his lantern." A different voice.

"Fiorello!" Signore Averlino called.

Silence. Light flared across the room.

"Well, if he was here," Signore Averlino said, "he didn't accomplish much. Let's to work."

There came a din of splashes, footfalls, thuds, scraping sounds, grunts. Renzo crouched low in the water, trying to make himself small. They must have passed him; they had moved to the back of the shop.

A dull ache spread across Renzo's legs and back; his feet had gone numb. He shifted, knocked a boot against the iron bars beside him.

The bars.

Underwater they wouldn't be noticed. But once the flood receded . . . An extra set of bars would be a puzzle, would call attention to the glass ones.

It would be best to drop them into the canal, but he

couldn't do that now. He'd better hide them somewhere in the shop.

But where?

He recalled seeing a chest flush against the wall beneath the windows.

He twisted round. There it was, not three paces away.

Slowly he picked up the iron bars, praying the men would stay where they were a little longer. He scooted on his knees through the black water, staying in the shelter of the table for as long as he could. When he came to the chest, he set down the bars in the water beside it. He reached his fingers to the bottom of the chest.

A gap.

He felt the bars.

Yes. They would fit.

Carefully he scooted the bars beneath the chest. They scraped the floor, loud as thunder in his ears.

Then they were in.

Renzo crept back beneath his table. He sat for a moment, plotting an escape route among the benches and tables. The men were at the back of the shop; with a head start he could beat them out the door.

All at once he realized that it had grown quiet. There was only a slow swish of footsteps, coming near. He crouched, kept his head down. Out of the corner of one eye, he saw a slick of yellow light glide across the water, illuminating floating flecks of sawdust.

Swish. Swish.

The flecks swirled before a new disturbance: a pair of tall, black boots.

Renzo peered up through the light—into the long, homely face of Signore Averlino.

A younger man appeared behind him. He lunged toward Renzo. "A thief! I'll show him—"

But Signore Averlino held out a restraining hand.

"Wait," he said. "I believe I know this boy."

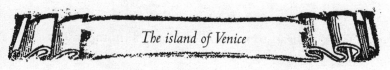
34.

Man to Man

Signore Averlino reached out a hand to help him to his
feet. Renzo, rising, ignored it. He was behaving like a
petulant child, he knew. But he couldn't help it. He glared at
Signore Averlino.

"Renzo." Signore Averlino sounded perplexed. There was
a questioning in his voice, an invitation for Renzo to explain
himself.

Renzo halfway wished Signore Averlino would berate him,
lay hands on him, and try to toss him bodily from the shop.
Then he could lash out; he could run. But this . . .

He'd better think of something quick, not just stand there
gaping like a fish. "You're such a . . . friend to my mother," he
said. "I wanted to see for myself what manner of man you are."

"And it's by my *shop* that you would know this?" Signore
Averlino raised an eyebrow, seemed to be amused.

Renzo bristled. "How else?"

Signore Averlino said nothing, only regarded him with
level eyes. The other man broke in. "Let me take care of him,
padrone."

"You go ahead to work. I'll be only a moment."

"But, *padrone*—"

"Go." Signore Averlino waved the man toward the rear of the shop, then turned back to Renzo. "Well?" he asked. "So what do you think? What does my shop say of me?"

Renzo's shirt and hose clung to him, frigid and clammy. He did not like this game, though he had begun it. Signore Averlino's tone was mild, but Renzo could hear the challenge in it. Still, he supposed that this was better than being accused of thievery—or having his true purpose discovered. Besides, Signore Averlino would no doubt report his presence here to Mama, so it behooved Renzo to play along and not make things worse.

He looked about. Light from Signore Averlino's lantern flickered through the workshop, illuminating work surfaces, ceiling, and walls.

Last time, Renzo had been impressed with the size of the shop. But now, as the light slid past, he marked the neat rows of pegs on which hung tools grouped by type and ranked by size: hammers, saws, rasps, chisels, awls. He marked the orderly tiers of shelves that held vises, planes, and tools of which Renzo didn't know the names.

There was nothing grandiose about the shop. The cabinets were unornamented, the windows unglazed. And yet it seemed the shop of someone who respected his craft.

"I think," Renzo said, "you are a man who cares well for his tools."

In the wavering light he could see Signore Averlino's

expression change, a shifting in the leathery creases of his face. Not a smile, precisely, but a softening.

Voices at the door. Renzo turned to look. Two more men, wading in through the doorway. Signore Averlino greeted them, motioned for them to help the first man.

Now it was four to one.

Renzo longed to run, make a break for the door, but something about Signore Averlino's steady gaze prevented him. Renzo recalled that he'd ever treated him with respect, even when Renzo had insulted his profession.

What would Papà have done if he'd found some intruder lurking about in his glassworks? Likely cuffed him about the ears, dragged him across the floor, and shoved him out the door—at the very least!

What would Signore Averlino do?

Rain tapped at the roof. A sudden wind gust rattled in the shutters. From the rear of the room came grunts, scraping sounds, swishes, splashes.

"Can you make it home safely?" Signore Averlino asked.

Renzo nodded.

"And what of your mama? Did you think of *her* when you embarked on this little escapade?" For the first time Signore Averlino's voice warmed with quiet anger. "No doubt your house is flooded too. You're the man of the family. She needs you."

Renzo's face burned. Who was there now to help Mama set up boards and trestles and stack the carpets and furnishings upon them? Who would help lift Mama's wedding chest,

Papà's chair? Pia? Uncle Vittorio, with his grievous wound? All Renzo had been worried about when he'd left was that Mama might catch him and scold him.

Like a little boy.

He made to go, but Signore Averlino blocked his way.

"I think your mama doesn't need to know of this. It would disturb her, and I think she doesn't need to be disturbed."

Renzo swallowed, met Signore Averlino's eyes. "Thank you," he said.

The older man yielded; Renzo started for the door.

"Renzo."

He turned back. "If you ever have questions about me, son, I'll be happy to talk with you. Just the two of us. Man to man."

◆   ◆   ◆

Outside, rowing back through the dark canals, Renzo tried to choke down the stubborn lump that had risen in his throat. So clearly had he conjured up the nightmare—that he'd be found out, perhaps beaten, perhaps released to the authorities.

Disgrace.

Signore Averlino's words echoed in his ears:

If you ever have questions about me, son . . . Just the two of us. Man to man.

Son.

So long since he had heard that word from a man's lips. What would Signore Averlino think of him if he knew that lying on a bench in his workshop was a set of bars that could destroy all he'd ever worked for?

Renzo almost hoped the bars would break before the dungeon doors were installed.

As they might.

Or the old ones might be discovered.

Truly, he could almost wish it.

Ahead now he could see the lagoon. An owl called from a nearby rooftop; Letta's face swam before his eyes.

Was she cold? Was she hungry? Was she ill? And the children . . . How long would they last in the dungeon?

His father would have told him to give up his plan right now. He'd say that a man shouldn't concern himself with the affairs of strangers. That his duty was to his family.

And yet . . . The children.

How were you supposed to know what was right to do?

How did a man decide?

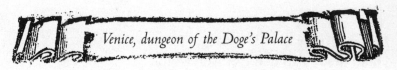

35.

Keys

The old woman woke to the sound of running water.

She shifted on the cold, hard floor, tried to ease the painful imprint of the rough stones against her hip. She felt feet pressing against her legs, and a head tucked into the small of her back, and a small body cradled in the curl of her chest and belly and thighs. She touched her owl with a light kenning and sensed him asleep on her knee.

Carefully she sat up. The bodies shifted to accommodate her, then leaned into her again. Her owl, now awake, flitted up to perch on her shoulder.

In the dim light cast by the oil lamp, she could make out the outlines of the sleeping children and their birds. She smelled the familiar dungeon reek of dank and sour decay; she heard breathing all around.

And the gurgle of water flowing.

Something damp on her hip, her legs. She touched the floor.

Not just damp.

Wet. Water on the floor.

She sniffed her fingers.

Salty.

Acqua alta.

"Letta," she whispered. "Wake up."

◆   ◆   ◆

They roused the children, sent all the birds away, and gathered close together, standing in icy rising water halfway to the old woman's knees. The two older boys hoisted Paolo and Ugo to their shoulders; Letta held Sofia. But how long could they go on like this?

Voices sounded through the corridors. Wailing. Shouts.

The old woman felt the children shivering against her; she felt them breathing—a trembling, many-stranded plant rooted deep in the stone floor of the dungeon.

Paolo began to cough.

"A rat!" Marina screamed. "'Tis swimming! It—"

The group lurched, gasping. "Just kick it away," the woman said. "Kick it away!" If a rat hooked its claws into Marina's clothing, it would climb up to get out of the water, and more of them would follow.

She shuddered.

Likely it was only a matter of time.

The littlest children were sobbing now. Some had begun to cough. The woman's feet had gone numb with cold. She felt the ghostly touch of a spider on her neck; she slapped it and shook it off her hand. Vermin of all sorts were on the move.

Light flickered brighter at the barred opening in their door.

"Shh," she said. "Everyone, hush!"

Voices. Water swishing, louder. The darkness thinned. And now she recognized Guido's voice, high and insistent — and Claudio's, grumbling and low.

". . . charged to keep 'em, not kill 'em." This was Guido.

". . . little water won't hurt." Claudio.

". . . sickly." Guido again. ". . . no shoes."

"*I'm* wearing shoes. Much good they do me."

". . . trouble for us if they die," Guido said. "The Ten want 'em alive."

A snort. "Aye . . . spectacle when the witches swing."

That one, the old woman thought. Scaring the children. She'd like to give him a piece of her mind.

The key grated in the lock. Guido entered, carrying a torch, and Claudio came in behind. "Everybody out," Guido said. "Come on, come on. Stay close together; nobody stray."

"Where are you taking us?" the old woman asked.

"You'll find out soon enough," Claudio muttered.

But Guido said, "Upstairs, to the cells just under the roof." He lowered his voice. "It's better there, Grandmother. You'll see."

The first of the children had nearly reached the door when Claudio let out a yelp. "A rat!" He thrashed about, stumbled backward into Georgio and Ugo, who fell against Federigo and Paolo, who crashed into one of the twins.

Splashes. Thumps. Screams.

The old woman helped the fallen children to their feet

and tried to calm them. Claudio was shouting, swearing at the children, at Guido, at the rat.

"Get 'em through the door, Grandmother," Guido said. "Tell 'em to wait in the corridor. Let nobody stray."

"My keys!" Claudio said. "Where are my keys?"

"Did you drop 'em?" Guido asked.

"They slipped out of my hand. If you hadn't made me come here . . ."

The old woman herded the children into the corridor as Guido and Claudio hunted through the water, arguing fiercely.

"Let's go," Guido said. "Those rats give me the twitchies. We'll lock the keys in here; you can fetch them when the water ebbs."

"This is all your fault. Why can't they stay down here like the rest of 'em? Upstairs is for prisoners of rank, not for the likes of these."

Just before Guido shut the door, the old woman flicked a last, regretful glance toward the stone behind which her quill and ink and paper lay hidden.

But there was no one left to receive her messages. Everyone she cared for in the world was right here in this accursed dungeon.

◆　　◆　　◆

They trudged single file down a narrow corridor, and up a staircase or two, then down another corridor. And then it was staircase after staircase after staircase—more staircases, the old woman thought, than she'd have imagined possible, even in the palace. Her knees began to protest, and then they rebelled—grinding, clicking, wobbling. Paining her something fierce. Claudio forced the children to move ahead, which vexed her—she didn't trust him—while Guido stayed behind, letting her lean on his arm. When at last she and Guido reached the cell, which truly was larger and airier than the last, the children had already settled in, and some of them were sleeping.

The guards left; the door clanged behind them. A single lamp flickered dimly at the center of the room, but it was nearly pitch dark in the corner where the old woman lowered herself to the floor. She felt a stir of quiet movement, and Letta came to sit beside her.

"Your knees?" Letta asked.

The woman nodded, rubbing them. "Stupid old things."

"Sorry," Letta said.

The woman shrugged. "No matter."

"Listen," Letta said. "Open your hand. Hold it out."

The woman did.

There was a *clank*, and the cold of curved metal crossed her open palm.

A large ring.

The old woman felt along it with her other hand. There, clustered together at the bottom:

Keys.

"Letta," she whispered. "How—"

"They hit my toe when they fell. I picked them up and wrapped them in my skirts."

The woman shivered. "This is dangerous, Letta! When they don't find the keys down there, they'll search here. Claudio will be enraged. No telling what he'll do."

"They won't find them," Letta said.

"What are you saying? They're too big to hide, 'less in somebody's clothes, and that's too perilous."

"The window."

The woman looked up. High up on the wall of this new, larger cell was a lighter darkness in the gloom. A small, barred window—a blessing. She could detect a hint of sea air and the freshness of rain. When the sun rose, there would be light.

"S'pose Georgio stood on Federigo's shoulders," Letta said.

"And they'd throw the keys out? But what if it's pavement down there? The guards'll look straight up at our window and know where they came from."

"Federigo's hawk could take them. It's carried heavier things before, for true."

"So . . . Georgio could stand on Federigo's shoulders and hold the keys out the window. And Federigo could ken his bird to come and take them?"

"And put them on the roof."

"The roof."

"Yes."

"Not in the canal?"

"No. Then we couldn't fetch them back."

"Fetch them? But they won't do us any good. We can't be

reaching the lock through the window in the door, and . . ."

Ah. Suddenly she understood. "Oh, Letta. 'Tis the boy, 'tisn't it? You're still thinking he'll come for us."

Letta didn't answer.

The old woman had hoped that Letta had given up on the boy. There had been two attempts to send him messages—once with the kestrel and another time with the owl—and both had ended badly. Neither Letta nor the old woman had been willing to put their birds in danger again.

The old woman reached for her hand. "Oh, Letta. Don't—"

Letta snatched her hand away.

The old woman sighed. Hope, she knew, could keep you alive . . . for a while. But in the end it could break your heart.

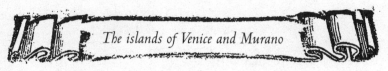

36.

The Beast

The captain stopped at the edge of the piazza, shielding his eyes against the glare. The *acqua alta* had nearly drained away from the stone pavements of Venice and back into the canals where it belonged. But a thin film of water collected in sunken spots and in the spaces between the stones, reflecting the dazzle of the morning sun. The captain squinted toward the dungeon entrance, at the mob that massed before the door.

They were a hundred strong, at least. Mostly men, but also women and troops of boys—an angry clot of humanity that seemed, to the captain, to be waiting for the slightest excuse to erupt.

Something odd about that door. He drew nearer, pushed a little way into the crowd. Above the ragged horizon of caps and hoods and shawls, he could see that a line of soldiers kept the mob at bay. And that the dungeon door stood wide.

No. Not open. It was gone.

Now, ahead and off to one side, he saw a group of men hefting something toward the dungeon entrance.

A door.

They were replacing the door.

With a low growl the crowd surged forward. The captain planted his feet, stood firm against the press of the mob. It was a thing of itself now, a feral animal. It smelled dank and sharp—of sweat and wet wool. Of bloodlust. Ahead the soldiers raised their pikes, drove back the beast.

"Witches! Hang the witches!" someone cried.

A single arrow arced up into the placid sky and clattered down on the roof of the dungeon, amid a gathering of birds. They rose up in a cacophonous cloud—not just the ever-present pigeons, the captain saw, but also crows, hawks, gulls, herons, a magpie, and other birds the captain couldn't identify.

The memory stirred again—the misty morning on the lagoon, the little boat . . .

The captain shifted, uneasy. He turned to a woman who stood beside him.

"What is this?" he said, gesturing at the crowd. "What witches do they speak of?"

"The foreigners. The bird people."

The beast lurched forward again, swallowing up the woman and her words.

The bird people. This was what he'd feared, though he wasn't surprised to hear it. In the captain's experience, traveling the world, he'd found that rumors of witchcraft often attached themselves to foreigners or those who seemed different. To people who were in some way *strangers*.

He questioned a well-dressed man and learned that the Council of Ten were said to be leaning toward a guilty verdict, and if they so decided, the witches would hang in the piazza on the day before Lent.

The captain swore. We humans! Blinded by our ignorance, consumed by our fears! Always looking beyond our own separate tribes for someone to scapegoat for our difficulties.

And yet, when he did business, man to man . . . With the artisans, with the traders . . . Especially when he broke bread with a man, seated at a table, warmed by the fire in his hearth . . . So often then—no matter how strange the customs of the place, no matter how far from home—he found little to fear and nothing to hate.

The beast surged forward again. "Hang the witches! Hang them!"

He saw her again, in his mind's eye. The girl who had looked at him from that small, overladen boat in the fog. The girl with the other children, and the birds.

Might she be a witch?

Who could know for certain? Not he.

But for his money, she was no more than a frightened child.

◆　　◆　　◆

As it happened, he had business at a glassworks in Murano later that day—the one where they made the glass falcons. He recalled the uneasy silence when he'd mentioned the bird children before, and against his better judgment he brought up the subject again. Again, the uneasy silence.

Why?

Would *no one* stand up for the poor waifs?

Unwisely, he persisted. "What have they done that they should be hanged? They're children, for God's sake!"

The *padrone* smoothly diverted the captain's attention to the glass birds he wished to purchase.

But when the captain left, a young apprentice came running after him, hailed him. They talked a little while, and then the boy told him a remarkable story.

And made him an offer he ought to have refused.

37.

The Tenth Falcon

Renzo's heart hurt.

He wanted to stop right there in the street and press both of his hands against it. He wanted to let his knees fold, sit back on the paving stones, and curl up like a sleeping bird. Just breathe there for a while. See if that would ease the pain.

But he did not. He kept his hands down by his sides. Kept walking. Made for home.

Hanged, the captain had said.

They were going to hang them. Almost certainly.

In twelve days, on the last day of *Carnevale*, right before Lent.

Not just the old woman but the children as well.

Renzo's feet dragged to a halt. A vast and terrible darkness welled up inside him. His hands moved to press against his heart. A woman, passing, looked at him with concern. "Can I help you?" she asked.

He shook his head, forced his hands back down.

Somehow he hadn't believed that they would do it. That they would actually kill the children. And *hanging* . . .

He started running then, moving through streets and alleyways, weaving in and out through patches of bright sunlight and shadow. He jostled an old man, dodged a fisherman, then bumped into a woman with a basket on her arm. Dried beans leaped from the basket and spilled across the cobblestones.

She called after him, cursing.

He should go back and help her gather them up. He should tell her he was sorry.

But there was so much, so much to be sorry for. Where would he even begin?

◆　　◆　　◆

When Renzo arrived home, he found Vittorio bent over the kitchen table repairing a wooden shutter. A large pot bubbled on the hearth; Renzo breathed in the rich aroma of rabbit stew.

"Is Mama here?" he asked.

Vittorio looked up. His bandages were gone now, replaced by a patch over his blind eye. The bruises on his face had faded but were still a lurid mass of purple and yellow.

"No. She had some errands and took Pia. We can talk."

Renzo related what he'd heard from the sea captain, about the dungeon door and the angry mob. About the Ten and the hanging.

Vittorio looked shocked. *"Maria santissima.* Hanging?"

Renzo nodded.

"In twelve days? I thought we'd have more time. "

"Listen. I've found a way to get them out of Venice, out of the lagoon entirely." Renzo told how the captain had agreed to take the children when he left. For the sum of nine glass falcons—one for each of the children and one for the old woman, should she wish to go as well.

"Do you know this man, this captain? Know anything at all about him?" Vittorio asked, his voice rising in alarm.

"Well, but . . . It was he who spoke of them first. He's angry about it. He wants to help. Anyway, what else can we do? *You* can't arrange it now. You—"

"You can take care! Don't go about risking your life so cavalierly! Don't—"

"You of all people should reproach *me* for risking lives!"

Vittorio gazed at him a long moment. The stew bubbled on the hearth. Outside, a seagull called. "You're right," Vittorio said at last. "This is my fault. And I'll make it good to you. I—"

"You can't."

"I will."

"You can't break them out of the dungeon. Your ankle's not healed yet; you can barely walk, much less outrun the dungeon guards."

"I'll do it," Vittorio said stubbornly.

The pain had come again to sit in Renzo's heart. There was only him to do it. If he did, and if he were caught, it would be a betrayal of Mama and Pia; it would be a betrayal of all Papà had ever wanted for him. But if he didn't . . .

Renzo pressed his hands against his heart. Something was crumbling there, shaking apart.

"I will go," he said.

There were many things to plan before Mama and Pia returned. They spoke of boats, and of masks, and of the configuration of the palace, and of when and where to meet. Renzo told Vittorio about the broken bars; Vittorio said he was sure he'd heard of a small, barred door somewhere near the canal on the east of the palace. "The door they take the bodies out of," he said. How could this door be found from inside the dungeon? Renzo didn't know. Though Vittorio couldn't go into the dungeon himself, he would steal into Venice the next day and make some arrangements.

"God willing, this will all work out, Renzo. You'll be back to the glassworks the day after, and no one will be the wiser."

Renzo nodded. But this was likely what Vittorio had told himself when he'd put his family at risk by leaving Murano.

"And what about Signore Averlino?" Renzo asked. "If it's discovered that the dungeon bars are made of glass, suspicion will land on him."

"I'll write out a confession for the authorities and leave it with you. I'll say I did it all—that Signore Averlino had nothing to do with it, and neither did you, or any other glassworker. I'll say that if the Ten want evidence of Signore Averlino's innocence, they should look for the iron bars in the carpentry shop. I'll tell them where."

"But that will make him look guilty!"

"Ah, but that's where you're mistaken. A guilty man would have gotten rid of the evidence long before. Only an innocent man would still have those bars in his workshop."

His reasoning seemed risky, thin. *God willing, this will all work out.* They'd had no right to put Signore Averlino at risk. And yet . . .

Night after night over the past week, Renzo had dreamed of Letta's kestrel, imprisoned in a block of solid glass but still alive, its heart trembling wildly in its breast. Sometimes the bird blurred and changed until it was Letta inside the block, or only his own heart beating. Each time, he took up a hammer and tried to break the glass, but it refused to shatter. Tiny chips and splinters flew off it. Spiderweb-like cracks penetrated deep. But the glass was strong, and he didn't know if he could break through in time.

Now he heard voices, outside. Pia, chattering out a question. Mama's calm reply.

Vittorio leaned forward, across the table. "Renzo," he said, his voice soft and urgent. "I hear things, at night."

"Hear things?"

"It may be nothing, but . . . I think it's time for me to leave."

"You mean leave our house?"

"Yes, that too. I'll leave tonight. Don't worry. I'm strong enough. I know places where I can hide. And after we rescue the children, I'll leave the republic altogether."

"But where will you go? Back where you were before?"

Vittorio shrugged. "Who knows? Maybe I'll find a new place, one more hospitable to strangers. But that ship — the one the children are taking — it could carry me well away from the lagoon. Make a tenth falcon, Renzo. That one will be for me."

38.

I Miss My Father

Twelve days.

Renzo worried that the days wouldn't pass quickly enough, that the mob would overpower the guards, that the glass bars would be discovered. He worried that the days would pass too quickly, that he wouldn't be able to finish the extra birds, that Vittorio wouldn't have time to conclude his preparations.

Sometimes he found himself imagining Letta, Vittorio, and the children on the ship, sailing away out of the lagoon, into the Adriatic Sea. Where would they go?

Once, many years before, Papà had spread out a great map on the kitchen table. He had drawn a finger across the map, showing Renzo all the places where the glass they made was sent. East, to Istanbul. West, around the boot of Italy and thence to Spain. Through the Strait of Gibraltar, then north to Portugal, France, and the British Isles.

Where would they disembark?

Where would they make a life?

Renzo didn't know. It was best, Vittorio had told him, that he not know.

In the meantime there were the ten extra birds to make. The new fire tender could bring him glass for the wings. The rest Renzo could manage on his own.

One night several days later, when the fire tender admitted him to the glassworks, he saw that someone was there at the furnace before him. Renzo crept forward in the dark and watched.

It was Sergio.

That afternoon there had been another ugly scene between Sergio and the *padrone*. Sergio had shown his father a falcon he had made. The *padrone* had ridiculed his work—loudly, so that everyone heard.

Though Sergio had feigned indifference, he had not been able to hide his bitterness and humiliation.

Now Renzo wondered: Would it be worse to have your father right there before you and still not feel his loving care?

But no. What could be worse than losing your father altogether? At least Sergio could hope.

Renzo watched as Sergio lifted the gather, as he rolled it on the *malmoro*, as he put his lips to the blowpipe.

Would this be another bird?

Yes. But when Sergio began to shape the beak, Renzo could see that he had it all wrong.

Sergio cursed. He struck the *pontello* against the edge of the broken-glass pail. The bird cracked off and landed with a crash.

Renzo approached the furnace. Sergio glanced his way. "What are *you* doing here?"

Renzo shrugged. "You're not the only one who needs to practice." He picked up a blowpipe and gathered a molten blob of glass from the crucible. He half-expected Sergio to object, but he did not. For a while they worked side by side in the heat of the furnace, with neither words nor looks of acknowledgment, like two cats sharing a patch of sun.

When it came time to make the beak, Renzo reached for the *borsella*. He began to murmur, as if to himself, not looking at Sergio: "Starting now, lifting up and up like so. Turning here, like so." Sergio turned to watch, letting his own work grow cold. When it was time for Renzo to make a wing, Sergio cracked his own piece into the broken-glass pail and fetched molten glass for Renzo's bird. He watched. At last Renzo cracked his bird off the blowpipe and bore it to the annealing oven. He returned to the furnace. Gathered more glass.

Sergio regarded him, said nothing. Renzo offered him the blowpipe with the newly gathered glass. Sergio hesitated, then took it and began to work. Renzo was silent until it came time for Sergio to make the beak, then, "Lift it now," he said. "Turn it now. A little farther. Yes, there, there, there — just there."

When the bird was done, they looked at it together. It was not perfect, but it was respectable. The beak looked nearly right, and the angle of the wings was much improved. Sergio cracked the bird off the blowpipe and bore it to the annealing oven.

Renzo gathered more glass from the crucible. Sergio watched him work. When it was time, he brought glass for the wings. Neither spoke.

But when the bird was nearly finished, Sergio said, "Why are you doing this? Why are you showing me how?"

Renzo shrugged. What could he say? *Because I'm stealing these birds from your father to give to the captain? Because I want to pay for them some way? Because I may soon find myself in deep disgrace, and I want someone to remember something good of me?*

Renzo cracked his bird off the blowpipe. Picked it up with the lifting irons. "I miss my father," he said. "I miss his teachings too."

◆　　◆　　◆

Signore Averlino had not come to mass the Sunday after he'd found Renzo in his workshop, but the following Sunday, there he was. He greeted Renzo without a hint that he had found him lurking there, crouching waist deep in water, in the middle of the night. He treated Renzo as he ever had, with kindness and respect.

But this time Renzo was different. He looked Signore Averlino in the eye; he smiled at him; he yielded his seat next to Mama without her having to motion him aside.

After mass Renzo watched Signore Averlino watching Mama. Renzo marked how he stood patiently aside as Mama greeted her friends, how he politely greeted them and listened to what they had to say. About the price of sugar and wheat; about a feud between two neighbors; about a graveyard rumored to have been robbed. About the death that had visited one of the parish households, and the birth that had blessed another. Papà, Renzo recalled, used to be at the center of every conversation—dispensing wisdom and advice, telling stories, making people laugh. Renzo had thought that this was so because Papà was an exceptional man. Everyone had wanted to be near Papà. He had drawn them in like a blazing hearth on a chill winter's night. But now Renzo saw that exceptional men come in varying hues. The man at the far edge of the crowd, the one whom people noticed least, could be every bit as remarkable.

Outside, Pia skipped across the walk and slipped a coin to her beggar. For the first time, Renzo approached him too. His face was hidden in the shadows of his hooded cloak, but the gnarled fingers spread wide as Renzo came near. Renzo's coin clinked against Pia's; the beggar murmured his thanks.

◆　　◆　　◆

The assassin closed his fingers about the coins. He did not like showing his hands to the boy. But it had been dark that night; there had been blood and pain and fighting; chances were the boy would not remember the specific geography of this handful of misshapen fingers.

The uncle had disappeared again. The assassin did not know yet precisely where he had gone, but he knew where to watch. Eventually the uncle would surface, and then . . .

Ordinarily the assassin would have dispatched him long ago. He would have stolen into the house; he would have finished it. But he had grown soft, he had grown weak, he had grown dangerously ineffective. Truth: He could not bear to frighten the little girl. He could not bear for her to feel unsafe inside her very home.

She would grieve for her uncle when he was gone. But that could not be helped.

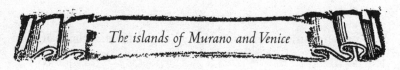
39·

Inside the Mask

L ate that night a heron, gliding low over the marshes in search of a juicy frog, saw three small boats moving through the curved ribbons of water that cut through the island of Murano.

The first boat glided down a wide canal and headed south across a moonlit stretch of open water.

The second made its slow way along a narrow stream, barely visible among the sedges. The third followed at a distance. The second boat hesitated before nosing out into the open, at the lip of the wide waters of the lagoon.

It did not, the heron saw, get far.

◆ ◆ ◆

Renzo moored his boat to the crowded dock in San Marco. On his way across the lagoon, he'd been grateful for the light of the full moon, but at the moment he longed for a nice, thick fog. He opened the bundle Vittorio had stowed beneath a strut and removed a ragged gown and a pair of women's slippers. He bent to take off his boots, then jammed his feet into the slippers and shrugged off his cloak, damp with condensed fog.

The hammer was still there, bound to his waist with a leather belt.

He pulled on the gown over his shirt.

Now for the mask — smooth and white, with full, red lips. The visage of a beautiful signorina. Fumbling with the tie strings, Renzo secured it over his face. He knotted the head scarf at his chin and slipped the shawl over his shoulders, then bundled up his cloak and boots and stowed them in the bottom of the boat. At last he picked up the basket and slipped the handle over one arm.

He gazed at the blazing lights of the Doge's Palace and summoned his will to move.

The night chill penetrated through shawl and shirt to shiver at his skin, still damp from the effort of rowing. Inside the mask his breath sounded loud. He felt leaden, unable to move. So many uncertainties to this plan. So many paths to disaster. He longed to turn back, to row north to Murano and tuck himself into his warm, soft cot.

And where was Vittorio? They weren't supposed to meet — not yet — but Renzo had hoped to catch sight of him. Vittorio had assured Renzo that he was well enough to do his part, but was he?

Abruptly Renzo stood and stepped onto the dock. If he didn't make himself go now, he feared he might lose heart altogether.

Stoop, Vittorio had said. *Walk as if your knees pain you, as if your feet ache and your hips creak.* It was a disguise inside a disguise: a boy dressed as an old woman wearing the mask of a beautiful girl. *The more mixed-up and confusing,* Vittorio had said, *the better.*

Bent over and shuffling, Renzo threaded his way through the *piazzetta*, still thick with jostling revelers even so late at night. He made for the Piazza San Marco, where he soon spotted the vendor Vittorio had told him of, the one who sold *fritole.* A man in a jester's mask bumped into him; Renzo stumbled into the path of a man on stilts, who wobbled, cursing loudly and long. A hand latched on to Renzo's arm and pulled him out of the way. Renzo looked up to see the mask of a long-beaked bird, looking strangely sinister. "Are you all right, Grandmother?" asked a kindly male voice.

Renzo nodded, shaken.

At last, with five warm *fritole* in his basket, Renzo turned toward the palace, toward the dungeon entrance.

And now, before him, he saw the mob of which the captain had spoken. Renzo held back — watching, moving his head side to side to take in the whole of the scene through the eyeholes of his mask. There were fifty, maybe seventy, people. Not angry and shouting but muttering, restless.

The sea captain had mentioned soldiers stationed near the door, but Renzo couldn't see them beyond the crowd. And the dungeon guard? He couldn't see him, either.

All depended upon the presence of the guard. He must mistake Renzo for a certain old woman who regularly visited her nephew in the dungeon. Vittorio had waylaid her and spoken to her days before. He had bought her shawl, her headscarf, her basket. He had paid her to stay away from the dungeon.

But suddenly Vittorio's plans seemed hopeless. How was it possible that the guard would mistake Renzo for an old woman? And even if he did, wouldn't he unmask him to make sure?

Again Renzo wavered. He could go back now. It wasn't too late. Not yet.

But he slipped between two women in the rear of the throng and made his shuffling way through—weaving, seeking out gaps between the bodies, sometimes clearing his throat or tapping an arm in a silent request. The crowd murmured and shifted. The inside of the mask grew moist and stale.

At last he found himself at the fore of the crowd, facing a flight of steps, the dungeon door, and a cluster of uniformed men. They looked like soldiers. Which one was the guard Vittorio had spoken of?

What now?

He studied the door. It was the larger one with the deeper window, as he had known it would be. The one with bars of iron, not glass. As to where the other door was—

"Grandmother! Come along."

Renzo turned his head, peering through the eyeholes. A man stepped forward, through the cluster of soldiers. He wore a uniform too, but it was different from the others.

The guard?

The man scowled and motioned impatiently. "Come *along*, old woman. Hurry!"

Renzo was seized with an urge to flee, to cast off his

disguise and run back to the boat. But he shuffled ahead, limped up the stairs.

The guard led him to the door, flicking a finger at the basket.

Renzo thrust it toward him; the guard took one of the *fritole* and popped it into his mouth. He rapped thrice on the door with his spear, a deep, hollow *thump, thump, thump*. He reached for the latch; the great door creaked open.

A shout: *Witches! Hang the witches!* The crowd surged forward. The soldiers fanned out before the door, hoisting their spears.

"Quick, you!" the guard mumbled around his pastry.

Renzo slipped inside; the door slammed shut with an echoing *clang*, leaving Renzo alone.

A long, dark corridor stretched out before him, dimming to blackness in the distance. He could make out the shapes of doorways recessed in stone walls. The air was eerily still, but a chill oozed out from the stone walls and crept deep inside Renzo's bones. It smelled different here — the mineral smell of stone and something else, something stale and sour.

Footsteps. A blaze of yellow torchlight bobbed toward him, the figure of a man beneath it. A second guard.

Belatedly Renzo remembered to stoop.

He twisted back to look at the door with its iron bars. No way out, unless the other glass bars had survived.

In a moment the second guard called, "Grandmother?"

His voice echoed down through the corridor:

. . . andmother?

. . . mother?

. . . other?

Renzo performed an exaggerated nod.

The guard drew quickly near. "I didn't know you at first, Grandmother, with you looking so young today." He smiled shyly at his own jest.

Renzo hoisted the basket. The guard plucked a pastry from it, took a bite, and smacked his lips appreciatively. *"Grazie!"* he said. "Come along, then. I'll light your way."

Renzo had thought he'd be left alone to find his "nephew." He'd thought he might have time to go searching for the little door. But now . . . what would he do when they reached the nephew's cell? Surely the mask wouldn't fool *him.* The bell of doom tolled again in Renzo's inner ear, but there was nothing to do but set one foot down after another, following the guard.

The floor was slick in places; puddles of muck collected in the corners. Renzo devoutly wished for his good, sturdy boots instead of these useless slippers. By the light of the torch, he saw a dark line on the walls — thigh high. A high-water mark. Had the children been down here during the *acqua alta?* Standing in the frigid water with no shoes at all?

The stench grew stronger as they moved deeper into the dungeon, a stench of excrement, piss, and fear. From time to time he heard mumbling, or groaning, or laughter. He wished he could see inside the cells as they passed, but the barred openings in the doors were too high. He'd have to stretch up out of his stoop—too much of a risk.

Thump, thump, thump.

Behind them. A knock at the dungeon door.

The guard stopped. Groaned. "Wait here, Grandmother," he said. "There's someone else wants in. I'll return directly."

Renzo watched the torchlight bobble away back toward the door, listened to the guard's echoing footsteps. Darkness closed in around him. He could hear a *drip, drip, drip* of water, and something scuttling along the stones.

Rats?

He shivered.

What should he do now?

The children might be in a cell farther along the corridor, or he might have passed them already.

But wait. Another sound, a run of clear, fluting notes. Familiar.

The little owl? From that day in the glassworks?

Renzo edged forward along the wall. The sound had not seemed close, but here in this echoing place it was impossible to tell. In a moment the wall dropped away to his right, and peering around a corner, he saw the dim outline of a flight of stairs.

He looked back the way he had come. The torchlight bobbed closer now. He could see the guard's shadow beside it and another shadow behind.

The owl called again. Nearer now. Somewhere above. And then . . . The *kree, kree, kree* of a kestrel.

Renzo ducked around the corner and crept up the stairs. Moonlight trickled through a small, barred window at the stair landing, giving him just enough light to see by.

Ahead, more stairs. To the left, another corridor, also lined with doors.

The kestrel called again—from above.

Renzo scrambled up the stairs. He tripped over his skirts; he grabbed them and hiked them to his waist. At the third landing something swooped past him from above. The kestrel. At the fourth landing the bird went pumping past again, heading back up. Renzo followed. His breath came hard; his legs were beginning to ache. Voices reached him from below. Shouting voices. Alarmed. He ignored them and pushed on up.

At last the stairs ended. On his right was an archway; on his left, a low, narrow corridor. This had to be a sort of attic, just below the roof. He crept a little way along the corridor, and saw that it was lined with doors. Doors with small, barred openings.

Cell doors.

A crow cawed from somewhere down the hall.

Renzo ran. He hurtled from door to door, the slippers skidding on the tiles. He stretched up to peer through the openings in the doors. The cells to his left were dark, each lit only by an oil lamp, dim and smoky. But the cells on his right had high, barred windows to the outside world; they let in enough moonlight to see by. A rotund man hunched on a bench, moaning. A tall woman pacing restlessly. A rag-clad heap of sticks on the floor — whether man or woman he couldn't tell.

At the next-to-last door Renzo stopped. Inside the mask his breath came labored and ragged.

There they were.

Huddled together, their backs rising and falling in sleep. Birds perched on shoulders, on heads, on arms. Somebody began coughing; somebody else joined in.

Renzo's vision blurred. All this time they had been here — in this hopeless, miserable place.

A head raised, turned slowly toward him.

Remembering his mask, Renzo yanked it off, blinking back the sudden moisture in his eyes. "It's me," he said. "It's Renzo."

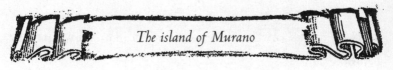

40.

Taste for Death

The assassin stood at the edge of the heat, near enough to the furnace to drive the chill from his bones but not near enough to make him sweat. He rubbed his aching hands, surveying his night's work.

Three bodies: One alive. One newly dead. One dead more than a year.

The first, lying well outside the open door, belonged to the guard. Useless man. So many of these guards were useless. It had been child's play to stop him, immobilize him. They'd surely find him in time, haul him away. He'd wake in a couple of hours, a little sore but none the worse for wear.

It would have been simpler to kill him, but the assassin had lost his taste for death.

As to the second, the assassin had had no choice. Though, to look at the man now — lying there so peacefully — you might think he'd settled down for a quick nap just inside the doorway. The assassin had left no mark. He had found out what he'd needed to know; he had been merciful; he had been quick. The man had come with him to the glassworks without a struggle; he'd seemed almost to welcome death.

With luck he would be recognizable later.

The third body, nearest the furnace, would be burned up entirely, except for the bones — and a cloak pin wrought of silver.

The assassin rubbed at his hands, at the painful, stiff knots of his knuckles. The stench of the long-dead corpse filled his nose. He pulled a torch from a bracket in the wall and moved to the white-hot furnace to light it. The heat seared his own skin, threatened to blister it black, threatened to melt the flesh from his bones. He hesitated, imagining: bones melting too, and the old, knotted knuckles, and the new wound above his heart that never ceased aching. He saw it all turning to liquid. Seeping across the floor.

But no. No more death here tonight. He still had much to do.

He moved toward the far edge of the glassworks. Touched fire to a dry, wooden beam. Walked a few steps. Touched another.

So many fires flared up in these glassworks. So easy for a wayward spark to waft into the rafters and catch. So natural for roof tiles to shatter in the heat. And then it all came crashing down.

People should be more careful.

Truly, they should.

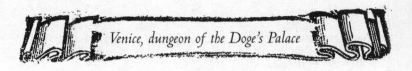
41.

Flight

R enzo?"
     It was Letta's voice. He recognized it, though the tone
of it, soft and wondering, didn't sound like her at all. A
figure rose inside the cell, haloed in the thin wash of moonlight. Yes. It was she. Renzo swiped a hand across his wet
cheeks as the others slowly rose as well. The children.

"Renzo!"

"Renzo!"

"Renzo!"

His name echoed faintly round the cell. He made out
Paolo, and the twin girls. Federigo and Georgio. Ugo, with
his magpie. And there, in the far corner, little Sofia.

One of them coughed, then another. Then a flurried
chorus of coughing.

Renzo knew he should say something, but his throat
seemed to have closed up tight. He hiked up his skirts, pulled
the picklocks from his belt, and felt along the surface of the
door, seeking out a lock. His fingers found the opening. He
inserted one of the picks, felt it nudge the tumblers inside—

A thump at the other side of the door. Letta's face appeared at the window, no more than a hand's breadth from his. "'Tis you," she breathed. "You came."

Her eyes held him; he couldn't look away.

"Well, hurry up!" she said. "We don't have all night!"

Now, *that* was the Letta he knew.

He put his head down, fumbled at the lock. "I come clear across to Venice, break myself in to get you out of here, and all you do is scold?"

"Ah, so this is Renzo."

His head snapped up. An old woman had taken Letta's place at the window. The grandmother, no doubt. "And what's your plan, pray tell?"

You would think that people would be grateful when you came to rescue them, Renzo thought, not pester you to hurry and demand to know every detail.

"Well?" the woman insisted.

The lock wasn't turning. Suddenly, despite the chill in this place, Renzo felt warm. He pulled out the pick and tried again. "Do you know how to get to the back door out of here?" he asked. "The small one that comes out in an alley?"

"I might. What's your plan?"

"I have a . . . friend outside. He'll take care of the guard in the alley and let us out."

It sounded so simple when he said it. Leaving out the fact that his "friend" was missing an eye and was still feeble from his injury. And that Renzo had no idea how to find the little door. And that if there were two guards stationed there instead of one, or if the little door was guarded on the inside as well, or if a passerby noticed anything amiss, Vittorio would fail, and then —

A shout. A distant reverberation of footsteps.

Letta's face appeared in the window. "Hurry!" she said.

He jiggled the pick. "I'm *trying!*"

All at once a commotion erupted from inside the cell. Birds calling. Clattering sounds. Voices. Footsteps.

A drop of sweat trickled down the side of Renzo's face. Still no movement in the wretched tumblers. Maybe Vittorio could spring this lock, but Renzo couldn't; he didn't have the skill.

Then, dangling between the bars of the opening in the door . . .

A hand, holding a ring of keys.

"'Tis the middle one, I believe," the old woman said.

Renzo gaped.

Keys?

"Hurry!"

He took them. Found the middle one. Thrust it into the lock. Turned it. The tumblers gave way with a satisfying *click*.

He pulled the door open.

From behind and below came a drumroll of echoing footfalls. Not one guard but many. Down the corridor Renzo saw a faint halo of light. They were somewhere on the stairs. They were near.

"Go, go, go!" the old woman cried. The owl pushed off her shoulder and glided toward the stairs, toward the voices. And then the air was filled with birds, creaking and flapping after the owl. They made for the archway on the far side of the stairs, and disappeared through it. The woman plucked Ugo from the floor and thrust him into Federigo's arms. To Letta she said, "You lead the way; I'll take care of stragglers."

Letta hesitated. "But, *Nonna*, your knees——"

"I'll be right behind you. Go!"

She went.

The children stumbled out of the cell, following Letta. The woman scooped up Sofia and pressed her to Renzo's chest. "The birds'll lead you to the door. Run!" she said. "Don't wait for me. I'll follow."

He didn't argue. He ran.

But in a few steps he heard her call out: "Renzo!"

He stopped. Turned back.

"She always knew you'd come. She never doubted. Now go. Get moving! Go!"

◆   ◆   ◆

He followed the children down the corridor, through the archway, and down another hall. Soon they came to a flight of stairs—a different one. He headed down, but then the stairs ended. He followed the children through a short corridor, around a corner, and then down another stairway. This one went on and on.

Sofia was bony and light, but she wiggled, kicking him with her one remaining boot, throwing him off balance. The hammer slapped painfully against his side, the keys rattled at his wrist, and the gown kept tangling between his legs. Soon it grew dark, so dark he could barely see. At last the stairs ended. He moved along a narrow corridor, following the sound of footsteps. The floor had become slippery again. The stones seemed to buckle and dip beneath his feet, making him lurch and stumble. He pushed himself to hurry, but Sofia jerked in his arms, and the blasted slippers slid out from under him. His hip cracked hard against the floor; he clung tight to Sofia; she landed on his lap.

He clambered to his feet and groped along the walls, limping now, straining his ears beyond the rasp of his own breathing for the sounds of the children ahead. Echoes reverberated all around him — echoes of voices, of footsteps, of coughing, of calling birds — but he couldn't tell for certain where they came from. Was the old woman coming along behind him? Were the guards?

Suddenly he slammed into something. It cried out. Paolo. Renzo found his hand, small and damp; they went on. A little way farther Paolo was seized with a fit of coughing. Renzo wanted to say, *Hurry, hurry, hurry* but could only wait until the coughing subsided.

Yet soon, as they walked, the air grew fresher; it smelled of water. The darkness lightened. Renzo turned a corner, and there they were, the other children, squatting on the floor, their birds perched on heads and wrists and shoulders. And down the corridor beyond them . . . a narrow door with thick black bars.

But were they iron or glass?

He set down Sofia; she and Paolo joined the others. Letta rose, came to him. "Where's *Nonna?*" she whispered.

"She's . . . coming," he said.

"You *left* her?"

"I did as she told me."

"Have you seen her? Have you heard her?"

Renzo shook his head.

"I'll find her, then. Your friend hasn't come yet. There's no one at the door, save for the guard."

Vittorio not there? But he should have been there long before. Maybe he was waiting for Renzo. "Stay here," he said. "Let me look."

"I told you, your friend's not there."

"There may be a way."

"But—"

"Would you wait, please? Just for a moment?"

She hesitated. Nodded. Stood aside.

Renzo picked his way among the children on the floor. When he came to the door, he reached up and touched one of the bars. Cold and smooth. Too smooth for iron?

He flicked it with a finger.

Glass!

Through the spaces between the bars, he saw the wall of another building. And in between . . . a narrow alley.

Footfalls outside. Renzo ducked. Above him a man passed on the other side of the bars.

A guard.

Vittorio was supposed to have dealt with him. Lured him away, or knocked him out, or . . .

Renzo hadn't wanted to know.

But where was Vittorio now?

Renzo crouched on the cold floor and put his head in his hands. He tried to *think*, tried to rise above the dragging pull of dread that lay heavy in his belly. Vittorio was still weak, had not fully recovered. And his eye . . .

A sound, behind him. Letta.

"Told you," she whispered. "Let's go back and find *Nonna*. She may have an idea. She — "

Renzo broke in. "I can get us out." He hiked his skirts and fumbled to untangle the hammer from his belt.

She raised her eyebrows, eyeing the gown. "That's very fetching, Renzo, but — "

"Be quiet, would you?"

"You couldn't even pick the lock of our cell; I don't know how you're going to — "

He pulled out the hammer, held it up.

"You're going to *beat* your way out?"

"Shh." The guard passed by again. Renzo waited. Then, "I can get us out. Trust me. But the guard is a problem."

"I can deal with him."

"You? What are you going to do, attack him with your fingernails?"

Behind them, a rumble of footfalls. No time to wait for Vittorio. They had to go now.

"How long d'you need him out of the way?"

"Not very long. Just — "

"I'll take care of him."

"How?"

"Trust me," she said.

Her face stilled, and in a moment Renzo heard a soft fluttering of wings. Birds streaked overhead, flitted between the glass bars.

A shout from outside. A cry. Renzo stretched up to peer through the window bars.

The guard was covered with birds. They funneled out of the sky and converged on him—on his shoulders, on his helmet, in his face. Not just the children's birds but masses of them—pigeons, seagulls, crows.

The guard tore at them, staggered away from the door.

Renzo drew back the hammer. "Step back, Letta! Everyone, cover your eyes!" He smashed the hammer against the bars. Glass exploded from the door, collecting bits of moonlight, spilling out in a bright cascading fan that, for an instant, blotted out the dark.

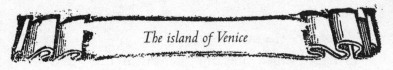

42.

Night Full of Trouble

The captain stood on deck scanning the legions of boats in the basin of San Marco, studying the crowds of revelers in the streets and on the stone pavements that bordered the canals.

No. Not there.

Hurry, would you?

He began to pace. The ship had been laded. Everything in place, everything lashed down. The flats of lace and bolts of silk had been stowed two days ago, the glass urns and tableware as well. Renzo's ten glass birds had arrived the day before; they slept snug in their crates with the other ones, deep within the hold. An hour ago the tide had turned. The captain felt it tugging at him, urging him to cast off. All lay in readiness . . . save for the last few passengers.

Who were late.

"Captain." The first officer approached. "Sir, ready to depart." It was not a question, but the captain heard the questioning in his tone: *What are you waiting for? The winds are favorable, the tide well turned, and the men are getting restless*

"Thank you, Fidelio," the captain growled, more abruptly than he'd intended. He dismissed the officer and searched the basin again.

Where were they?

He couldn't wait forever. If suspicion were aroused, if he were caught with them . . .

But wait.

A fleet of shadows shivered across the face of the moon. They poured into the darkness somewhere near the south end of the Doge's Palace.

Birds?

A distant crash.

Shouting.

Something was going on. He swept his gaze across the crowded pavement near the palace. But of his passengers . . .

No sign.

"Damnation!"

But now an odd brightness in the sky caught his notice; he pivoted north.

The horizon glowed orange.

Fire?

Yes, it had to be. Was it a ship? Or something on one of the islands?

This night, it seemed, was full of trouble.

He should cast off now, before trouble came to find him. And yet . . .

He'd given his word.

Just a moment longer, he thought, and then we'll go.

43.

Vittorio

Renzo smashed out the last of the glass. He turned to Letta. "You first."

She was gaping at him. "What . . . What'd you do, Renzo? How—"

"Hurry! I'll help you out and hand them through to you."

"No. Hand them t' Federigo. I'm going back for *Nonna*."

Renzo grabbed her arm. "Listen!" he said. The footsteps were louder now, thundering in the corridor behind them. "She'd want you to go. You know she would. What use are you to anyone if you're dead?"

She wrenched out of his grasp. Her eyes gleamed bright with unshed tears. "I'm going back."

"The others won't leave without you. Is that what you want?"

She glared at him.

He bent and made a stirrup with his hands. "Letta, come on! Please?"

She hesitated so long, he feared she'd turn back after all. But then she stepped into his clasped hands, boosted herself up, and twisting like an eel, slid through the window. Her hands caught on the sill; they released; he heard her feet crunch down on glass on the other side.

He called the children and, one by one, lifted them up and through the opening into Letta's waiting hands: Sofia, Ugo, Paolo. Marina, Ottavia. Georgio, Federigo. Just as Federigo disappeared, the footsteps suddenly surged behind Renzo, and a swath of light swept across the door.

"Hey! You!"

Renzo didn't look back. He grasped the edge of the window and jumped. With a grunt he hauled himself up. He squirmed through the opening, which dug into his belly and pressed against his back, and then tumbled headfirst into the narrow alley. His elbows hit with a *crack*, his hands skidded on broken glass, his body thumped down hard, and all his breath came whooshing out.

For a moment he lay there gasping. He heard the dungeon door rattle and looked up to see a guard's head and shoulders suddenly fill the window from inside. The man began to shout at him. Renzo was afraid he would jump through too, but he couldn't; he wouldn't fit.

Someone was shaking him. Letta. "Get up, get up, get up! Where do we go now?"

Renzo sucked in a juddering breath. He wobbled to his feet, looking for the other guard, the one the birds had attacked. Beyond the shouting he could hear a clamoring of birds down the alley to his left, but neither they nor the outside guard were anywhere in sight. Renzo ran a few steps to his right, to where the alley ended at the little canal that ran flush with the east side of the palace. Vittorio was supposed to be waiting for him there. He was supposed to have dispatched the guard, but . . .

He hadn't come.

Well, the ship would still be there, waiting, anchored somewhere in the basin of San Marco. At least he hoped it would. He scooped up Sofia and headed left, down the alley. They'd have to go the long way about, but they'd find the ship somehow.

But when he had gone only a few paces—

"Renzo!"

He whirled around. There, in a small boat in the canal, was a man wearing a mask. A mask with a long, thin nose and an absurdly jutting chin.

Papà's mask.

Vittorio! Rowing straight across the water toward them.

Renzo went weak with relief. He had feared . . .

"This way," Renzo said. He motioned the children toward the canal. In a moment the boat scraped against the wall. Renzo stepped inside, set down Sofia. He held the boat fast to the bollard as the rest of the children tumbled in, packing the boat full.

"Wait," Letta said. She twisted back toward the alley. "Maybe she'll come."

Her *nonna*. Renzo didn't know what to do, what to say. Vittorio pushed off; the boat moved away from the wall. Letta kept her gaze fastened on the alley. A soldier appeared at the edge of the canal. Two soldiers. Three. All shouting at once.

Letta pressed her lips together, hard. Her hands rose to cover her mouth.

The clamor dimmed behind them, muffled by the calming gurgle and swish of water. The palace glided serenely by. In a moment Vittorio's little craft slipped under the bridge, around the corner, and into the basin of San Marco.

A sparrow alit on Marina's shoulder. Vittorio paused in his rowing. He gestured for Renzo to cover the children beneath a rolled-up tarp stashed in the bow of the boat.

Renzo began to unfurl it; Letta wiped her eyes and nose and came to help. "Can you keep the birds away?" he asked.

She nodded, murmured to the children, tucking them all beneath the tarp. The sparrow darted off.

She turned back toward the palace as they wove among the other boats — small fishing boats and plain, black gondolas; pleasure boats alight with torches, tinkling with bells. The strains of a lute welled up as their boat passed a canopied gondola; masked revelers sang and laughed.

Renzo inspected his scraped and bloody hands and knees and elbows, suddenly realizing that they stung. He pulled the gown over his head, wadded it up, and stuffed it into the bottom of the boat. Good riddance! He looked about for soldiers but couldn't see a single one. Surely they must be searching, and yet . . . He breathed in the fresh night air, feeling his body begin to unclench.

They had escaped. Escaped from the very dungeon

of the Ten! Except for the old woman, Letta's grandmother.

"Listen, Letta," he said. "Maybe they'll only banish her. Lent's nearly upon us. Maybe they'll lose their appetite for . . ."

For hanging.

She didn't look at him. Didn't reply.

And now, low in the sky, past an odd brightness to the north, Renzo made out the dark outlines of tall masts and rigging. "Is that the one?" he asked Vittorio.

Vittorio nodded.

"I've met with the captain of that ship," he told Letta. "He'll take you away with him. He'll leave you in the care of friends of his; they'll look after you for a while, maybe until it gets warmer . . ."

He trailed off, hearing in his voice the thinness of the thread he held out to her. He had thought that breaking the children out of the dungeon would be enough. But now . . .

She turned to regard him gravely, and he couldn't tell what she was thinking. Could she get past her grief to attend to this? Was she afraid? Was she worried about life in another place where they knew no one, another place where people would find them odd and maybe threatening? Was she silently reproaching Renzo for not having saved her grandmother along with the rest? Was she leery of the captain?

Was the captain trustworthy?

"It's the best I could do," he said.

"I'm grateful," she said. "And those bars . . . they were a miracle, for true." She picked up the edge of the tarp.

"Letta, listen . . ."

She gave him a long, impenetrable look, then disappeared under the tarp with the others.

Why wouldn't she talk to him? The old, scolding Letta, he had known how to deal with. But this new Letta—the *grateful* Letta, the Letta who turned away and said nothing—perplexed him utterly.

A wind gust ruffled his hair; he shivered, suddenly uneasy. The danger was far from over for her and the children. As for himself . . .

He recalled that one of the guards had seen his face. But he would stay on Murano from now on; the man would never lay eyes on him again.

And Vittorio . . .

Renzo scooted past the children to the stern of the boat. "Did you run into trouble?" he asked softly.

Vittorio shrugged.

"What happened?"

Vittorio looked straight ahead. Kept rowing. Didn't answer.

"Uncle?"

Something prickled at the back of Renzo's neck. He peered up at Papà's mask. There was the familiar chip at the right temple. There was the stain on the chin. He tried to see into the dark spaces beyond the eyeholes. The hood covered his uncle's head and neck, but his hands . . .

Renzo gazed down at the hands on the oars. Large, scarred hands, with knotted fingers.

He knew his uncle's hands. Small and smooth, with tapering, well-formed fingers.

Not these.

Fear poured through him, icy, sickening.

These hands, he had seen them somewhere.

A memory blinked into his mind: a raised hand in the starlight. A noose.

The assassin.

44.

The Lives of Strangers

Renzo started to rise.

"Don't . . . move," the assassin said. Renzo sat back down. Softly, so only Renzo could hear, the assassin murmured, "I have no business with *these*." He turned the long nose of the mask toward the children. "I'll take them to the ship, and then we'll talk."

"What of Mama? Pia? Do you have *business* with them?"

"No."

"Vittorio?"

The assassin lifted his masked chin, pointed it to the north. The flickering brightness bloomed orange in the sky above Murano.

A fire.

Renzo didn't know what had happened, nor how, but he *knew*.

Vittorio was dead.

And likely *he* would be dead soon too. He leaned toward the assassin, suddenly fearless. "And my father?" he demanded. "Was that you?"

"It was," the assassin said, "an accident."

"An accident?" Renzo rose to his feet. He didn't care if the man had a noose. He didn't care if he had a knife. "An *accident?*"

"Renzo!" came a voice from behind him.

Renzo twisted back to see the ship looming there, the captain hailing him from on deck. "Where are they?" the captain shouted.

Renzo took a deep breath. He glanced at the assassin. "They're here," Renzo called.

"Well, pull alongside, and be quick about it!"

Renzo began to lift the tarp off the children. The assassin wouldn't kill him now, not with the captain and crew looking on. In a moment sailors were securing the lines, helping the children onto the dock. Letta turned to him.

"Maybe . . . you should be coming with us."

Her gaze flicked to the assassin, then back to Renzo.

How much had she heard?

But he couldn't leave. He was a glassmaker. They would find him and kill him for certain if he left . . . and maybe Mama, too.

"I can't."

"Why not?"

"Family. You should understand that."

She leaned in close to him. "What use are you to anyone if you're dead?"

All at once it struck him that, no matter what happened, he would never lay eyes on her again. Something jarred loose at the center of him; he felt as if he were coming apart.

"Get moving!" the captain shouted. "Shake a leg!"

Abruptly Letta turned away. "I see you've made your choice," she said. "Federigo, take Paolo. Georgio, take Ugo. Now go! All of you!" She scooped up Sofia and shooed the rest of them toward the gangplank, then followed without a backward glance.

She was hurt. That was what he'd failed to understand earlier. She'd wanted him to go with them.

The children trudged single file up the gangplank. One by one they turned back to look at him. Sofia waved, and then all of them were waving—all save for Letta.

He wanted to jump out of the boat, run up the plank, and join them. Join *her*.

But he couldn't.

He watched as the ship shrank behind them, as the assassin rowed out into the basin. Heading east, toward the lagoon. He was still watching as the ship slipped away from the dock.

"With your uncle," the assassin said.

Renzo turned to look at him.

"With your uncle it was quick, without pain."

Renzo swallowed. Why was he telling him this?

"I think," the assassin said, "he was expecting me."

Well, maybe so, Renzo thought. There'd been something of the ghost about Vittorio ever since he'd returned.

"With your father . . . I intended to ask him about Vittorio. I was prepared to inflict pain, but that was all. But when he realized who I was, he came after me with a blowpipe. He was strong and he was quick. He surprised me, and I had no choice."

An accident.

It was worse, somehow, that Papà's death had been unintended. Unnecessary. A waste. Renzo looked back across the basin to where the lights of Venice shimmered in the water in streaks of liquid gold. He wondered if this was the last night he'd ever see them. Their loveliness struck him so hard, it made him ache.

"What happens now?" he asked. "Do you kill me?"

The mask was hard and blank. Unreadable.

"No. I'm done."

Renzo drew in breath, taking back the lights, taking back his life.

"But," the assassin added, "you have a choice to make."

A choice?

"Listen very carefully. They will find a burned body in the ashes of the fire, the body of a boy your size. He's long dead, but they won't know that. They will find your silver cloak pin."

His cloak pin? And a boy . . . long dead? "But—"

"Listen! If you were to disappear at this moment, there would be no search, no repercussions. They would think you dead."

What did he mean, *disappear?* "You mean, leave the republic?"

The assassin nodded.

"And Mama and Pia?"

"Safe. Because as far as anybody knew, you wouldn't have absconded with secret knowledge. You'd be dead."

"But I don't want to . . ." *Leave Murano*, he'd been about to say. Though, a moment ago he'd been ready to leap off the boat to join Letta.

"Did any of the guards see you?" the assassin asked. "After you took off the mask?"

"One of them did."

"They know now that the bars were made of glass. Do you think they won't scour the ranks of glassworkers, looking for connections with the bird children? The Ten already know you've been suspected of harboring them in the glassworks. Not from me. But they know. And now there's a guard who can identify you. You might well come through it, but there would always be questions. And if this night's work were ever known . . ."

"But you said you were finished."

"I am. But there are others like me, and always will be."

Renzo couldn't still his mind to think. It was a restless wind, sending one thought after another fluttering past him, until at last he latched on to the pin.

"My silver cloak pin. You . . . planted it. Why would you do that? Why would you help? Why should I trust you?"

The assassin set down his oars and moved to sit opposite Renzo. "If you knew my face, I'd have to trust you, too. Perhaps we might trust each other." He reached up his crippled hands to his face and pulled off the mask.

It was an older face than Renzo had expected. A scar

slashed across one cheek, looking dangerous and harsh, but the thin line of the mouth, to Renzo's eyes, seemed to hold more pain than cruelty. The man's eyes, rimmed with dark circles, seemed tired and sad. Not the face of a man who had triumphed in life but of one who had been beaten down.

The man reached into his purse. Pulled out five copper coins. Held them out in his twisted hand.

"She reminds me of *my* sister," he said. "Though that was long ago."

Renzo stilled. Did not breathe.

"I watched you. At first my aim was to find your uncle through you. But even when I did, after he came to your house . . . I couldn't take him from there. Didn't want to violate *her* house. Didn't want to make her afraid."

"Pia," Renzo whispered.

"I was no one to her — just a beggar, a complete stranger. And still . . ."

He gazed at the coins, then funneled them back into his purse. "You might well come through it, but *she* will be safer if you go."

Papà's voice came swimming up through the long, bending stream of memory. *There will never be a greater glassmaker than you; you have the eye and the hand and the heart for greatness; you will bring honor to the family; they will build on your legend for generations.*

Gone now, Papà and his dreams. Ashes. And Vittorio, gone. And Mama and Pia . . . Not gone, but lost to him?

Signore Averlino would step in and take his place as the man of the family. Which wouldn't be such a bad thing. Not for Mama. Not for Pia. Especially since Renzo might be a danger to them if he stayed—a danger to *family*.

But how could he bear to leave them?

And the glass itself, spinning at the end of the blow-pipe, transforming into small miracles at his touch . . . What would his life be without it?

Suddenly Renzo remembered Vittorio's confession. He slipped the parchment from beneath his shirt. "The carpenter. He had nothing to do with . . . the glass bars. My uncle wrote out a confession—"

"So he told me." The man took the paper. "I'll give this to . . . the ones who hired me. And I'll tell them I know it to be true."

They sat for a moment in silence. A wind gust brushed at Renzo's cheek; it ruffled the surface of the water. A wave rocked the boat with a soft, gurgling splash. He gazed at the reflected lights of the city, trembling and golden. How had he come to this place? he wondered. How had his heart become so entangled in the lives of strangers that he'd been willing to risk all he'd ever cared about? How had it happened? He could not say.

He tipped back his head and searched the stars—familiar, clear, and bright. Did they shine just the same in other places? Could they still guide you when you were far from home?

Behind him he heard shouting. The ship strained toward

them, the wind beginning to fill her sails. And another voice came to him: *She never doubted. She always knew you'd come.*

Something heavy rolled off his heart; he felt himself grow calm.

The man sighed, stood, took up the oars. "Have you decided?" he asked.

Renzo nodded. "Take me to the ship," he said. "I'm ready to go."

EPILOGUE

The ship appeared in the distance in the soft pink glow at the rim of the world. The little owl veered toward it, pumping hard beneath fading stars. Although he was light—for he bore no message—the flight had spanned a great length of land and sea, and weariness dragged at his wings. When at last the ship's sails loomed above him, the owl swooped low across the deck, seeking the one he'd been sent to find.

He heard a rustling somewhere below—then a drowsy, chuckling *coo*. His heartbeat quickened; he spied an opening and dived down into a deeper darkness, where the air lay heavy and still.

She was sleeping among the others—the smallest of the companions. Feathers ruffled; the sounds of human breathing stirred the air. The owl lit down on the girl's knee, called softly. Her eyes opened; she sat up; she gazed at him. Slowly she held out a hand.

It was a tiny hand, and smooth—unlike the hand he'd known so long and well. He hopped onto the back of it, stretching up in alertness, feathers shut tight. They gazed at each other, the owl and the girl, until a strange new kenning went shivering through him. Thinner and weaker than the kenning he'd known, yet oddly sweet and musical.

He blinked.

At the same time she blinked too.

The little owl fluffed his feathers. He settled down on her small, soft hand and knew that he was home once more.

AUTHOR'S NOTE

In 1291, after a series of destructive fires, an edict went out from the authorities in Venice banning all glassmaking furnaces from the city. From that point forward the island of Murano became the center of glassmaking in the Venetian lagoon. Murano glass came to be renowned for its beauty and originality and was much sought after across all of Europe.

Glassmaking, like many crafts, has a vocabulary all its own. In this book I've taken all but one of the glassmaking terms from *Murano: Island of Glass* by Attilia Dorigato, who derives his terms in part from documents dating from the Renaissance. (I've taken *malmoro* from *Glassmaking in Renaissance Venice: The Fragile Craft*, by W. Patrick McCray.)

During the Renaissance the authorities made many efforts to keep Murano's glassmakers from taking their secrets to other countries. Numerous decrees were passed, imposing fines, banishment, or prison sentences on glass artisans who left Murano to practice their craft beyond the Venetian lagoon.

According to some historians the authorities went even further in their attempts to protect trade secrets: If a glass-maker left the lagoon, agents of the state would seek him out, wherever he was, and kill him.

At the time in which *Falcon in the Glass* is set, Murano was part of the Republic of Venice, which was governed by a doge — or duke — and the Council of Ten, a group of noblemen who had extraordinary powers and a fearsome reputation. Sometimes they were referred to simply as "the Ten." If a citizen wished to denounce someone to the doge or the Ten, all he had to do was slip a written message through a slot in one of several Lion's Mouth boxes that could be found scattered across the city of Venice.

Visitors to Venice today can tour the prisons, located across a narrow canal from the Doge's Palace. But these prisons had not yet been built at the time of this story; most prisoners were then housed on the ground floor of the Doge's Palace itself. However, prisoners from elite classes or people not yet convicted might be taken to cells high up in the palace, cells called "the Leads," from the sheets of lead used to cover the roof just above. It was from the Leads, much later, that Giovanni Giacomo Casanova famously escaped, managing somehow to scramble onto the roof and then climb down through a skylight into an attic. He passed through a number of rooms and at one point leaned out a window, where he was seen by a guard who mistook him for an official and let him out.

I was surprised to learn that at least some prisoners were

supplied with oil lamps, which they kept burning day and night. Apparently many of the cells were subdivided into chambers with wooden walls. I've chosen to use stone walls for the purposes of this story, and I've invented some details regarding the prison doors.

The Doge's Palace, situated in a low-lying part of Venice, is particularly vulnerable to a lagoon-wide phenomenon called *acqua alta*, or "high water." These seasonal, exceptionally high tides tend to occur with the conjunction of a new or full moon, rain, and a sirocco wind. Although episodes of *acqua alta* are becoming more and more frequent in modern times, many such inundations have been documented back to the Middle Ages. Today visitors walk on elevated planks when an occurrence of *acqua alta* floods the palace and Saint Mark's Square.

Carnivale (or Carnival) was the annual celebration wherein citizens wore costumes and masks, staged plays, ate heartily, danced, and made merry before the privations of Lent. The festival of *Carnivale* began in the Middle Ages and continues in the present day.

On a final note, if you go to Venice, you'll notice that people usually stand while rowing their boats — one oar per person. However in the past there was a type of small fishing boat in which a single man, with the aid of a central oarlock, rowed using two crossed oars. Renzo and Vittorio travel in such a boat when crossing from Murano to Venice. Some readers may be surprised when Renzo encounters the island of San Cristoforo, which is not in evidence today. Originally,

San Cristoforo and San Michele were two separate islands, but the area between them was filled in during the nineteenth century, and the combined island is now known as San Michele.

If you'd like to know more about Murano glass, I recommend *Murano: Island of Glass* by Attilia Dorigato and *Murano: A History of Glass* by Gianfranco Toso. If you'd like to delve even deeper into the historical and technical aspects of Murano glassmaking, I recommend *Glassmaking in Renaissance Venice: The Fragile Craft* by W. Patrick McCray.

If you'd like to know more about the old Venetian prisons, I recommend *The Prisons of the Doge's Palace in Venice* by Umberto Franzoi and *The Medieval Prison: A Social History* by G. Geltner.

If you'd like to know more about how people lived in Venice during the Renaissance, I recommend the elegant and richly illustrated *Private Lives in Renaissance Venice* and *Art and Life in Renaissance Venice*, both by Patricia Fortini Brown.

If you'd like a more general view of Venice and its history, I recommend the incomparable *The World of Venice* by Jan Morris.

—Susan Fletcher

ACKNOWLEDGMENTS

I'm grateful for the generosity of so many people who helped me with this book.

Ellen Howard, Winifred Morris, Kathi Appelt, Marion Dane Bauer, Linda Zuckerman, and Kelly Fletcher read and commented on the manuscript; each one helped immeasurably. My critique group—including Carmen Bernier-Grand, Nancy Coffelt, David Gifaldi, Eric Kimmel, and Pamela Smith Hill—patiently listened to chapter after chapter on Wednesday evenings and showed me how the manuscript might be improved. Cynthia Whitcomb taught me a joyful way to move through the first draft.

Patricia Fortini Brown read the entire manuscript for accuracy and directed me to resources that told me just what I needed to know. Patrick McCray and Charlene Fort checked to make sure the details about glassmaking were correct. Dr. John Morrison lent me his expertise on injuries to the eye. Doris Kimmel set me straight on both glassmaking and birds and kindly lent me books from her personal library. Silvana Hale brought her knowledge of Venice to bear on the manuscript and helped me with words and phrases in Italian and the Venetian dialect. Jim Nolte, head librarian at Vermont College of Fine Arts, gave me invaluable research assistance. Nina and Laurent Rochette and Janice Simnetta went out of their way to find resources for me. Jerry Fletcher advised me on many matters, most notably those involving the carpentry shop.

Thanks so much to Emily Fabre for her help and enthusiasm for the project. Most especially, I want to thank my agent, Elizabeth Harding — for taking me on, getting this project on the road, and smoothing the way — and my editor, Karen Wojtyla, for her wisdom, humor, and trust.